TIME'S
CHARIOT

www.**davidficklingbooks**.co.uk

To Kerstin, who shapes my future

Also available by Ben Jeapes:

THE XENOCIDE MISSION
THE NEW WORLD ORDER

BEN JEAPES

TIME'S CHARIOT

David Fickling Books

OXFORD · NEW YORK

A DAVID FICKLING BOOK

Published by David Fickling Books
an imprint of Random House Children's Books
a division of Random House, Inc.
New York

Originally published in Great Britain as *Wingèd Chariot* by
Scholastic Ltd. in 2000

David Fickling Books and colophon are trademarks
of David Fickling.

Visit us on the Web! www.randomhouse.com/kids

Educators and librarians, for a variety of teaching tools, visit us at
www.randomhouse.com/teachers

Library of Congress Cataloging-in-Publication Data
Jeapes, Ben.
[Wingèd chariot]
Time's chariot / Ben Jeapes. — 1st American ed.
p.   cm.
Summary: In an overcrowded future, Earth's surplus population
is dispersed throughout history, but the system that makes this
possible is about to collapse with deadly consequences.
ISBN 978-0-385-75167-4 (trade) —
ISBN 978-0-385-75168-1 (lib. bdg.)
[1. Space and time—Fiction. 2. Science fiction.] I. Title.
PZ7.J356Ti 2008
[Fic]—dc22
2008004694

Printed in the United States of America
September 2008
10 9 8 7 6 5 4 3 2 1

First American Edition

'But at my back I always hear
Time's wingèd chariot hurrying near,
And yonder all before us lie
Deserts of vast eternity.'

Andrew Marvell, *To His Coy Mistress*

One

They had drugged him and now his body twisted lazily as it tumbled through the air.

Body. Somewhere in one corner of his drugged mind was a feeling of annoyance, because he wasn't a *body* yet, but that was how they had referred to him. And, looking at the ground creeping closer, he felt the description would soon be accurate, which annoyed him even more. He hadn't even been given the choice of whether or not to die.

The wind was a booming, rushing noise in his ears. He had fallen for a long time. He had fallen off a mountain, he recalled, though he wasn't sure what a *mountain* was. Perhaps it was that shining blur. They may have drugged him into compliance and a fatalistic acceptance of death, he thought, but he wasn't stupid.

Another corner of his mind wondered about the emergency agravs – necessary equipment when you lived over a mile above ground, designed for just such eventualities as this. Even now they should be picking him up and reducing his rate of descent so that he would land as smoothly as a feather. Somehow he had got past their reach.

He frowned because something wasn't making sense. This was the Home Time and murder was meant to be a thing of the past, and yet he was reasonably certain that murder was what had just happened to him.

And then the ground, once so far away and approaching slowly, was suddenly coming quickly up towards him, and there was no time for terror before all his worries abruptly ceased.

Two

Isfahan, 1029

'Help! Help me!'
The Correspondent paused and cocked his head, still fingering the halter of the camel tied up beside the road. He had stopped to inspect the animal because a camel saddled for a rider, but riderless, aroused his curiosity. He was in the middle of what was still called Persia and it was shortly after his arrival at 08:00, local time on 13 May in the year the faithful called 407, the Christians called 1029 and his masters called 1564 pre-Home Time. He was on the road between Qom and Isfahan and so far, apart from the camel, he had seen no sign of anyone else around him.

'Help!' The voice was more desperate and, turning up his hearing, the Correspondent could hear the sounds of conflict, heavy breathing, metal on metal. The noise came from the other side of a small hill beside the road through the desert, and he set off over it at a slow jog.

There was a fight going on round the other side

of the hill, three against one, and the one was tiring. The Correspondent had no idea of the rights and wrongs of the situation and no especial desire to intervene, so instead he began to record the scene, sucking the information in through his eyes and storing it in the special areas at the back of his brain.

In his final despair, the one man below raised his eyes and saw the Correspondent at the top of the rise. 'In the name of the Prophet, help me!' he cried. Still, the Correspondent might have stayed put if one of the three others hadn't turned round and spotted him. Immediately he charged with an angry bellow, scimitar raised.

The Correspondent stood where he was and watched the man approach. Something inside him assessed a threat to personal safety and he shifted to defence mode, without showing any external change. The attacker's yell peaked as he drew close and brought the blade down.

With one hand the Correspondent swatted the blade aside. The other he jabbed deep into the man's throat. The man staggered backwards and fell, eyes bulging, choking on his crushed larynx.

The two remaining attackers stood over their now motionless victim. They ran at him as one, and again the Correspondent let them get close. Then his foot came up at the end of a straight leg, catching the first under the ribs and crushing his heart. The second man got the Correspondent's rigid fingers in his solar plexus and his spinal cord was severed by a chop to the back of his neck.

The Correspondent looked down at the three bodies, stored the scene in his memory and then went down to see if the one they had been attacking was still alive.

He was – a young man only just out of adolescence, with a scraggly beard. He had propped himself up on one arm and he gazed at the Correspondent with awe.

'You just stood there!' he said. 'I have never seen someone dispatch three bandits so quickly. You have my eternal gratitude.'

The bandits had actually posed little threat. The Correspondent still didn't know much, but he knew that. Provided he avoided immediate trauma and kept himself in more or less one piece, his body could overcome virtually any threat to it from war or disease, and regenerate itself indefinitely. He was packed full of added organic components and he possessed skills and senses that evolution had never given *Homo sapiens* and never would. He could even remould his features if desired, given a day or so to himself. At the moment, he appeared like any other man of the region in his mid thirties.

The young man in the sand would not have understood, so the Correspondent just asked: 'Who were they?'

'Infidel worthless bandits,' the young man said casually. He looked up at his helper. 'And who are you, friend?'

Who was he? A good question. *Your memory will be affected by the transference.* They had told him that, though he couldn't remember who they were and he still had no specific memory of the Home Time. He did know that he had a function: to observe, to comment, to survive. He was Correspondent RC/1029 – any further identity that he took would be up to him.

'My name is of no importance and I am going to Isfahan,' the Correspondent said – slightly to his surprise, because until that moment he had had no idea which direction on the road he was taking. Meanwhile, he guessed what might be worrying his new friend. 'I am no bandit. If I were, you would be dead by now.'

'A worthy point. I am Ali Salim Said and I have the misfortune to be scouting for my father's caravan, which will pass this way shortly.'

'Scouting?'

'For bandits,' Ali said with feeling. He began, very gingerly, to climb to his feet.

'Then I would say you are good at your job,' said the Correspondent, holding out his hand. Ali burst out laughing as he took it and pulled himself up.

'I am good at finding them but not at detecting. One of them lay by the road, as if already waylaid, and two waited behind a rock.'

'Is that your camel, then, back by the road?'

'It is.' Ali had finally found his feet, only to fall over and clutch at the Correspondent.

'Then I had better help you back there,' the Correspondent said.

An hour later the caravan finally passed by and the Correspondent was taken in, helped by a glowing introduction from Ali and the mute testimony of the three graves which the Correspondent had been digging. And that was how the Correspondent came to enter Isfahan.

Isfahan hustled and bustled with the activity and purpose of a major metropolis. The city was a place where trade routes converged and it thrived in its business of producing cotton, silk and wool, with hundreds of individual shops turning out carpets and metal goods. The wind shifted and the Correspondent quickly deduced the location of the animal market.

'Is this place not magnificent?' said Ali. He and the Correspondent strolled side by side through the bazaar, as best as two men could stroll in a place packed with such a number of people and animals.

The Correspondent made a non-committal noise. To his surprise, an item of knowledge about Isfahan dropped into place in his mind. Isfahan was already doomed, but it would soon recover from the fate that awaited it. In 1051 it would be conquered by the Seljuk Turks and as compensation it would become the capital of their empire. But by 1051, the Correspondent would be long gone. After 1037 he would have no further reason for staying here.

1037: another rationed scrap of memory. As a correspondent he knew he was a free agent, but apparently not that free. He hadn't been dropped in eleventh-century Persia on a whim. Thirty seconds ago he had been a casual wanderer but now he knew he was here to meet someone, and that this particular someone would die in 1037. The man was known to have spent the last fourteen years of his life as scientific adviser and physician to the ruler of Isfahan, so that gave the Correspondent somewhere to start his search.

'Are you well?' Ali was looking at him with anxiety. The Correspondent realized his expression must have been blank, his thoughts miles away.

'Yes, I'm well,' he said. 'And yes, Ali, this is a marvellous city indeed. Do you know where the palace might be?'

Ali gave him a strange look but, yes, he did know where the palace was and he was happy to act as a guide. It was an impressive structure and the two men stood a safe distance off to observe it.

'Do you have business in there?' Ali asked.

'I've come to meet a man.'

'Then ask to be announced to him.'

'He's never heard of me,' said the Correspondent, 'but I know how to get his attention. I need parchment, and charcoal, and ink – black, red and blue.'

Later he lay on his bed in his room, hired with money he had taken from the dead bandits when

8

Ali wasn't looking, and composed his report. His eyes stared blankly towards the ceiling, and though it was dark he could easily see the plaster above him. He had turned all his senses to maximum while he prepared his report; should anyone come by, they would find him apparently in a coma, and he had no intention of letting that happen.

First he put in the straightforward sensory data of the day. The air, unpolluted but also hot and dusty. The terrain, tough and unyielding, only just begrudging a living to the locals. The precise temperature, the shade of blue of the sky, the texture of the rock and the sand.

Other things – things that made him feel good. The friendship of the caravan, and of Ali. The gratitude of Ali's father. The vitality of Isfahan outside his window; a city of only a few thousand but still more alive, more animated than the Home Time with all its billions ever could be. The taste of the food, the smell of the people and animals.

(*And how did he know what the Home Time was like when he had such a poor memory of it? He just . . . did.*)

When the report was finished, he breathed a sigh. His first! Now it just needed filing. The moon was up, so . . .

He *thought*, and a tone that only he could hear sounded in his head.

'*RC/1029, stand by*,' said a voice. Then, '*RC/1029, transmit.*' He *thought* again and in a couple of seconds it was over.

'*Report received, RC/1029*,' said the voice.

His first report was filed. A big moment! He got out of bed and strolled over to the window to look at the moon. Somewhere up there was the station, awaiting retrieval by those who had put it there, centuries from now. It was comforting to consider. He had no doubt that sooner or later in his career he would feel very lonely and it would be good to know that up there was something else from the future. A link to the Home Time. As long as the moon was up, he would be able to make contact with it. That was another item in the innate knowledge he had brought back with him.

He had a thousand years to go before he could return to the Home Time. In a thousand years' time, in the twenty-first century, the world would be sufficiently advanced technologically that the Home Time could send the recall equipment back without it appearing anachronistic. A thousand years until Recall Day. No doubt he had had his reasons for volunteering for this assignment, but thinking about it now, it did seem rather a long time.

But he was at the start of his career; he was alive and well and surrounded by thousands upon thousands of facts and minutiae waiting to be noted and reported on. And tomorrow he would start by seeking out the man in the palace whose philosophies would help carve out the path of western science, centuries hence, and who would one day be known in the West as the third Aristotle – but that of course lay in the future, and the

Correspondent had better reason than most to know that there was a great deal of future ahead.

'Are you looking for someone, my son?'

Ali Salim Said started when his father spoke. He had been searching around the caravan fruitlessly and his expression had grown more and more baffled.

'I'm looking for Salim, Father,' he said. His new friend yesterday had eventually yielded a name, but only after his father had asked for it three times. 'He has vanished.'

'Isfahan is a large place,' his father said with a shrug.

'He is not in his room, which he hired,' Ali said. That point still smarted with him. To have the hospitality of the caravan, yet to turn it down like that . . . And then to vanish . . .

'My son.' Ali's father put a friendly hand on his shoulder. 'Your friend Salim was . . . strange. Did you not notice?'

'He saved me from three bandits! I told you that!'

'Indeed you did. You also told me he saved you when you called to him in the name of the Prophet, blessings be upon his name, but first he stood by and watched. Now, do you recall how I had to try and get his name out of him? Indeed, do you know a single thing about the man other than what he has grudgingly told you? For saving your life he has my eternal thanks, but when you have my years and

11

my experience, you too will notice these things in strangers. They are not always what they seem. Did Abraham not entertain three angels without realizing it?'

'You think he was an angel?' Ali wasn't sure whether to scoff at the idea, or be awed.

'I think he was a man whose life's path only briefly crossed yours, my son. If he wants you to find him again, he will let you do so. If not, accept it as the will of Allah. I only ask that you be prepared for the possibility that you will not see your new friend again.'

The Correspondent sat on a cushion and sipped his coffee in the calm of the palace while his host paced round and round him, feasting his eyes on the document with which the Correspondent had gained entry. They were completely alone.

'Fascinating. Truly fascinating.' Abu Ali al-Husayn ibn Abd Allah ibn Sina was forty-nine years old but looked older – he had never seen eye to eye with more orthodox Muslims on the subjects of drink and sex. The Correspondent had found the way to his heart, and if there had been any doubt as to its location, Abu Ali was holding a map. 'I have always known the blood circulates within the body, because it will flow from a wound in the head just as easily as from a wound at the feet, but to see this . . . where did you get it?'

'It is common knowledge where I come from,'

12

said the Correspondent. 'The complete circulatory system of the human being.'

Abu Ali looked again at the maze of lines drawn in blue and red over the black, androgynous outline of an adult human. His eye traced the course of the wrist artery, and holding the diagram in one hand he felt for the beat of the blood in his own wrist with the other. Then his hand moved to his neck and again he felt his pulse.

'And where is it you come from?' he said. 'Cathay?'

'A good guess,' the Correspondent said.

'Why did you send this to me?'

'I wanted to show you my intentions were sincere. I wanted to talk to you and I would have you assured in advance that I am no charlatan.'

'You wish to discuss medicine? I am your obedient servant.'

'Actually, no, not medicine,' the Correspondent said. Abu Ali was a polymath, a fluent thinker in many subjects including medicine – indeed, his medical works would still be reprinted as authoritative in Europe in the seventeenth century, though before long orthodox Islamic theologians, more worried by his heresies than his habits, would have his work very well suppressed in the Arab world. That wasn't why the Correspondent was here. 'I would talk to you of the *Kitab ash-Shifa*.'

'You have read it?' Abu Ali leaned forward eagerly.

'I have.' It was a white lie – Abu Ali's *Kitab*

ash-Shifa, the misleadingly titled *Book of Healing*, was a collection of treatises on Aristotelian logic, metaphysics, psychology and the natural sciences, amongst other things, and the Correspondent had a full copy of it in his head. 'I am interested in your thoughts on Actuality and Nothing. Or to be more precise, the Potentiality that lies between the two.'

No one comes an unknown distance, perhaps from Cathay, seeks out the author of an obscure book, draws an accurate and precise map of the human circulatory system to get his attention, and then asks to talk about Potentiality. From the tilt of Abu Ali's head it was obvious he didn't believe it, but he went along with the game, perhaps out of curiosity.

'An interesting subject with which to while away the hours,' he said. 'Potentiality? Well, we know that nothing truly changes.'

'Do we?'

'Of course! For change to be real, something must come out of nothing, which is plainly nonsensical. The only change can be in an object's substance –' *a reasonable description of the conservation of energy*, the Correspondent thought – 'yet before the change there is no sign of it.'

'So the object must have the potentiality in it for that which it is to become?' the Correspondent said.

'Precisely!' Abu Ali was forgetting his curiosity and talking for the love of it. He leaned forward and his eyes gleamed. 'Potentiality is what does not exist but which could—' He stopped. The Correspondent waited politely for him to continue, but Abu Ali was looking over the Correspondent's shoulder. 'Who are you?' he said. 'I . . . I did not see you come in—'

The Correspondent turned quickly to see the newcomer for himself. He was considerably more worried than Abu Ali because even his enhanced senses had not detected anyone's approach.

The newcomer was dressed like someone from Isfahan but he had skin paler than either Abu Ali, who was a native Arab, or the Correspondent, who looked like one. He had not come in by door or by window – the Correspondent would have heard him. The man opened his mouth and the words that came out would have been babble to Abu Ali, yet to the Correspondent they made perfect sense.

'Is this Avicenna?' It was the language of the Home Time, and he gave the name – a Western corruption of *Allah ibn Sina* – by which the Arab philosopher would one day be better known, by those who knew of him at all.

'Why, yes.' The Correspondent made to stand.

'Stay seated,' said the man, and it was as if a heavy weight had fallen on the Correspondent's shoulders. The man raised his hand towards the philosopher and a light shone from a small, dark globe that he was carrying. Abu Ali froze, then brought his feet slowly together, letting his arms dangle limply at his sides. Hypnotized, perhaps, but not knocked out. The newcomer walked forward,

15

took a crystal from his pocket and held it to Abu Ali's temple. The crystal changed from blue to red. 'He won't remember this.' The man pocketed the crystal again and studied the chart of the circulatory system that remained in Abu Ali's hand. 'This was a good idea, RC/1029. You had better get on with your interview.'

'Who . . . who are you?' said the Correspondent, echoing Abu Ali but still more uncertain. 'Are you another Correspondent? Why—'

The man smiled a mirthless smile. 'Enough questions,' he said. He held up his hand once more, the light shone again and the Correspondent's mind went blank.

Three

Ricardo Garron woke from a dream where someone was calling his name over and over again.

Someone was. A familiar voice pulsed by symb into his thoughts.

'Rico? Come on, Garron, wake up. I can't believe . . . Rico! *Wake up—'*

'Su?' he mumbled into the pillow.

'You're asleep, aren't you?' He could only hear her voice but he could picture his partner perfectly. Su Zo was a dark, Asian woman and her short frame would be trembling, unsure whether to laugh or be angry.

'I was.' He shifted in his bed and wrapped the quilt more firmly around himself, determined to get at least another ten minutes.

'I'm coming to get you. Taxi says I'll be there in five.'

'Here?' Rico frowned. Something was nagging at the back of his mind. Normally he and Su met up at the College at the start of their shift, but . . .

'Oh, frak,' he shouted as he jumped out of bed. 'Just let me shower . . .'

'*You forgot, didn't you? I can't believe you actually forgot . . .*'

'I remembered when I went to bed,' he said, defensive.

'*Five minutes, Rico.*' Su cancelled the symb.

The entfeed started automatically on his favourite channel as he went into the shower and he just caught the last few minutes of one of the leading soaps. He loved counting the anachronisms which he could then compare with Su once they got to work. Imperial Romans in motor cars, medieval knights with computers, that sort of thing. Today it was a Victorian lady going off to join a free love commune.

'Load of crap,' he muttered, angling his head into the flow of warm air to dry his hair. The College that he worked for made all the resources of humankind's rich and glorious heritage available to a waiting world, and rubbish like the soap opera was the result. A Fossil Age writer had once used the term prolefeed, and to Rico that perfectly summed up ninety-nine per cent of everything the College's data was used for. Yet he couldn't avoid a feeling of professional pride that he was partly responsible – he, Su and others like them. Most people in the Home Time were content to lap up what the College supplied, but he and his colleagues went out and got it.

He was fully dressed and dry when the door chime went. The gelfabric of his suit slid around him and styled itself into the College uniform of

18

yellow and red. He symbed for the door to open and drew himself up with a proud beam when Su stepped into the suite. She looked him up and down as if checking he had remembered to clean his teeth and put his shoes on.

'You only just made it, didn't you?' she said.

Rico grinned. 'Been ready for the last ten minutes. Where were you?'

'Come on, then,' she said, and they went out to the taxi together.

The taxi, a hollow sphere with a transparent membrane and a padded bench all around its circular cabin, rose up, and up, and up. Azania ecopolis, Rico's home, fell away and spread itself out below: a fully self-sustaining, environmentally enclosed city of fantastic shapes and colours; parks, lakes and buildings sculpted from the artificial land coral that covered most of the inhabited Earth's surface. Sparkling in the subtropical sunshine, it was a beautiful sight.

Within a minute the taxi was too high for small details to be picked out. By the time it reached the forcefield that officially marked Azania's upper limits, the shape of the southern end of Africa – a riot of greens, browns and blues set into the darker, royal blue of the sea – had become evident. Above them the sky was dark and the brighter stars were showing. Then the taxi was through the forcefield and had gone hypersonic, and the end of Africa fell away with noticeable speed.

A few minutes later it braked down from transit

speed as it arced down through the atmosphere towards Antarctica. Its passengers felt only a slight deceleration pressure. They knew the invisible barriers that the flying sphere was passing through. It was targeted by missiles and plasma bolts and several terawatts' worth of anti-aircraft energy weapons, and every quanta emanating from it was subjected to extreme scrutiny by the College's defences, for a sign of bogusness. The College took its security seriously.

The dark bones of Fossil Age oil stations passed beneath them and then the College itself came into view, sparkling white like the land around it and perched like a miniature city overlooking the Ross Sea. A city, not an ecopolis; the College had been built in the era of old-time cities, before the first ecopolis had been grown. The College was made of old-fashioned steel and concrete and plastic, not land coral, and the outlines were straight and regular: the truncated pyramid that was the transference hall and a host of smaller shapes, like a child's collection of play bricks.

It never seemed quite right to Rico. For the last four hundred years, and for the next twenty-seven, men and women had been able to walk in the same streets and breathe the same air as Shakespeare, Al-Nasir, Einstein, Kennedy, Genghis Khan, the Director, Beethoven, Persaud, Mozart, Galileo, Dabrowski. All those journeys started and ended in this place. Yet where were the streams of taxis bringing time-travelling tourists from their ecopoloi to the holiday of a lifetime in Imperial Rome? Where were the bold hunters going on safari among the dinosaurs? Where were the eye witnesses to the Five Bomb War? They were there, but they were either College employees or rich patricians with time on their hands. The people of the Home Time were happy to feed on the correspondents' reports and to enjoy the vicarious pleasures of Earth's myriad civilizations, but only in the sanitised safety of the Home Time; only in their cosy, regulated, artificial homes. When it came to real history, the people just weren't interested.

Two minutes later Rico and Su had arrived; ten minutes later they were no longer in the Home Time.

Some hours earlier, Marje Orendal too woke to a symb signal, an alarm pulsing into her mind.

'Wha—?' she mumbled. 'OK. I'm awake. What is it?'

'*Dr Orendal.*' A voice she might have recognized. '*May I project?*'

'If you must . . .'

Marje symbed the lights of her suite to come on, and sat up in bed. The eidolon of a man appeared on the other side of the room, and his eyes widened when he saw her.

'I'm sorry! I didn't think . . .'

'Where did you imagine I'd be, ten seconds after waking up?' Marje squinted at him. Awake, and with a face to put to the voice, she recognized him. 'What is it, Hossein?'

Hossein Asaldra's face showed a certain hesitation before he spoke. 'I've been asked to ask you to come to the College at once,' he said.

'Whatever for?'

'Something I'd rather tell you face to face, Dr Orendal. May I meet you in the transference hall in twenty minutes?'

'Are we going somewhere?' She saw just a brief shadow of irritation cross his face. 'Yes, certainly,' she said. 'Twenty minutes.'

After he had gone, she took a quick shower and field massage, though not too quick to avoid going through her daily ritual of reciting Morbern's Code. Some things were just too important.

The first tenet:

I will deny to no one to whom the universe has given it the right to existence. I will respect all human life, for even that which only lives in my memory will accuse me.

Jean Morbern and his Creator had had a special relationship. She often wondered what it had been like for him when he realized the godlike responsibilities he had suddenly acquired over millions of people, in creating the Home Time; worse, when he finally accepted he was dying and had to hand over that responsibility to the College he had founded. But he had done well; the Code had lasted four hundred years, as had the College that maintained it.

The fac presented her with her clothes and she let them settle and seal themselves around her. She checked her appearance one last time in a mirrored field as she waited for the taxi to arrive. A former lover had called her slight: she preferred slim. Blonde hair in the style she wore for work: prim, no-nonsense. Dark trousers, yellow and red tunic, high collar. She liked to be formal for work – it emphasized that at the end of the day, when she shucked off the College clothes and put on the casual ones, she was then in her own time, account- able only to herself.

A chime told her that the taxi was waiting. She took one last look at the reflection, then cancelled the field and went out to the waiting sphere.

'Swishville,' Rico murmured as they stepped into what was technically an apartment. He and Su stood on the edge of a small courtyard with a colonnade running around the edges, and a chuck- ling little fountain in the middle. Through the arches opposite they could see a vast space of empty air and, beyond that, the stark dark rock and sparkling white snow of a Himalayan mountain, shoulder to shoulder with its neighbours in the range. Rico and Su had to crane their necks to see the cloud- and snow-shrouded tops. Rico peeked behind him and saw a similar mountain towering right over them – the courtyard was carved into it.

This was the Himalayas, 5000 BC. Warmth and air provided by the Home Time and kept in place by an invisible forcebubble around the premises; setting and scenery provided by Nature. Or God. Just one perk of being a patrician of the Home Time, and a lot bigger than the little box Rico lived in.

'Out of our league,' Su agreed.

'Oh, come on. You and Tong will end up somewhere like this in another twenty years.'

'I doubt it.'

'May I help you?' The eidolon of the apartment's intelligence appeared in front of them, the standard blue outline showing that it was the projection of an artificial personality, not a real human. It was in the form of an old man, bald head, white beard and robe. Rico wondered who it was meant to be.

'You're the household?' he said. 'Ops Garron and Zo. We made an appointment with you to collect something from Commissioner Daiho.'

'Of course.' The eidolon bowed, and turned into a glowing ball that hung in mid-air. 'Please follow the light.'

The light led them over to the valley side of the courtyard, where a gap in the balustrade led onto a suspended staircase that curved out into the open air, then round and down to the level below them. The apartment was set into the side of a mountain and the drop below was sheer. Rico savoured the view, and when his instincts protested at the amount of solid ground that wasn't beneath his feet, he told himself the apartment would naturally have agravs to catch him if he fell.

Still, it was a relief to step into what was presumably the apartment's main chamber. A split-level sitting room, one side open to the view and the rest of it carved out of the native rock. There was an unusual number of people there – more than Rico had expected Commissioner Daiho to have around. Being a patrician and a Commissioner of the College would mean a busy life, but this number of staff was unexpected.

As his foot touched the floor a voice symbed into their minds. *'This area is under the jurisdiction of the Security Division. Please state your business.'*

Security? He and Su looked at each other, then Rico glanced back at the others already present. Some were waving instruments here and there, others seemed to be just lingering and chatting in small groups. So, these were Security Ops.

'Ops Garron and Zo,' he said. 'You can check our business here with the household.'

Presumably the voice did just that. *'You may proceed.'*

'Did the Commissioner leave instructions for us?' Su asked the ball of light.

'I'm afraid not,' said the house's voice.

'Can we see him, then?' Rico said.

'I'm afraid not,' the light said again. 'The Commissioner died this morning. He fell from his balcony.'

Rico and Su glanced at each other, then Rico edged back to the stairs and peeked into the abyss, trying to imagine the drop. The whistling of the wind, the ground looming, the awful knowledge that in just a few more moments that would be it, the end, no comeback, body so smashed that no surgery could repair it.

'Ouch,' he said. Suddenly he felt a lot less secure in the apartment's agrav safeties and he stepped back into the security of the room again.

'It was tragic,' the light agreed.

'I think we should go,' Su said.

'Go?' Rico protested. 'But we haven't got what we came—'

'Rico, I don't think now is a good time for removing items from the late Commissioner's apartment, do you?' Su murmured.

Rico glanced around, then back at the light. 'We'll see ourselves out, if that's OK,' he said.

'Of course.' Rico watched as the light moved away, then turned back to Su.

'Look,' he said, 'the place is crawling with Ops . . .'

'*Security* Ops,' Su hissed.

'. . . so who's going to notice a couple of extra?'

'Rico, we're *Field* Ops. Completely different thing.'

Rico grinned and plucked at the tunic of his own uniform. The cut and colours – yellow, with red piping – were just the same: Security and Field Ops all worked for the College. 'If you've got it,' he said, 'use it. Su, the sooner we find what we're after, the sooner we can leave, right?' He blocked any further argument by swinging round on his heel and

heading off for where he assumed the study was.

Rico paused in the doorway because the room was already occupied. A slight, blonde woman a few years older than him, and a man his age; dark hair, pale eyes. They were talking closely to each other, voices barely more than a murmur, and Rico almost apologized for interrupting. Then he remembered he was masquerading as a Security Op and didn't have to apologize to anyone, so he sidled in without announcing himself. He sneaked a look around: where to start?

The study was decorated with a typical Home Time eclecticism. Fake bookshelves lined the walls, the carpet glowed with 1960s psychedelia and in an alcove there was a bust of Jean Morbern, founder of the College. Rico chose a shelf at random and started to examine what was on it.

'. . . suicide,' said the woman behind him. 'He was so . . . so alive, Hossein. He enjoyed existing so much. And look around you – he was so *tidy*! If Li had wanted to kill himself he'd have used one of the bureaux.'

'I know how much he meant to you, Marje . . .'

'And retirement! Li was going to retire any day now! He had it all arranged . . .'

Retirement? Rico thought, with another glance around at this mini-palace in the Himalayas. Retirement meant moving out into space, to one of the retirement worlds; the one concession the space nations made to their native Earth to prevent their home world from being completely overrun.

Well, if Daiho had to chuck all this in . . . maybe the suicide idea had something to it.

The man sounded like someone who wasn't used to having to sound sympathetic. 'Let's not jump to conclusions,' he said. 'We should wait for the autopsy report.' Rico carefully didn't think of how much body there would be left to perform an autopsy on, after a fall from that height. 'For now, Li would want you to get on with the job. Who are you?'

Rico was only half listening and it took a moment to realize he was being addressed. He turned round, fingers pressed innocently to his chest. The man and the woman were both looking at him. The woman's eyes were red and damp: she had taken the loss of the Commissioner hard. The man's pale eyes were just hostile and his head was tilted to one side, as if Rico looked familiar in some way.

'Op Garron,' Rico said. He remembered he was playing Security. 'And you, sir?'

The man was taken aback. 'Hossein Asaldra. I'm the personal assistant to—'

'Me, Marje Orendal,' said the woman. 'I'm Head of Psychological Profiles at the College . . . and apparently I've been appointed Acting Commissioner to replace Li. Commissioner Daiho.'

'Have we met before?' Asaldra said. He still had that quizzical look on his face.

'You're the new Commissioner for Correspondents?' Rico said to the woman, caught off-

guard. He hadn't expected to bluff with this level of seniority. On the other hand, she was sufficiently senior that he could ignore Asaldra's question quite safely.

'Acting,' the woman repeated.

'What are you doing here?' Asaldra said, apparently deciding, as Rico already had, that the answer to his last question was 'no'. 'You people have already been over this room.' He spoke blandly, almost sounding bored, but still managed to convey animosity.

Rico decided the truth was called for. 'I'm looking for a field computer,' he said. 'Comm . . . the late Commissioner booked it out and never returned it.'

The woman rolled her eyes to the ceiling. 'Bureaucracy goes on. Well, carry on looking, Op Garron.'

'It will be returned to Fieldwork when the Commissioner's effects are cleared,' the man said. 'Why is a field computer any concern . . .' He paused and his face went blank for a moment. He was symbing into the copy of the College database held somewhere in the apartment and Rico knew the bluff had just evaporated. 'There is no Security Operative Garron,' he said. 'There is a Field Operative of that name. You're not Security, are you?'

'My partner and I made an appointment with the household,' Rico said. 'We were expected.'

'Why's a field computer so important?' Orendal said.

Rico gave an embarrassed grin. 'I, um, stored data on my last field trip and never downloaded it,' he said. 'I thought it might still be there . . .'

'Your sloppy work is your problem, not ours,' Asaldra said. 'I think you had better leave and stop intruding on the Acting Commissioner's grief.'

Since the Acting Commissioner was standing five feet away from him and perfectly capable of speaking for herself, Rico felt his blood rising.

'Of course,' he said directly to her, 'you have to ask why the Commissioner would check out a field computer if he was going to—'

'That will do,' Asaldra said. 'I've had enough of this. I'm calling Security.'

'Just shout,' Rico said. 'They're everywhere.'

But a Security Op was already in the doorway. She shot Rico a curious glance before addressing the other two.

'Acting Commissioner, Secretary, I thought you should know the autopsy report is in.'

'And?' Orendal said quickly.

'Commissioner Li Daiho died of an aneurysm, ma'am. An artery in his head must have burst and killed him immediately. He was probably dead when he fell off the balcony.'

'It was definitely him?' Orendal gave the impression of a woman desperately clinging onto hope.

'The body was smashed badly but we got residual brain patterns. It was him.'

Orendal's shoulders sagged. 'The poor man.'

'It could have happened at any time,' said Asaldra, nodding wisely.

'So why didn't the agravs stop his body falling?' Rico said to the Security Op. 'Someone would have to turn them off.'

'The agravs haven't been touched since their last routine maintenance . . . who are you?' the Op said.

'Someone who shouldn't be here,' Asaldra said. 'Kindly see that this man is escorted off the premises. Now.'

'You're Su! Su Zo!' Orendal exclaimed suddenly. She was looking past Rico when Su, who had been trying to lurk in the background, reluctantly came forward.

'Marje?' she said.

'You know this woman, Commissioner?' Asaldra sounded somewhere between disapproving and disappointed.

'We did our basic induction together,' Marje said. 'How are you, Su?'

'I'm doing OK,' Su said.

'You went into Fieldwork, I heard?'

Su nodded. 'Senior Field Op. I heard about your promotion, Marje, I'd say congratulations, but . . .'

'I know.' Orendal pursed her lips but managed a smile. 'Thank you.'

'I'll take my partner and leave, if that's all right with you?' Su said. She plucked at Rico's sleeve and didn't let go.

Orendal's smile grew slightly less forced. 'It might be wise. I'll see you around, Su.'

*　*　*

'That went well,' Su said as they stepped into the courtyard. It was the first time she had trusted herself to speak since taking their leave of Orendal and Asaldra.

Rico grunted.

'It's not often you get the chance to be rude to one of the most senior people in the organization that employs you,' Su went on.

'She was Acting and I wasn't rude to her.'

'Her friend seemed to think you were.'

'Yeah, well, her friend was another matter.' Rico thought back to those pale eyes, the hostile tone, and decided he could live with the knowledge that he had made an enemy. 'Pair of tossers anyway. Wait here.'

'Now what are you—' Su said, but Rico had already scooped up two handfuls of pebbles from the gravel that surrounded the fountain. He walked back to the balcony and the drop down the mountainside, held out his left hand and opened his fingers. The pebbles fell three inches, then stopped in mid-air, spinning gently. They floated back over the stone parapet and fell at Rico's feet.

'Yup, the agravs work all right,' Rico said. Then without warning he drew back his right hand and flung the other handful as far as he could into the abyss. The pebbles flew out in a scattered arc and plunged into the depths below. Rico followed them with his eyes, leaning out over the stonework as far as he could.

'Aha,' he said.

'Just what are you doing, Garron?' Su demanded.

'Just testing a theory.'

'And?'

'It works but it doesn't make sense. Come on.' They walked back across the courtyard to the recall area, and thirty seconds later were back in the Home Time.

The time display set into the wall of the spherical transference chamber showed it was fifteen minutes after they had left – precisely the time they had spent in Commissioner Daiho's apartment. The apartment had a constant and timed stream of transmit and recall fields going under the control of the Register, the artificial mind that governed transference, and this was the Register's arbitrary way of handling the flow of cause and effect. It could have brought them back a second after they had left, but the rules were that however long you spent upstream, that was how long elapsed before you were back in the Home Time. One of the tenets of Morbern's Code:

The span of my life is synchronised to other lives around me. I will not abuse the power of the College to break that synchronisation.

. . . as Rico and Su could have recited without even thinking about it.

'I know you don't like the correspondents,' Su

said as they stepped out of the chamber. Outside, the transference hall would have dwarfed a cathedral. The chambers were silver spheres set into walkways – row upon row, above, below and beside them.

'It's not that.' Rico scowled at her. 'It's not that she's replacing the Commissioner for Correspondents. That's a job for politicos who might not have had anything to do with the College.'

'Then what?'

'It's what she was. Still is. Head of Psychological Profiles. She's the one who decides if someone's suitable for being a correspondent or not. She's the one who sends them out to their deaths in the first place.'

'Funny,' Su said, 'I could have sworn you worked for the College. You know, the organization that employs her and pays her to send them out to their deaths.'

Rico growled. His relationship with and feelings towards the College were complex, and she knew it.

'Not everything the College does is bad,' he muttered.

'Oh, Rico.' Su took his hand and looked into his eyes. 'Look. You blew it once and you were lucky. Please, please don't do it again.'

'I won't drag you down,' Rico said.

'It's not me I'm worried about, you cretin.'

Rico changed the subject. 'We should get to work. What does the Register have planned for us today?'

'Escort duty. A professor and some students to Amazonia, C14, alpha stream.'

'Off we go, then.'

They went off to change into their fieldsuits and to meet up with the group they were to escort. An hour later they had again left the Home Time.

Four

The air was warm and close under the canopy of trees, and the ground was speckled by the sunlight that beamed through the leaves. The hum of life was everywhere – the humus on the ground, the leaves up above, and the thriving chain of eco-systems around the tree trunks that linked the two. Life was engaged in a constant, to-the-death battle with itself and yet was involved in an intricate balance, every organism depending minutely on every other.

It was also sauna-bath hot and the group of humans who materialized out of the shadows began to sweat buckets the moment they appeared. But that was OK, Rico Garron thought, because they were probably taking the same water back in with every breath of the humid air.

A monkey swung through the branches over-head and Rico was sure it had noticed them, but it wasn't concerned. He and the rest of the party were doused in neutral pheromones and they had been inserted into the timestream with minimal disturbance, so the monkey might have had a brief disorientation but was otherwise un-disturbed. As it should be.

He returned his attention to the group and listened to Su ending her Senior Field Op's spiel. Her sleeve was rolled back and she was studying her forearm. Her field computer was embedded there and data symbols ran over her skin. Field Ops had to travel unnoticed amongst bygoner people and their equipment had to be as unobtrusive as possible, though in this case that wasn't an issue. They were in the middle of uninhabited jungle and their fieldsuits were in their natural, non-camo state: slick, dark grey gelfabric.

'We are at sixty degrees west, four degrees south,' Su said. 'In the Home Time this is the middle of Brasilia ecopolis. There's a tributary of the Amazon ten miles north of us.'

'Are there predators?' said one of the students. He was a pale, nervous young man.

Rico showed his teeth in a smile without humour. 'Almost certainly. Everything around here preds.' The student went even paler. Rico symbed a command to his own field computer and a display appeared in his vision. 'But there's nothing dan-gerous at present within a quarter of a mile, and certainly no bygoners. Your repulsion field is keyed to the local fauna and it'll come on if anything predatory approaches you.'

'You've had your training.' Professor Onskiro took charge and she sounded irritated at students who obviously hadn't listened to their briefing.

'Thank you, Field Ops. When do you want us back?'

'We'll be recalled twelve hours from now,' Su said.

'Then we return to this location no later than eleven hours from now,' Onskiro said. 'Give us time for a debrief. Activate your beacons now, get into your teams . . .'

The students huddled round their leader and, apart from seeing that no one interfered with the ecosystem, or wandered off into the jungle and got lost, or removed anything other than the plant specimens they were authorized to collect, Su and Rico were suddenly redundant. Assuming no emergency in the next twelve hours, their next job would be tagging the specimens that were to be taken back to the Home Time, sensitizing them to the probability frequency of the recall field.

Rico tilted his head back again to admire the leaf canopy. He lived in a community module which had no natural views at all – he remembered with envy the view from Daiho's place – in a block with five million other people, and he had grown up in a crèche, an orphan taken in and raised by the College. Here it was hot and sticky, despite the cooling action of his fieldsuit, but he loved it. This wasn't the regulated and balanced ecology of an ecopolis – this was real. Once it had been the artificial world of the future that had been real to him – it was where he had grown up – but then he had gone on his first trip upstream and become a convert to the joys of nature.

Su swung the pack off her back. 'Drink, Rico?'

'Thanks. Don't mind if I do.'

They sat cross-legged on the mulch and Su poured out two cups. She handed one over. 'Brazilian coffee.'

'Appropriate.' They sipped their drinks. 'Su?' Rico said.

'Yes?'

'Tell me about your friend Marje.'

'Why do you care? I thought you loathed her on principle.'

'Humour me.'

Su shrugged. 'We don't see much of each other and I wouldn't say she's my friend. We just joined the College at the same time.'

'She looks older than you.'

'She is. She's a psychologist and she was a partner in a practice, but as I recall she felt she wasn't contributing enough to . . . I don't know, the common good. She wanted to contribute more, and what organization contributes the most? The College. So, she joined, and by all appearances hasn't done too badly for herself.' Su pierced Rico with a look. 'Now, why do you want to know?'

Rico grinned. 'It's just that she's high up. Higher up than that prick who was with her, and I wouldn't ask him anyway.'

'Higher up for what?' Su said cautiously.

Rico put his cup down and lay back, propping himself on one elbow. 'Why would a Commissioner want a field computer?' he said.

'Did it ever occur to you it might not be any of your business? Perhaps he wanted to show it to one of his grandchildren.'

'And then there's the agravs. They should have stopped him falling . . .'

'Here we go again . . .'

'It's my old-fashioned scientific mind,' Rico said, and Su almost choked on her coffee. 'One tiny little fact which doesn't fit the theory, and I dismiss the theory rather than the facts.'

'So what does this have to do with Marje?' Su said.

'She has authority we could never get even if we asked,' Rico said. 'If we could raise her suspicions and get her to do some investigating of her own, she could find out more than we ever will.'

'We?' Su said.

'Aren't you even remotely curious?'

'No.' Su took another swig of her coffee and put the cup down. 'Look. Ever since you got bust down, you've made a point of not caring about anything. Why are you so worked up now?'

Rico narrowed his eyes. Su was one of the few people – correct that, the only person – in the whole of the Home Time whom he would allow to refer so casually to his being busted. But she had a point. Why was he so fixated?

'It just bugs me,' he said. 'That's all.'

A scream echoed through the jungle, inspiring a responding chorus from the bird life, and immediately Rico and Su were on their feet and

running towards its source. They knew the difference between animal noises and terrified humans,
and they knew which sort that scream had been.

'*Go to agrav,*' Rico symbed at Su. Their fieldsuits
had in-built symb units and they could communicate as easily here as in the Home Time. The agrav
harnesses beneath their fieldsuits came on and the
two Field Ops leaped through the undergrowth,
covering ten or twenty feet with a bound.

'*Stay low. You'll just get tangled if you get into the tree
tops,*' Rico added. He could have flown with the
agrav but there just wasn't room.

'*How lucky I am to have you,*' Su symbed back, not
breaking her step. The irony was just strong
enough to remind Rico that she was the senior, not
he. But he had been trained for harder and dirtier
missions than this, and old habits died hard, and
she knew he was better than she was at this sort of
thing.

They were near their target and the symb display
in Rico's vision indicated three Home Timers surrounded by a large group of smaller primates. And
then he was through the leaves and in sight of the
scene, and he saw the mistake the sensors had
made. It was three Home Timers and a small group
of larger primates: human beings, to be precise.
One student writhed on the ground with an arrow
sticking from his shoulder and the other two
cowered under the spears of the natives. They were
small men, barely coming up to the shoulders of
the Home Timers; naked but for loincloths; nut

41

brown skin decorated with paint; dark knots of jet black hair.

Rico let out a wild whoop at the top of his voice and symbed the command '*full radiance*' at his fieldsuit so that it immediately blazed with white light. Su followed his example. It was stage one of the standard operating procedure for frightening bygoners from primitive cultures, and the sight of two whooping, yelling, shining beings leaping and bounding through the trees towards them made most of the natives turn and flee.

Three of them, visibly terrified, still stood their ground and brought their weapons up. For stage two, Rico raised his right hand and sparks flew from his fingertips, stinging two of them painfully. They yelped, dropped their spears and followed their friends.

The last man was made of the sternest stuff of all, which perversely made Rico take an immediate liking to him. He was pale beneath his naturally dark skin, but he shifted his feet into a slightly firmer position, braced himself, looked Rico in the eyes and brought his spear to bear as the Field Op touched down in front of him. Rico cancelled the blazing light and smiled, holding his hands out: *look, no harm.* The man feinted, then lunged at him. Rico didn't even need the fieldsuit: he twisted to one side, caught the man as he ran past and rendered him unconscious with a simple jab at the right spot on the neck. The man crumpled, face down, next to the student.

Sorry, thought Rico.

Su was already tending to the stricken, groaning Home Timer so Rico turned the native over, checking him for damage. He would live.

'Kill him!'

Rico looked up in surprise at one of the other students. A young woman, late teens or early twenties.

'Kill him!' she spat. She could have looked attractive if her face hadn't been twisted with hate. 'He's an animal!'

Rico stood up slowly to face her, then, more quickly than she could react, tapped her lightly on the cheek. 'He's as human as you are, and he's probably an ancestor, so show a bit of respect.'

'He killed Veci! He could have killed us!' Back in the Home Time, her social preparation would have taken over. Her symb would have transmitted her mental condition to the central systems and positive images of peace and calm would be pumping into her brain right now. But here, her fear and anger could go unchecked.

Rico glanced down at Su, still kneeling beside the boy. She shook her head. 'They used a curare dart on him, but he'll live,' she said.

She rose to stand next to Rico and glared at the other two students, waving the dart she had pulled from the boy under their noses. 'Not that he deserves to: his suit's neutralizer and defences were switched off. The poison would have killed him in another minute if we hadn't got here. Weren't you listening?'

Su and Rico had carefully briefed the students on fieldsuit protocol and a host of other issues before the transference. Properly managed, the suit would have detected the incoming arrow and switched on its repulsion field. And if any dangerous toxins had made it into the bloodstream, the neutralizer would have taken care of it.

'They attacked us!' the girl repeated, ignoring her.

'I'm not surprised.' Rico had just noticed what was hanging in the bushes behind them. He didn't know exactly what the carved bits of wood were meant to be but he recognized a shrine when he saw it. 'You're probably blaspheming against their gods, or something, just by being here. We should move.'

The girl turned to follow his line of sight. 'Oh, that,' she said with a complete lack of interest.

'You don't think much of it?' Rico said.

The other student, a young man, spoke for the first time.

'We have the greatest respect for their religious practices,' he said: smooth, calm, *patronizing* in a way that made Rico grit his teeth.

'But . . . but we know they're a load of superstitious bygoner nonsense,' Rico said with a friendly, baffled smile. The student chuckled, a bit strained after his shock but trying at sophistication.

'Well, of course, we know that . . .'

'Don't have a lot of respect for them, then, do you?' said Rico, leaving the student stranded by the abrupt turn.

'Where were you, anyway?' the girl demanded. 'You're meant to be protecting us.'

'Are you dead?' said Rico.

'No, but . . .'

'Then what's the problem?'

'Our sensors misinterpreted the threat,' Su said quietly. 'With all this biomass around us they can get confused.'

'I'm suing the College when we get back!'

'Fine.' Su finally lost patience. 'We'll leave you here. As for the moment, your friend's laziness nearly cost him his life, and you three's disregard for bygoner sensitivities probably provoked the attack in the first place. As Senior Field Op, I'm abandoning this mission. When your friend can walk, the three of you are coming with me. Rico, round up Onskiro and the rest and rendezvous at the recall point.'

'I love you when you're angry.' He quickly touched a knuckle to his forehead when Su glared at him. 'Right away, ma'am.'

There was the usual disorientation as the shadows of the fourteenth-century Brazilian rainforest faded out and the lightly glowing walls of the transference chamber appeared around them. It was a hollow sphere with a floor provided by a carry-field that sliced it in half. The top hemisphere in which they stood could have held fifty adults. Even experienced transferees like Rico and Su always needed a moment to collect themselves,

45

remember where they were and what they were doing.

Rico was amused to see looks of relief on the faces of some of the students, which they tried to hide, when it finally dawned on them that they were back home. He knew they were slaves of their conditioning. The past was officially a nasty, dirty place where people had no social preparation and were cruel and mean to each other, as recent events had shown. For these poor sods, Rico thought, when the past was compared and contrasted with the controlled environment of an ecopolis, coming back to the Home Time was like returning to the womb.

And that was why the authorities were happy to let the impression abide. For Rico, on the other hand, returning to the Home Time was more and more depressing every time he did it.

Su was discharging the last of her duties. 'All of you, shut your eyes until I tell you to open them.' They all did so, and felt the warmth of the decon field flow around them, making them safe for re-entry into the Home Time. 'You can open them now. Place your specimens in those containers there, please, for scanning . . . Thank you. I now declare this excursion to be over. Walk slowly through the exit . . .'

They were the last two to leave. Like Su, Rico held up his arm and touched the 'release' icon that appeared there. By his elbow a small flap of skin appeared, which he took between thumb and forefinger and pulled. There was a tingling as the computer disengaged from his nervous system and what looked like the skin of his forearm peeled away, leaving the real skin reddened but healthy beneath it. His arm was shaved but still he winced as it snagged on a couple of budding hairs.

'Thank you for the trip, Register,' Su said as they walked out of the chamber and into the huge, multi-tiered vault of the transference hall.

'My pleasure, Op Zo,' said a friendly voice out of the air.

'But before you go . . .' said another voice behind them. Rico groaned beneath his breath, and they turned to face the red-outlined symb projection that had appeared in the middle of the room. The eidolon showed a short, squat man: Rico had heard him called 'Toad Face' and had never understood the epithet, until he had actually seen a toad on a field trip. Then he had understood perfectly.

'Supervisor Marlici,' said Su, taking the initiative as senior partner. 'What can we do for you?'

'I'll come straight to the point,' Marlici said. He had full, wet lips which, Rico reflected, seemed made to quiver with indignation. It was the state in which he usually saw them. 'No beating about the bush, no prevarication. I've received a formal complaint from the office of the Commissioner for Correspondents about you, Op Garron, and by extension, you, Op Zo. Well?'

The vindictive bitch! Rico opened his mouth—

'May we know the substance of this complaint?'
Su asked.

'The complaint,' Marlici said, 'is that Op Garron
bothered the Acting Commissioner in the late
Commissioner Daiho's apartment this morning. I
won't go into details –' he smiled thinly – 'but the
words "absurd speculation" and "grotesque
fantasies" were heard to be uttered.' Rico's cheeks
began to burn. 'None of this would be my concern,
of course, if you were off duty, but at the time you
were on duty. I'm consumed with curiosity as to
what you were doing in the Commissioner's suite,
and why Op Garron impersonated a Security
Op, and why you, Op Zo, let him. Well?'

Something inside Rico snapped and he took a
step forward. 'This is—'

Su put a hand on his arm. 'We were there on official business, sir,' she said.

'Re-ally?' Marlici seemed to enjoy drawing out
the word. 'Do tell me how, when I knew nothing of
it.'

'Rico?' Su said. Rico breathed deeply, twice,
before answering.

'On my last but one field trip,' he said, 'I failed
to download all the information I had stored in my
field computer. I needed to get the computer back.
When I asked for it, I learned it had been signed
out again.'

'You think you have a special right to equipment?' said Marlici. Rico suspected that his explanation was sounding far too reasonable and

48

Marlici was determined to find fault somehow.

'I don't recall saying that, sir,' he said. 'It had been signed out again by Commissioner Daiho. I tried to contact him so that I could copy the data over. He wasn't available but the Register arranged things with his household so that we could go there and retrieve the computer ourselves. Which we did, and met the Acting Commissioner.'

So there, he added silently. *Stick that in your chamber and transfer it.*

'I see.' The smile had left Marlici's face the moment Rico mentioned the Register. What the Register chose to do was not subject to the whims of any supervisor. However, Marlici rallied quickly. 'And impersonating a Security Op?' Su opened her mouth. 'I was addressing Op Garron,' he said.

'I identified myself as Op Garron,' Rico said. 'I said nothing about Security.' He tried not to smile. Two points down: Marlici was running out of ammunition. 'Now, sir, if you'll excuse us . . .'

'One moment. The last thing.' *Damn.* 'These, ah, theories with which you regaled the Acting Commissioner?'

'Theories, sir?' Rico said with reluctance. Su was looking at him and very slightly shaking her head.

'Apparently you speculated as to whether the agravs were sabotaged.'

'I did not!' Rico exclaimed. 'I just said—'

'Op Garron,' Marlici said, 'you're a Field Operative. You escort away parties upstream. You

49

are a hired gun, you are not a detective and you don't pursue your paranoid delusions on College time, is that understood? And you, Op Zo, as senior partner should know better than to let this ... this spoo—'

Marlici caught himself, though Rico was wishing him on. *Go on, say it! Spookboy! And then I can report you for abusive language, and won't that be fun?*

'Individual,' said Marlici – and Rico thought, *damn!* – 'get into situations beyond the capacity of his atrophied brain cells to comprehend.' He drew himself up and looked down his nose at Su, the only one of the pair he *could* look down at. *Official prat pose number one*, Rico thought. 'Op Zo, unofficially, you are warned. Op Garron, officially, you are reprimanded.' He paused to savour Rico's expression. 'Do you know, that's a total of two reprimands on your record,' he murmured in an aside to himself. 'Dear oh dear.'

The eidolon vanished, leaving them both looking at the space where it had been.

Su spoke first. She reached out and touched Rico's shoulder. 'I'm sorry, Rico.'

'Bitch!' The word burst out and Su looked taken aback, until she realized it wasn't directed at her. 'That spiteful, malicious . . . *bitch!*'

'Rico . . .'

'A reprimand? A reprimand, for . . . for what? Was I rude to her? Did I insult her? Did I assault her? Su, did I even mention Security? Can I help it if she got it wrong? I thought maybe, just maybe she might be a teensy bit more human than the other high-and-mighties, worked up through the ranks and all that, but no, she's Acting Commissioner for five minutes and suddenly she's as bad as the rest of them.'

'Rico . . .' Su said again.

'And I wanted her on our side! Well, forget that—'

'Op Garron, shut up,' Su said. 'We don't have a side, remember? You'd love there to be foul play but there wasn't. He died naturally and if there was something about the agravs, Security will find it. For us, it's over, Rico.'

Rico was silent for a moment. He reached up and fondled her hand that was still on his shoulder. 'Yeah, it's over. Su, there's two reprimands on my record now. I can't afford a third.' A third, they both knew, meant automatic suspension pending a formal enquiry into conduct.

'You won't get it if you behave.'

Rico snorted. 'Yeah, easy to say, Su. How many have you had? Somewhere between nought and none, isn't it? But not me. The spookboy makes another balls-up. You noticed that, didn't you? He almost said it.'

Spookboy. Or *spookgirl*, of course. Someone not born in the Home Time, and in certain quarters, a term of purest contempt.

'Oh, Rico . . .'

'I'm sorry I got you into it too, Su. Next time my paranoid delusions start to take over, say to me, "Op

51

Garron, your paranoid delusions are taking over." I promise I won't mind.'

'I'll remember that. Shall we get the Register to witness?'

Rico twitched the corners of his mouth, but it was more to make an effort for her than to show genuine mirth. 'Nah. I enjoy getting paranoid. Senior Field Op Su Zo, I believe we're off duty?'

'We are now.'

'Then I'm off to pursue my fantasies. Should be safe as long as it's not on College time.'

'Fancy a drink?'

'Thanks, but . . .' He shook his head. 'Go and see your family, Su.' He walked towards the exit of the hall with his resentment like a dark, heavy lump, deep inside him. It was festering nicely.

Rico was still angry as the taxi approached the sheer white coral cliffs of Azania ecopolis. The breathtaking view as the taxi passed over the ecopolis' organic building clusters and parks, lights glowing in the night, had a slightly pacifying effect. It reminded him of how far he had come in his life. To keep his ire going, he started to mutter 'bitch, bitch, bitch' under his breath.

The taxi threw itself at the land coral cliff that was the residence cluster where he lived, and dropped effortlessly into one of the taxi ways that ran sponge-like through and around the structure. After another minute, it drew to a halt as close to his community module as it was going to get.

Door-to-door service wasn't an option at his social level. Community modules in this section were arranged around a large mock Aztec plaza, complete with looming jungle in the background and insect noises, which at this time of night was empty, so he was spared having to mix with his neighbours. He and they never really got on: technically their memeplexes all contributed equally to the consensus running of the module, but when you're in a minority it's easy to be overruled and overlooked by the majority. It is especially easy when that majority is afraid of you because they know full well you have more relaxed social preparation than they do and that you actively prefer not being in the Home Time.

His anger was nicely peaking as he reached the door of his own module. Externally, it seemed to be an adobe hut. The suites here were all for single persons and he shared the module with nine others, but they too were all asleep and he could get to his own place without breaking his pace or train of thought.

'Aggression therapy,' he said out loud as he walked into his main room. Inside was very different, comfortable and minimally decorated in a completely Home Time style. 'Level five.'

'Welcome home, Rico. Would you not rather shower and change first?' The voice of the household made him look down at himself. He was still in the fieldsuit he had worn for the Brazil trip. Normally he would have showered and changed back at the College; indeed, normally he would have showered, changed, and had a meal and a drink with Su, or perhaps been invited back to the Zos' suite in a Pacifican multi-family module where Uncle Rico was already a hit with the next generation, in his capacity as mobile climbing frame.

Normally. Today was different.

'I'm already hot and sweaty,' he said. 'Let's go.'

'Very well,' said the module.

Rico walked into the aggression room, which was white, sterile and padded, without anything hard to fall against. The dummy was waiting for him, poised for combat. Level five meant it would make at least a few moves to fight back. He hurled himself at it without warning, bringing it down in a tackle around the hips. While it wriggled to get free he pinned it down, sitting astride its chest, and proceeded to pummel its blank, yielding face.

This was no good. Too easy.

'Stand and go to level ten,' he said. He and the dummy squared off, and this time the dummy came for him. He seized its arm, twisted round and sent it over his shoulder. The dummy recovered and spun round, and its foot came for his head. He ducked under it and kicked both feet out at the dummy's groin, breaking his fall with a roll that brought him back to his feet again.

'Full attack and defence,' he said. This would be no holds barred and he spent a joyous five minutes blocking, parrying and lunging, occasionally letting one of the dummy's safely padded blows get through his defence. He had programmed it with the full course that any Field Operative had to undertake – a blend of the best of the many forms of unarmed martial arts from humanity's history. It was as good as any machine was allowed to get when it came to possibly hurting a human; in other words, it was as close a match as social preparation would ever allow him to have with anyone.

'Enough,' he said eventually, with a broad grin on his face. He collapsed against one of the walls and slid down it, panting. On the other side of the room the dummy did likewise. Even at those times when the victory was clearly and distinctly his, it somehow diminished the triumph of the moment to have him lying panting on the floor while the dummy stood passively over him. 'Assess,' he said.

'Blows that connected: seventy-two per cent of your own, forty-eight per cent of the dummy's.'

'Pretty good. Pretty bloody good.' If he had actually tried to hurt a human being within the Home Time then social preparation and his symb connection would have done their best to immobilize him, but there was nothing to stop him *pretending* that the dummy had been Acting Commissioner Marje Orendal.

'Now,' he said, 'about that shower.'

After a stinging hot needle shower, a massage and a light meal, and with a drink in his hand, he felt much better. Warm, relaxed, contented. He lounged in his favourite chair, legs stuck out so far in front of him that he was almost lying down, and looked around him with a dour smile. Maybe he could get used to it here. His recent demotion had meant moving to a smaller suite, but even the last had been smaller than Daiho's Himalayan pad, which was practically a module in its own right. But in this (slightly smaller) suite of which he was master there was a main room, a bedroom, a bathroom and an aggression room – four rooms that were *entirely his*. Not bad for a spookboy from the crèche; a child no one wanted to adopt, to give some kind of start in life to, because – well, because he was a spookboy, he came from the past and the past was bad. By sheer hard work and without any kind of sponsorship, he had worked up to this.

He had done all right, and two reprimands weren't going to change that.

But as he undressed for bed, another thought struck him. The fact was, he still didn't have that computer. Maybe he would just have to write it off: fate seemed to be against his getting it back. But he also still didn't have an answer to a question he had put to Su in fourteenth-century Brazil. What did the Commissioner for Correspondents, who never did any fieldwork of his own, want with a field computer?

Five

For Jontan Baiget, a biotech journeyman on the Holmberg-Chabani-Scott plantation, the journey to the Dark Ages started like a perfectly normal day, five thousand feet below the surface of the Pacific, north-east of the Marquesas. It was the day before Union Day.

Jontan left the dormitory that morning and headed with his friends to the foreman's office to be given the day's tasks. His group and the women's contingent got there at about the same time, to the strains of the usual repartee.

From the men:

'Wha-hey!'

'All right, girls?'

'Over here, love, over here!'

From the women:

'Do your mummies know you're out, boys?'

'Too small for me.'

'Any three of you, OK? Any three of you.'

Back home in Appalachia ecopolis the journey-men could mix with whom they liked. On the plantation they were kept apart, except for their professional duties and carefully chaperoned off-duty get-togethers. Journeymen were expected to keep their minds on their work. Jontan glanced up. Was she . . .

Yes, she was. Sarai Killin was there and looking as fed up with the catcalls as he felt. She met his eye for a moment, half smiled and looked away again.

They had known each other since childhood days in their module crèche in Appalachia. As they got older he had become aware of two disturbing factors: she was becoming more and more attractive, with her dark eyes and short brown hair and slender figure that always lurked at the back of his mind and just wouldn't go away, and he was becoming less and less so with what he considered his quite unreasonably big ears, general gangliness, hair that just wouldn't do anything . . .

But tomorrow was Union Day, and all the journeymen would be going to the same party, so there was hope.

'Baiget.' The foreman called his name and he stepped forward. 'Sector twelve, abnormalities at cellular level in nutrient solution.'

Two other journeymen and a supervisor were assigned to the same job and a grounder took them there, skimming along the path that ran through the golden corn. It was a sight that cheered him up and took his mind off the non-chances of ever getting closer to Sarai. The ground beneath was reclaimed sea bed, the 'sky' was pitch black – not much sun got through five thousand feet of water – and the plantation existed in a forcebubble, full of artificial air and light, but Jontan felt completely at home there. And happy, and proud. The world around him held twenty billion people and the Holmberg-Chabani-Scott plantation helped feed them, and he, in his own small way, was helping with the process.

Their destination was a pumping station that looked over a thousand acres of reclaimed sea bed. The grounder approached in a curve to avoid the gaze of a nearby UV pylon that faced safely away from them and poured its beneficent ultraviolet rays into the force-grown corn.

Inside the station the journeymen got to work. The station supplied the solution that was meant to be nourishing the seed germs, and 'abnormalities at cellular level' essentially meant mini-cancers above the usual rate of cell division. The solution was notoriously unstable and could go bad at the slightest unwanted variable – the proportion of chemicals in it, the ambient heat, a slightly pro-longed filtration session. The solution suffered, the corn suffered and the crop suffered.

The job was split between the three journeymen. One looked at the solution that entered the station, Jontan studied the mixing process and the third checked the output. The supervisor hovered in the background, somehow seeming to be looking over the shoulders of all three of them at once.

An hour later they had made progress, or at least

they had eliminated possibilities. There was nothing contaminating the solution in the station and the supervisor was getting redder and redder in the face.

'Nothing wrong at this end. Nothing at all. But the solution is cancerous when it gets to the far end. Well, laddies, looks like we're going to have to check the pipework . . .'

Oh, goody, more work, Jontan thought. He pushed himself back in his seat and stretched, gazing out of the window at the corn that was the ultimate beneficiary of their hard work. He frowned, then smiled slowly and stood up.

'Going somewhere, Baiget?' The supervisor stopped him with his hand on the door.

'Sir . . .'

'It's at the back, Baiget. You don't go outside. That'd really foul up the solution.'

The other two journeymen sniggered.

'Sir, that pylon's directly between us and the field,' Jontan said.

'So?'

'I'll bet the pipeline from this station runs straight from us to the field, too.'

The supervisor frowned. 'It can't be . . .' He turned to a display and called up a schematic of sector twelve. Sure enough, a red line ran from the square that was the station to the shaded yellow that was the edge of the field, and the UV pylon stood right over it.

'Which moron moved that there?' the supervisor

bellowed. The pylons weren't fixed and they got moved around according to the whims of the agronomists. Radiation spillage was quite enough to upset the cell chemistry of the solution passing through the pipes.

The supervisor symbed Control. 'Request shutdown of pylon 12-UV-970. Don't worry, won't take long.' A pause, then: 'Right, you two, get over there and shift it. Stay here, Baiget.'

When the two other journeymen were gone, the supervisor shook his head. 'How long had you known about that, Baiget?'

'Um, I saw it just now, sir . . .'

'And you were going to move it all by yourself? Did it occur to you you'd get fried? And if it did, did it occur to you that you don't have the authority to shut it down to prevent frying?'

'Um . . .'

'You're talented, Baiget,' the supervisor said grudgingly. 'You can think laterally – you don't just go through the motions that the book says you should. Just learn to play in the team, OK? It'll do you a world of good.'

A symbed call broke into both their thoughts. '*Journeyman Baiget report to the foreman's office immediately.*'

Jontan looked at the supervisor in surprise. The supervisor looked back. 'Still here, Baiget?'

There was another man in with the foreman – tall, dark-haired, bearded and immaculately dressed.

Jontan immediately began to feel self-conscious on behalf of his working clothes.

'This is Baiget, sir,' said the foreman.

'I see.' For some reason Jontan expected the bearded man to walk around him and study him, but all he did was say, 'You did well in your exams, Baiget. Congratulations.'

'Thank you, sir.'

'Where's the other?' The man was talking to the foreman now.

'Should be here soon, Mr Scott.'

Mr Scott! And this was the Holmberg-Chabani-Scott plantation. Jontan doubted he was *the* Mr Scott, head of the family, but he was a Mr Scott and that was enough. He would be a patrician, no doubt about it. And he was here.

The door opened and there were footsteps behind him. 'Come in, Killin,' said the foreman.

Jontan's heart leaped and he hardly dared look round in case it was another Killin. But no, it was Sarai Killin, standing next to him and ignoring him completely; as he should be ignoring her, in the presence of a Scott and the foreman. With an effort he turned his attention to the front.

'Now you're both—' said the foreman.

'Now you're both here,' said Scott, not even looking at the foreman but immediately silencing him, 'we'll start. I have a job that requires two biotech journeymen capable of working in unusual conditions. The best equipment will be made available but there will be no possibility of replacements or resupplies. I need people who can work with what they have and make sure that what they have works. Your aptitude tests suggest you are the two. I cannot say how long the job will last, so I have to ask, are you capable of getting on with one another? Be honest.'

Jontan and Sarai looked at each other. For a moment it occurred to Jontan that Scott shouldn't have to ask journeymen – journeymen were told, not asked – but the doubt was swept away with the thought of working with Sarai, indefinitely. And with the worry that she might say no.

'I can work with Sa— Journeyman Killin, sir,' he said. He was pleased to see one corner of her mouth twitch in a slight smile.

'I can work with Journeyman Baiget, sir,' she said.

Scott nodded. 'Good. As of now you're detached from your duties. You won't need to pack anything, just meet me at the surface port in half an hour. That's all.'

'Um, yes, sir.' Jontan and Sarai turned to go, uncertain. It hadn't been a formal dismissal such as they were used to, so . . .

'Get going,' said the foreman for their benefit.

'Yes, sir!' they said together, and went.

Phenuel Scott was pleased that the two journeymen were suitably silent as the taxi flew swiftly south-wards. It was as it should be. He had no real desire to travel with journeymen at all but he was determined to keep them in his sight at all times until they were safely ensconced at the College. He had nightmare visions of the two of them arriving at the College unaccompanied, and innocently getting lost and somehow coming to the attention of some official who would wonder why Scott had hired two biotech journeymen . . .

It didn't bear thinking about and he shook the vision away.

'We are heading,' he said, 'for the College. That is, the College of Advanced Manipulation of Probability and Chronotic Transference.'

He wasn't surprised to see a hint of awe in the looks. Aside from the plantation they'd probably never left Appalachia before.

'As well as helping with the family business, I'm the assistant to the Appalachian consul there, and you are officially on the staff as well,' he said. 'Remember that – you shouldn't have to meet any College personnel, but if you ever do, your work is Appalachian business only. You will discuss it only with consulate personnel. You will just be doing biotech work, nothing else, and you are under my sponsorship.'

That last line, he thought, should buy their loyalty if nothing else did.

'*Attention*,' the voice of the taxi symbed into their minds. '*College Defence Systems request information concerning the two unknown individuals on board this taxi.*'

'Individuals are Journeymen Killin and Baiget,

staff for the Appalachian consulate.' Scott couldn't avoid giving their titles but he had no compunction about doing so to a machine – it was unlikely any human with a sense of curiosity would hear about this. 'Visitors on authority of Phenuel Scott until due residence authorization is given.'

'Visitors are requested to identify themselves verbally.'

Scott nodded that they should do so, and they symbed their names and citizen numbers accordingly.

'Please wait,' said the taxi, and it slowed down and stopped and hovered.

'This will take a couple of minutes,' Scott said. 'There's Antarctica. Make the most of the view because you won't be seeing much of it.'

With his permission given, they pressed their faces to the membrane. The continent of Antarctica was spread out before them. It was summer in the southern hemisphere and the pure white of the land below them would have been painful to look at if the membrane hadn't been tinted.

The taxi was hovering in mid-air a mile above the snow, three miles away from the geometric shapes of the College. Scott stood with his arms folded and feasted his eyes on the unattainable prize three miles distant. It was insane. Down there was the Earth's most valuable resource. Used properly, it would set the people of Earth free from the grip of the space nations. Instead of saving up a lifetime to be allowed to emigrate in old age, as a grudging concession from the established powers of the former colony worlds, young men and women could head out into space instead. They could set up an empire of Earth in space that was new, not a superannuated copy of Earth that was old.

But the College had the monopoly on transference, and the College had Morbern's Code, and the College would never allow what Scott and his friends had in mind. Well, that would change.

The taxi announced that clearance had been given, subject to the visitors checking in with Security upon arrival, and began to move again.

'Stay by me when we arrive,' Scott said. 'I'll escort you to Security, then to the place where you'll be given your first assignment.'

The College was a severe disappointment to Jontan, who had been hoping to see the transference hall, or at least a Field Op. It wasn't grown like an ecopolis, so there was a strange oldy-worldy feel to walking down corridors that were straight and smooth and not very interesting, but otherwise there was nothing new. After Security they reached the offices of the Appalachian consulate, which could have been anywhere on Earth. Then, instead of showing them to their quarters, Scott whisked them away and stopped halfway down a corridor, next to a maintenance access hatch. He spoke a code word and it opened.

'Follow me,' he said, and ducked inside. Sarai

went next and Jontan followed, shutting the hatch behind him at Scott's command.

They entered the maintenance tunnel, which for a while ran parallel with the main corridor they had just exited, then veered to the left. It was narrow and the roof was low, and they had to walk in a crouched single file. The lights were spaced at wide intervals along the ceiling. Jontan, bringing up the rear, admired the way light would flare around Sarai's silhouette in front of him, gradually revealing all of her, then vanish again as they moved on and his own body blocked the light out.

They turned abruptly left, then right again into an identical tunnel. They seemed to have ducked through a hole cut in the wall between the first tunnel and the second – not a door, not a hatch, not even a planned junction, to judge by the rough look of the edges, but a definite hole.

Then they came to a ladder and had to climb down it into the darkness. The lights at the bottom were much dimmer and, wherever they were now, Jontan was sure it was old. Possibly the foundations of the College. The walls weren't artificial any more – they were stone, the carved bedrock of Antarctica.

Then light began to grow around them and suddenly they were in a high, smooth-walled cavern. It was well lit and well ventilated, and a shining metal dome took up most of the centre of it. Two clam-doors were set into its side, gaping invitingly open. The dome was empty, though a jumble of crates was piled up next to it. Banks of antiquated-looking machinery with lights and displays glowing merrily lined the walls, broken here and there by the black rectangles of doors that led only into darkness. Jontan got the impression they were at the inhabited heart of quite a large, unlit and otherwise empty complex.

'You'll be here until tomorrow morning,' Scott said, encompassing the whole room with a gesture. 'There's a couple of cots set up in the next room, foodfac over there, washing facilities through there. Your first job is to check these crates against this inventory, and when that's done, get them loaded into there.' He pointed at the shining dome. 'Keep me informed of your progress. Here's my symb code.' He turned to go, then half turned back.

'By the way,' he said, 'if you had any Union Day plans, cancel them.' Then he was gone.

Cancel them! Indignation welled up in Jontan but was swept away in a moment by another thought. His hopes had been high for getting near to Sarai at the Union Day party, but this was even better – no one else but each other in this strange labyrinth beneath the College. Things could be worse.

So, he checked the inventory he was holding. 'Biotech kit,' he said.

'That makes sense,' Sarai said, 'if they want biotech journeymen.'

'Yeah.'

They looked at the crates some more. 'Do you think,' Jontan said, 'that we'll find out what all this is about after this?'

'It'll be fun to guess, won't it?' said Sarai. Neither of them yet knew why Scott had had them whisked away from the plantation, but it was enough of an adventure for them not to worry. And the sponsorship of a patrician didn't come your way every day.

'S'pose we'd better get started, then. Crate one, item one . . .'

It took the rest of the day.

When the last crate was resealed, they looked at each other.

'It's what we'd expect,' said Sarai. 'I mean, it's our job.'

'Yeah, but why bring 'em here?' Jontan shrugged and opened a symb link. 'Mr Scott, please.'

Scott's eidolon appeared in front of them. 'Yes?' he said abruptly.

'Journeymen Baiget and Killin, sir . . .' Jontan said.

'I can see that. Report?'

'Um, everything present and correct, sir.'

'Good, good. Got it loaded yet?'

'Loaded, sir?'

Scott's impatience was almost tangible. 'Have you put the equipment in the cham— the, uh, dome yet?'

'Um, no sir . . .'

'Then do it! I'll see you tomorrow. Out.' The eidolon vanished again.

'So then what does he expect us to do?' said Sarai.

You have to ask? Jontan thought. 'Ah . . . um,' he

said. Sarai looked at him thoughtfully. Was she maybe thinking . . . ? he wondered.

As it turned out, no, she wasn't. 'He said we wouldn't be doing anything for Union Day,' she said.

'Uh-huh?'

She smiled. 'He said there's a foodfac.'

'Yeah, but . . .'

'Think it could produce a sort of mini-feast? Booze, too?'

Jontan's eyes widened. 'Um, yeah.'

'So we have our own party a day early.'

His heart pounded. 'Great! That'd be great. Oh. No music.'

'We symb the music. Take me to the ball, Mr Baiget? When we're done loading.'

He grinned. 'I'd be honoured, Ms Killin.'

Jontan and Sarai woke up the next morning to the same symbed time signal. Jontan stirred and rolled over in his cot and looked at Sarai, in her own cot across the room by the other wall. Bleary eyes, tousled hair: she had never looked more beautiful. He could feast his eyes on her forever.

So, part of him chided, *you were alone in a room all night with the girl of your dreams and what did you do? What happened? You slept. Oh, won't the lads back home be proud of you . . .*

We didn't just sleep, he answered himself, just a touch defensive. They had . . . well, danced. It had been quite a satisfactory two-person Union Day

70

party, complete with low lights, slow music and cheek-to-cheek dancing towards the end ... after which Sarai had pointedly kissed him on the cheek and retired to her own cot.

And they had talked. They had a lot to talk about. The advantage of being madly in love with her was that they had so much of their shared childhood to talk about. The disadvantage ... was that they had so much of their shared childhood to talk about.

'Hi,' he said.

She smiled sleepily. 'Hi,' she said.

'Time to get up.'

'Yep.'

While Sarai was washing, Jontan wandered idly into the main chamber and ordered up a breakfast sandwich from the foodfac. He munched slowly as he walked into the large dome that dominated the place, and looked around him. Apart from the lights that were set in a circle around its highest point, flush with the metal, it was featureless. Standing inside it, he could see it was actually a complete sphere – the floor was a metal mesh that cut the globe in half. It seemed there was a faint vibration, a hum, at the back of his mind, only noticeable when he thought about it. The crates were stacked inside, put there by himself and Sarai the previous day.

'Any guesses?' Sarai stood in the wide doorway.

'None,' he said. 'Is it some kind of vault?'

'I remembered something,' she said. 'Look.'

Jontan symbed with her and an image came to mind of hundreds of shiny metal balls in racked layers, one above the other, stretching into the distance. Then he noticed people moving among them and realized the balls were spheres like this. The place where this was happening must have been huge.

'What's that?' he said.

'The transference hall at the College. I saw a picture of it once.'

'Then this . . .' Jontan did a double take and looked around, as though expecting the sphere to have changed somehow. If this was like the spheres in the picture then it could only be one thing. 'But if all the transference chambers are in that room . . .'

'Yeah, I know.' Sarai shrugged. 'Maybe it's a mock-up or something. We could ask the Register.'

'What's the Register?'

Sarai looked askance at him. 'It's the intelligence in charge of the College, Jontan. It handles all the transferences and everything and nothing works without it.'

'Oh.' Jontan wasn't really listening. It had dawned on him that Sarai was standing closer to him than at any time since last night and his mind was racing with possible ways of rekindling that romantic mood.

'Impressive, Ms Killin. Tell me more about the Register.' They both jumped. Phenuel Scott stood in the entrance to the sphere, arms folded.

'Oh, um . . .' Jontan was pleased to see that Sarai's assurance fled just as fast as his own in Scott's presence. 'It's, um, like I said to Journeyman Baiget, sir. The Register handles all the details of time travel, and . . .'

'Who created it?'

'Oh, Jean Morbern, sir . . .'

'And no one can travel through time without it?'

'No, sir.' Sarai was beginning to look confident again. 'The banks were very clear on that, sir. No one can travel without the Register knowing. It makes sure no timestreams cross and no one meets themselves and—'

'So how did Morbern manage it, before he created the Register?' Scott said. Sarai went quiet, with the stricken look of an advocate who has suddenly found a gaping hole in her own case.

'I, um, don't know, sir,' she whispered.

'Nor does anyone, Ms Killin. Morbern was a genius who worked by luck and intuition and serendipity; the Home Time was an accident and Morbern destroyed all his records. Come out here, you two.'

Two more men were waiting out in the cavern. One was Asian and old – almost old enough for emigration, Jontan thought – and was dressed in casual slacks. The younger man was dressed in the yellow and red that Jontan knew was the uniform of College staff. The College man spoke first.

'Everything's ready. The charges are set so you'll be untraceable.' He handed Scott a green crystal.

'Here's the lingo. These two . . .' He looked at the journeymen.

'These two won't need it,' Scott said. 'I'll do the talking.'

'They'll need this, though,' the man said. He took a medfac from his pocket and entered commands into it. After a moment it beeped to show it had synthesized the correct drug. 'Your shots. Hold still a moment.' He walked around them all and pressed the medfac to each neck. Jontan heard it hiss and felt a slight tingle which meant he had just been injected with something, but he had no idea what. He felt slightly annoyed that someone would pump something into him and take his consent for granted, but – as he reminded himself yet again – he was a journeyman, Mr Scott was a patrician.

The younger stranger was speaking again. 'On arrival, just ask for Ms Holliss. She's in charge there and she's expecting you.'

'Excellent. Now?'

'No time like the present.'

They filed back into the dome – Jontan, Sarai, Scott and the old man, while the younger man crossed to a control panel outside. He was the last thing Jontan saw, and hearing him wish them luck was the last thing Jontan heard, before the doors swung shut. He swallowed as his ears popped with the changed pressure.

'Don't be alarmed, my dear.' The old man spoke for the first time, addressing Sarai, who was looking

74

just as unsettled as Jontan felt. He was smiling like a benevolent uncle. 'Transference involves manipulation of probability within the chamber, and for that reason no quanta of any kind can get in from the outside. We're completely isolated from the control room. Everything is powered internally.'

'Transference?' said Sarai, too surprised even to add the 'sir' which the man surely merited. So it wasn't a mock-up, it was real, but where was the Register, and why was this chamber all on its own down here, and . . .

'I told you Morbern destroyed his records, Ms Killin,' Scott said as the background hum in the chamber changed in tone, beginning to ring like a bell. 'No one said he destroyed his original equipment.'

And then complete disorientation took Jontan's mind and the walls of the chamber faded away.

Six

'Last case,' said Hossein Asaldra, in a bored monotone. 'Alicia Gonzales/Zeng.'

Marje Orendal stretched her arms out and arched her back with a sense of accomplishment. One more of these and the backlog that she had been hacking through ever since taking over Li Daiho's job would be cleared. 'Let's see it,' she said.

Alicia Gonzales/Zeng had worked for the civil administration of Cuzco ecopolis. She was twenty-seven years old and four months previously she had locked herself in her suite, refusing to come out or let anyone – including her bond partner – in. Security had cut their way in and found her catatonic, curled up in a foetal ball in the corner of her bathroom.

The case was depressingly familiar, and the equally familiar and depressing routine had swung into action. Gonzales/Zeng was remanded for psychological evaluation. Reports indicated a complete mental freeze-up and inability to face living a normal life in an ecopolis any longer. Enhanced social preparation hadn't worked and, not having committed any crime, she wasn't eligible for personality reinforcement. She was too young for the retirement worlds, even as an exemption case. Inevitably her case had been referred to the correspondents programme.

'We get the dregs again,' Marje said.

'Academic.' Asaldra waved the problem away, clearly impatient to get this over with. They both knew Alicia Gonzales/Zeng would be a new woman after passing through their hands. The difference was, in her previous job, Marje's responsibility had ended at this point, with the psychological profile prepared and all appropriate recommendations made. For the first time, now, she would be the one to speed the woman into her new existence.

Marje studied the specs. The woman was physically robust – correspondents were remodelled to a great extent, but it helped if they had a good frame to hang the extra work on in the first place. That wasn't really her concern. Her problem was: if this woman's social preparation had broken down once, could her mind retain the far more intense conditioning required of a correspondent? The fact that social preparation hadn't taken wasn't necessarily a bad sign – a correspondent's personality, such as it was, was practically rebuilt from the bottom up anyway, while social preparation was just a gloss laid down on top of an existing human mind. But experience had shown that the deepest layers of the human mind persisted, despite all attempts to eradicate them, and could sometimes push themselves up even through a correspondent's conditioning.

Marje felt sorry for the subject and she felt sorry for the other half of the Gonzales/Zeng partnership, the woman's husband; very likely neither would ever see the other again, and even if Alicia did make it to Recall Day at the end of the Home Time, it would be the new correspondent's personality that would be in charge. The woman had had her go at life in the Home Time and she had been found wanting, yet here was her chance to make a real contribution. The data she supplied would be snapped up by the people of the Home Time: the entertainment networks would base shows on it, fashions and trends would derive from it, society would be enriched by the understanding gained from this peek into its past. Terrible things had happened in humanity's history when people lost sight of their past – where they came from, what mistakes had been made on the way. The College, and the correspondents especially, helped prevent that happening ever again.

Marje spoke. 'Subject Alicia Gonzales/Zeng accepted for the correspondents programme. Authorization Orendal.'

'Witness Asaldra,' Asaldra said. The business was done. 'If that's all . . .'

'Apparently.' Marje herself still had to catch up with a lot of her predecessor's affairs, but the end was in sight. And she could tell from the way Asaldra was, well, hovering, in the polite way that all assistants had, that he had more in store for her. 'Well?'

'Just that the Patrician's Guild would like to send someone to introduce you to your responsibilities as a member of the patrician class. No time has been set but you have a free slot at 14:00 tomorrow.'

'Patrician's Guild?' Marje exclaimed.

Asaldra raised an eyebrow. 'Naturally. A Commissioner must be a patrician.'

'I ... I had no idea. And I'm only Acting.' Marje's thoughts were whirling. She had known she could bring something to this job, but *patrician*! The perks – and responsibilities – of a patrician were enormous. A vastly increased salary, which she would be expected to use to sponsor and support deserving individuals. Close social contact with the great and the good of the Home Time, an apartment like Daiho's, increased allowances of just about everything – and the expectation that she would allow the power and privilege that accrued to her to trickle down to the sponsorees she took under her wing. Being a patrician could be a full-time job in itself.

'Even so,' Asaldra said. 'What answer should I give?'

Thus bringing Marje back to the matter in hand – the Patrician's Guild. 'Delay them,' she said. 'Same excuse – I'm waiting to see if it's permanent or not. They'll understand.'

'Of course.'

The conversation had reminded Marje of a question that had occurred to her earlier.

'Hossein, I have to ask . . . um, I'm sorry, there's no easy way: is there a reason why you weren't considered for this position? You'd have been a far more logical choice than me. You were Li's assistant, for one thing.'

Asaldra smiled. 'Not a problem, Acting Commissioner. My wife works for the World Executive – she's on the Oversight Committee. There would have been a clash of interests.'

'Oh.' Marje sighed in relief. So, no hidden Asaldra skeletons – just the fact that his wife helped run the College. 'I wasn't aware. But it seems unfair. Why should I jump to the head of the patricians queue?'

'Ekat – my wife – is a patrician,' Asaldra said, 'and I'm happy to serve the College. I'll get my due reward.' He stood decisively. 'I'll be off, if I may.'

Marje waved a hand. 'Of course. Will I see you at the ball tonight?'

'We'll be there,' Asaldra said with a nod. 'My wife and I.'

'Of course. I look forward to meeting her.' Apart from anything else, Asaldra could be so unresponsive that Marje looked forward to finding out what kind of woman could put up with him, but she kept quiet about that thought.

Asaldra smiled with his mouth, but his eyes stayed the same. 'I'll see you later, then.' He bowed slightly and left.

Marje stood up and began to pace around the

conference table. It wasn't much but her legs and her spine welcomed the exercise. She would have to deal with this office, she thought, looking around her. Li Daiho had decorated his office as he had decorated his Himalayan home, with books and shelves that gave it an almost dusty feel clashing with that ghastly twenty-first-century carpet. There was also a real-time window giving a view of the Ross Sea outside, and on one wall an hourglass – the logo of the College. It was cleverly arranged so that the sand appeared to be rushing from the top to the bottom, yet if one looked closely it seemed the sand wasn't moving at all. And yet again, Marje knew it was moving, but too slowly for the eye to detect. The top half was almost empty and the sand would be completely gone in another twenty-seven years. To remind the onlooker of this fact, the hourglass was superimposed over a large 2 and a 7, side by side. They too changed with each passing year, as Marje knew from previous visits to the office.

It was twenty-seven years until the end of the Home Time, but the thought had never really bothered her. By then she would be comfortably settled on a retirement world.

Enough daydreaming, back to work.

'Display incoming,' she said, and the latest batch of in-mail that was yet to be dealt with appeared in front of her as she walked. She frowned at one of the items; she had already seen, and ignored, several like it. 'Query: why do I keep getting reports from this correspondent?'

All the reports of all the correspondents had of course been logged long before she was born, but the Register only released them little by little, giving them the illusion of news just in. It was one of the quirks programmed into it by Jean Morbern, and something no one had the know-how to alter. This correspondent had begun reporting in the eleventh century and its stories had so far been of negligible interest to her.

The voice of Records spoke to her through her symb. *'Commissioner Daiho asked to be apprised of all reports coming from this particular correspondent. Do you wish to discontinue?'*

'I do,' Marje said. Clearly the correspondent had had a pre-programmed disposition which had been of interest to Daiho, but she was more interested in cutting down on the workload. 'No further reports as of now. Move this one and all previous to archive.'

'So noted,' Records said.

Pre-programmed dispositions. That was something else she would have to get her head around. There was always a pile of petitions from various societies and interest groups to have one or more correspondents from the next batch to go upstream predispositioned to their own particular concern. Right now, for instance, the Technological History League of Russkaya ecopolis wanted a correspondent who would seek out the great engineering thinkers of their day. The Association for Atonal Composition had supplied a list of musicians and composers that it wanted interviewed. And so on. Selecting which groups to favour and which not was a politically fraught occupation and Marje decided to put it off until she had more practice. Maybe she should investigate that patrician thing . . . make friends, get an idea of how it was done . . .

'*Marje Orendal, may we talk?*' said another symb voice.

'Commissioner Ario,' she said. 'Of course.'

The full red-outlined eidolon of Yul Ario, Commissioner for Fieldwork, appeared in front of her. 'Marje,' he said. 'We have been remiss in not welcoming you into our midst yet.' He had a wide smile that seemed quite sincere.

'I've been busy . . .' Marje said.

'Of course, of course.' Ario held out his hands. 'Anyway, welcome to the office of Commissioner. Did you know we have monthly briefings? The next is tomorrow and we'd like to see you there – you know, get to know you socially . . .'

'I'd be delighted.'

'Good, good! Tell me, how's young Hossein coming on?'

'He's doing nicely, thank you,' she said. 'You know him?'

'Oh, yes.' Ario looked surprised. 'Didn't you know? I'm his sponsor. He used to be with me in Fieldwork. Miss him, sometimes. Surprised he transferred. I was going to give him a timestream. I suppose he just wanted a change.'

'Yes,' said Marje, surprised. She hadn't known. Maybe Asaldra had felt he was going to be promoted too high. Perhaps being an assistant was simply his preferred station in life.

This conversation was going somewhere: she could feel it. Ario was the kind of man who had to spiral up through the pleasantries to get to the point.

'So, Marje. Have you been thinking about sponsorship yet?' Ario said.

'Yes, I've been thinking,' Marje said, with a sinking feeling. The patrician thing again. A good patrician was expected to take on at least twenty sponsorees, though she knew some who had something like fifty. From those to whom much was given, much was expected.

The question was, where to start?

'The one thing you don't do,' said Ario, 'is take on unsolicited applicants. Well, you can, if you want the extra work. But you want to make sure you can take on people you can work with and approve of, and that usually means people you know. Of course, I've got some overflow sponsorees that I could let you have to get started.'

'That's very kind of you,' Marje said.

'And . . .' Ario gave a reluctant frown, the kind that said he really didn't want to have to interrupt the flow of bonhomie with something distasteful. 'Marje, I thought I should give you a word of advice, just between the two of us. There's a friendly bit of rivalry between the wings of the College, you know,

Fieldwork and Correspondents and Social Studies and . . . but by and large, if you're actively dissatisfied with the actions of one of our staff, you should come straight to us. Don't have your office issue a complaint. It's bad form and, well, it detracts from the mystique of being a Commissioner. It shows us up to our juniors.'

'Well, thank you,' said Marje, baffled. 'I'll remember that if I ever want to complain about someone.'

'It's –' Ario gave a dry little laugh – 'it's a little late for that, Marje.'

'It is?'

'Isn't it?'

'Isn't what?'

They looked at each other for a few seconds in the silence that comes from a complete lack of communication. Marje broke the silence.

'Yul – I may call you Yul? – what exactly are you trying to say?'

'I'm trying to say that your office recently issued a complaint against one of my Field Ops, and I'd really rather you had brought it straight to me.'

'Is that a fact?'

'The Op in question has . . . well, a reputation for difficulty, but if he's to get into trouble I'd like it to be because of his professional conduct, not what he does in his time off duty.'

'I'm not dissatisfied with one of your Ops!' Marje said. 'I don't know any of them.'

'But if a complaint came from your office . . .'

'Who was this Op, anyway?' Marje said with a sudden surge of intuition.

'One Garron. Ri—'

'—co Garron,' said Marje, shutting her eyes. She had just about got him out of her mind.

'So you do know him?'

'No! I mean, I've met him once, for about a minute. I could probably walk past him in the corridor without recognizing him again. And I certainly haven't made a complaint about him.' Ario still looked sceptical. 'I haven't!'

'In that case, Marje, someone in your office is taking your name in vain,' Ario said. Marje cast her mind back to all the people who would have known about that brief meeting – and found there was only one. A cold anger welled up inside her.

Marje was already annoyed, and was made more so by the fact that Hossein Asaldra could only blink as she gave vent to her feelings. From his typical expression of ennui there was no way of knowing how much of it was getting through. It would probably be the same even if he had been physically present, instead of just being projected.

'If I want to reprimand someone, or even just complain about them, I'm perfectly capable of doing so!' she said. 'I don't need help or assistance and I don't like my name being used without my permission.'

'I was out of order.' Asaldra still sounded bored. 'I apologize.'

'You had no right to try and read my mind! That Field Op has been reprimanded. Have you ever had a reprimand on your record? Do you know how difficult it is to get rid of? People ask questions for years afterwards . . .'

'I apologize,' Asaldra said again. It was probably the best she was going to get. 'Perhaps I should apologize to Op Garron too. Though if he hadn't tried to masquerade as a Security Op, this wouldn't be happening now.'

'No!' Marje could think of nothing likely to offend Rico Garron more than a wearied, monotone apology from Hossein Asaldra. 'No, don't bother. The complaint came from this office so the apology comes from me. And he wasn't masquerading, he was there by appointment to retrieve an item of equipment. He probably doesn't want it docked from his pay. Had that occurred to you?'

'As you will.' Asaldra seemed to dismiss the subject for something he found far more interesting. 'If you've got a moment to project, Commissioner, there's something I thought you might like to see.'

Marje was infuriated by the complete lack of interest shown in his change of subject. 'What?' she snapped.

'Only something that could clear up a mystery several centuries old. Are you interested?'

The cavern was still hazy with smoke, and the

technicians and Security Ops moving around in it, studying the slagged remains of the equipment, wore breathing gear. The eidolons of Marje and Asaldra were unaffected.

'That's . . .' Marje said, gesturing at the object in the centre of the cavern.

'It's a transference chamber, yes.' Asaldra actually had a hint of excitement in his voice. 'Essentially the same as the type we use nowadays, though the design is more basic.'

Marje looked around her. The walls were smooth but still had the look of having been hacked out of bedrock, and were lined with equipment. It reeked of antiquity, if antiquity was the word – it couldn't pre-date the College, and the College was only four hundred years old. 'What is this place?' she said.

'I think it's where Morbern did his original experiments.'

Marje let out a whistle. It made sense. Jean Morbern had come to the Antarctic in the first place because he wasn't sure how dangerous his experiments might be to other people; going underground as well would be one more sensible precaution. 'And it's been running all this time?'

'Apparently. But all the machines were just ticking over, and everyone thought the power was being used by something else so no one ever checked. All the tunnels to it were blocked off, which helped.'

'What changed?' Marje said. She should be getting back to work – she oughtn't to have time to spare to investigate strange caverns that had suddenly been discovered – but she was caught up by the mystery nonetheless.

'This.' Asaldra indicated a nearby bank of equipment which was still gently steaming. 'A sudden power surge was picked up and Maintenance sent some people to investigate. They found this place. Something must have given and this meltdown resulted.'

'That's some surge,' Marje said. 'Didn't Morbern use a clever twenty-sixth-century device called a fuse?' Asaldra just shrugged. 'Well, there goes the museum exhibit.'

'A lot of the equipment seems to be duplicated,' Asaldra said. 'If the museums want a console that Morbern sat at, there's plenty more left.'

'Hmm.' The suspicion growing in Marje's mind was so inevitable she couldn't believe she had been the first to have it. 'Hossein, could this equipment have been used?'

'All College personnel are accounted for,' he said. 'I checked.'

'They're all here?' Marje said sceptically.

'They are either in the Home Time or they left it via an authorized chamber.'

'There are non-College personnel at the College.' It was a ghastly thought, but it had to be said. Non-College personnel, non-adherents to Morbern's Code, unleashed on the past . . . a nightmare scenario.

He paused. Perhaps that point hadn't occurred

to him. 'I don't think anyone else would have been able to work it, Commissioner. Look at this.' Their eidolons moved towards one of the panels. 'We're all too used to asking the Register to set co-ordinates. Could you work out how to do it manually this way? It would be difficult enough for one of us, and for someone not trained in the theory . . .' His gaze moved to a point behind her and he drew himself up more smartly. 'Good day, Commissioner.'

'Good day, Hossein,' said a man's voice. Marje turned to see Yul Ario's eidolon standing there, looking about him appreciatively. 'Quite a place you've unearthed here.'

'Maintenance unearthed it, sir,' Asaldra said. 'I just reported it.'

'Yes, why?' Marje said, suddenly curious. Fascinating though it was, it was nothing to do with her job, or Asaldra's. Asaldra looked artlessly at her.

'I thought you'd be interested,' he said.

'Quite right. This is history, Marje!' Ario threw his arms wide to encompass the cavern. 'A capsule of history right under the College, and we head the College. Of course we had to know about it. Well done, Hossein.' He squinted up at the ceiling. 'Speaking of under the College, which bit are we under?'

'Residential and administrative. The Appalachian consulate and various others,' Asaldra said.

'Really? Well, I can see you've got everything

90

under control, Hossein,' Ario said. If he had spoken to Marje in that patronizing tone, Marje would have hit him, but it seemed to go down well with Asaldra, who didn't show the least sign of irritation. And the subject of irritating people led Marje inevitably to think of Op Garron, so she made her apologies and withdrew.

Marje had only met Garron once before, but still she hadn't been entirely accurate when she had told Ario she could pass the Field Op in the corridor without recognizing him. In the eidolon the blond stubbly hair and burning eyes hadn't changed. It was satisfying to note that when she had seen him in Daiho's apartment he had looked smug; now he just looked wary.

'Yes?' he said.

'Acting Commissioner Orendal,' Marje said.

'Yes,' he said. 'I remember.' His voice was a lot colder than it had been before.

'I hope this isn't a bad time to call?'

'I'm just off on a field trip.'

'I'll be quick, then. I owe you an apology, Op Garron.'

That took him by surprise. 'Really?'

'I gather a complaint was made against you that resulted in a reprimand. I'm sorry and I apologize on behalf of my office. The complaint didn't come from me.'

'Really?' Garron repeated. 'Could I ask who, then, Commissioner?'

'An over-zealous subordinate. It won't happen again.'

Garron didn't say anything but his expression made clear his opinion of that particular promise. 'Is my record going to be altered?' he said innocently.

The thought had occurred to Marje, but it was a sad fact of office politics that such things didn't happen. A really serious mistake would have led to an enquiry, Asaldra's disciplining and the altering of the record, but this sadly wasn't that serious and Asaldra didn't deserve that level of rebuke. And the system didn't allow for the correction of more minor errors.

Op Garron, she suspected, knew all this perfectly well, so she didn't answer the question. 'I'd like to make up for it in some way,' she said.

'Well, you could find my computer . . .'

'You mean, you never did?'

'Didn't have time before Security kindly showed me the way out. Some other Field Op will have it now, and the data'll have been erased anyway.'

'Have you tried chasing it up?'

'I keep checking at the wrong time. All I ever get is a "that item is not presently located in the Home Time", any time of day or night. I can take a hint.'

'I'll find it for you,' Marje promised. 'That's the least I can do.'

Garron still looked unimpressed. 'Can I go now, Acting Commissioner?'

'If you like.' Marje was struck by inspiration,

remembering her conversation with the other Commissioners about sponsors. 'Listen, it's possible I'm going to make patrician, and I'll have vacancies for sponsorship . . .'

She almost flinched at the sheer hate in his expression. 'Thank you, that won't be necessary,' he said. 'Out.' He vanished.

Well, up yours too, Op Garron, she thought bitterly. So much for trying to help. She half stood, then sat down again. No, she would find that computer. She had decided she would help Garron, and she would, and if he got even more annoyed then so much the better.

She didn't know when Garron had had the computer, so she symbed into the College records.

'Request number of field computers signed out by both Field Op Rico Garron and Commissioner Li Daiho in the last month.'

'There is one field computer matching that criterion,' said the voice of Records.

'Request its present location.'

'That item is not presently located in the Home Time.'

'To whom is it signed out?'

'Commissioner Li Daiho.'

'Commissioner Daiho is dead.'

'Commissioner Daiho was the last individual to sign the computer out.'

'So where is it?'

'That item is not presently located in the Home Time.'

'Request details of the last transference involving that computer.'

'*That computer has not been involved in a transference since Field Op Garron returned it to Stores.*'

'So where is it?'

'*It is not presently located in the Home Time.*'

'This is ridiculous.' Marje realized she was pacing about the room, and she made herself stop. There was a way of breaking this loop . . . but no, surely it was abuse of power . . .

But she was a Commissioner, so . . .

'Register, please,' she said.

The Register's eidolon appeared in front of her, looking quizzical. It was outlined in blue to show it was a projection of an artificial personality, and the appearance it took was of a middle-aged white male. It was as Jean Morbern had looked at the height of his career. 'Marje?' it said.

'Register, I'm sorry to use you for such a trivial matter . . .'

The Register smiled. 'You're a Commissioner. Rank has its privileges.'

'I thought I'd use them,' Marje said, relieved. 'I'm tracing a computer signed out recently by Li Daiho and Field Op Garron.'

'Records can't help?'

'You try it!' Marje said with feeling.

'If you like.' The Register paused for half a second. 'I see your point. How annoying.'

'So where's it got to?'

'I have no idea. Records would try and trace it through the symb network. It's not responding to the signal, so it must be faulty. It was last seen with

94

Commissioner Daiho, so perhaps you should check his things. His apartment has been reallocated but his effects will have been stored.'

'That's been tried,' Marje said.

'By Op Garron. I know – I gave him the authorization. But that is all I can suggest.'

Then Marje remembered. Garron had indeed been there, but he had said, *didn't have time.*

'Where are the things stored?' she said.

'Here at the College.'

'Right,' Marje said. She knew how she could help Garron and she was going to, whether he liked it or not.

Seven

'And then,' said Rico, 'just to really rub it in, she offered me sponsorship.'

'Shocking,' said Su.

Looking like a man and woman of the reasonably prosperous merchant classes, they strolled arm in arm in the July sunshine along the footpath beside the Danube Canal, through the Prater park in the Vienna of 1508, capital of the Khanate of Austria.

This was the gamma stream, one of several parallel Earth histories inadvertently created by Jean Morbern on his first trips into the past. The alpha stream was the 'official' history, the one Morbern would have recognized. In both alpha and gamma, the Golden Horde of Batu Khan had overrun eastern Europe in the thirteenth century. In the gamma stream, they had stayed.

Here, Paulus Khan, many-times great-grandson of the original Genghis, was the latest Khan to hold sway over the Khanate of Austria. The new empire was a happy blend of east and west, having made its peace with the Christians, and Rico and Su were often chosen for missions to this particular time: a Caucasian and an Asian together, apparently husband and wife, would raise no eyebrows. No one would have guessed that her flowing robes and scarf, his tunic and breeches weren't the work of the best tailors of the city but were imitations wrought by the gelfabric of their fieldsuits.

By this world's twentieth century, the College would be openly running the place. Eventually it would take over all the worlds. After the creation of the Home Time in the twenty-sixth century, they would all be spliced back into the alpha stream and the populations of all the streams merged. But that was a long time in anyone's future. For now, the people of the College kept their heads down.

'I mean,' Rico said, 'insult or what?'

'Terrible,' Su said.

'She calls me up, she . . . yeah, OK, she says sorry, that's good of her, but then—'

'Appalling,' said Su.

Her tone was finally seeping through Rico's indignation. 'Su, why do I think you're not taking this seriously?'

'I don't know. Why do you think I'm not taking this seriously?'

'You're not, are you?'

Su smiled sweetly and nodded at a couple passing in the other direction, then turned her head to glare at him. 'A Commissioner of the College contacts you, off her own bat, and apologizes for a wrong that was done to you, and offers to find your precious computer, and offers you something that others would kill for, and you're angry with her?'

'Well . . .' Rico suddenly became aware of how ephemeral his indignation was and became doubly resolved to hang on to it. 'She thought she could buy me off that way.'

'No, she didn't.' Su jabbed a finger into his chest to punctuate each word. 'She was trying to help you!'

'Ow.' Rico rubbed his sternum resentfully.

'Your record probably doesn't mention that you're the prickliest man on Earth so she couldn't have known that. She doesn't know a thing about you and in the absence of a large sign saying "I've got a massive chip on my shoulder" she made the mistake of treating you like someone normal. Like herself, really.'

Rico was silent for some seconds. 'So what do I do, then?'

'Apologize to her. You don't have to do it face to face, you can leave her a message. Thank her for her generous offer, tell her that it's really appreciated but it's not necessary. And don't sound like you're saying it by rote, try and put some meaning into it.'

'Right.' Another pause. 'This generous offer thing – are we talking computers or sponsorship here?'

'You let her work that out.'

'Oh.'

A symbed chime sounded in both their minds,

and Su pulled a face. 'Work, work, always work. Come on, let's go.'

They walked towards the Innere Stadt, using the spire of Saint Stephen's Cathedral as their guide through the narrow and irregular streets. The inner city of Vienna enfolded them. It felt odd to be surrounded by buildings so small and yet so crowded.

The bulk of the cathedral loomed over them. The Bishop there no doubt thought he was master of all he surveyed, second only to the Khan: he had no idea that one of his junior priests was the Home Time superintendent for the area.

Superintendent Adigun exuded his usual bonhomie to such an extent that his moustache quivered when they entered his front room in one of the small cottages in the cathedral's shadow. 'How are you? How are you?' he said, as if he hadn't seen them two hours ago. 'Did you enjoy your inspection?'

'Everything is satisfactory,' Su said formally, though the inspection hadn't taken long. Her powers only extended to checking that none of the bygoners were being abused in any way and that basic health and safety regulations (very basic, in this period) were being observed. After that, it was just a case of carrying the latest set of figures back to the Home Time for the Social Studies department to fuss over. Less formally, she added, 'You run a good establishment, Superintendent.'

Adigun beamed. 'I'm glad to hear you say that,

I really am. Are you sure I can't offer you something?'

'The recall field comes on in fifteen minutes, Superintendent.'

'Of course, of course. I suppose you'll both be at the Union Day ball? Lucky things, can't have one here, of course, the bygoners will notice . . . let me get you those figures. Must observe the protocols, eh?' He peered into the next room. 'Sanja? That little gem I showed you, could you bring it . . .?'

Sanja was a bygoner and she glided into the room under Adigun's approving gaze. Her hand brushed the Superintendent's when she handed the crystal with the figures over; Adigun's slightly glazed look followed her out of the room and it seemed to Rico that no, the Bishop would *not* approve.

He raised an eyebrow at Su; she pursed her lips but shook her head slightly. Disapproved of, but not illegal, and not something she as Senior Field Op could rightly include in her report. But she could make it known that Adigun let his bygoner woman play with data crystals and make out that they were jewellery. Social Studies could perhaps draw their own conclusions.

Superintendent Adigun, Rico decided, was an out and out bastard, however pleasant and affable he might appear. He would only be a few years in this job before moving on to something else, probably nice and cushy and secure back in the Home Time. And was there any question of Sanja coming to the Home Time? Nor did Adigun look the type to volunteer for mind-blanking and re-settlement in the gamma stream. He was playing with the woman.

'Enact symb,' said Adigun, tuning his mind into the local symb junction that would be hidden some-where in his house – isolated from the Home Time symb network, barely more than a poor, crippled relative, useful only for managing such data as was available to it. After a couple of seconds he handed the crystal to Su.

'All updated with my latest reports. Social Studies will find it interesting,' he said, and pro-ceeded to hurl fact after statistic at them. Rico tried to look interested and Su held up a hand.

'We're just couriers, Superintendent. We'll pass this on, don't worry. Good day, it's been inter-esting.'

Rico could contain it no longer. 'You're sitting pretty,' he said, just as Su turned to go.

'I beg your pardon?' said Adigun.

'Lord of all you survey.' Rico tilted his head in the direction Sanja had gone. '*Droit du seigneur*, I think it was called back home. Maybe there's a word for it in Mongol-German.'

'Rico . . .' *That* tone was back in Su's voice but he ignored it. He took a step forward.

'We're here to observe, Superintendent Adigun,' he said. 'Observe, not break hearts. Does Miss Bygoner know you plan to vanish from her life in a couple of years?'

'I really think you're out of order.' All good humour had vanished from Adigun's expression. 'You have about ten minutes until the recall field comes on. Use it, Op . . . ?'

'Garron. Rico Garron.'

'Rico Garron.' Adigun's eyes widened. 'Weren't you—' He chuckled. 'I don't think you can afford to get into trouble, Op Garron. Why don't you leave now?'

'Rico, what am I going to do with you?' Su said quietly as they headed back to the recall point, a patch of clear ground outside the city walls, hidden by trees.

'It just happens,' Rico muttered.

'The supervisor in beta-Rome . . . and now this.'

'What else was I supposed to do? Su, we're meant to protect bygoners, we're meant to uphold the Code . . .'

'You leave well alone, Rico, and let me pass on any complaint through official channels.'

'Would you?'

Su was quiet for a moment. 'Probably not,' she said.

'See? See?'

'Rico, he's a *superintendent,* which means he's senior to us and he's probably got better sponsorship. Anyway, I've never understood women who can't see through creatures like him. They deserve everything they get. If Tong tried to use me, I'd

102

know in about a nanosecond. Two, if he was clever and got up early enough.' She symbed into her field computer to access the crystal's data. 'Still and all, Rico, he's a good administrator. Output's up, I can tell that. And lots of gobbledegook which will only mean something to Social Studies, but it looks good.'

'I hope someone appreciates it.'

Su glanced thoughtfully back at the city. 'You know, I wouldn't mind a job like his.'

'Lord and master and petty tyrant of a smelly bygoner town back up the gamma stream?' Rico said with disbelief.

'Not specifically, but with that level of skill and challenge. Tong and I have been talking about this a lot, Rico.'

'Talking about what?'

'Well, has it occurred to you that our generation's unique?'

'How so?'

'There's a gap looming in the future and we've no idea how it's going to be filled. How old will you be in twenty-seven years, Rico?'

Twenty-seven years. The magic figure. The time when the singularity that created the Home Time was due to collapse and suddenly transference wouldn't be possible any more.

He pulled a face. 'Old enough.'

'But not old enough for retirement. And what job will you be doing in twenty-seven years and one month, Rico?'

Rico trudged on in silence. 'I'll think of something. It's quite a while,' he said.

'It pays to think ahead. That's all.'

'Whatever happens, I don't think it'll be a case of life continuing as normal, minus the College. A lot'll change, Su. You can't plan for that.'

'No harm in thinking about it,' she said. 'I just want a job I *want*, rather than one that's allocated to me. I'm thinking of applying for retraining.'

'Su!' Rico stopped in his tracks in genuine dismay. Su laughed even more at the look on his face.

'It'll be in my time off, Rico. But I don't want to be a Senior Field Op until I drop, and sooner or later I'm going to have to change jobs. And so are you.'

'I like this one,' he muttered, but started walking again.

The recall point was in a small glade in the woods, quiet and unobserved. They stood there in silence, waiting for the field to come on, and Rico looked idly down at his shoes. There was mud on them. The mechanics of transference had been explained to him and he had sat through the required courses on theory, but he had never claimed to understand. He knew in principle that the mud on his shoes would be transferred with him but the ground he stood on would not be. Somehow the universe knew that the mud, and the food he had eaten in this time, and the air in his lungs, and all that was closely associated with him should be transferred with him. Everything else should stay.

Somehow it happened. It worked – that was good enough for him.

But a future without transference? Of course he knew it was coming – who didn't? – but it was a bit like death. It would happen, one day, but polite people didn't talk about it.

He was still thoughtful back in the Home Time. Su, as usual in her capacity as Senior Field Op, declared the excursion over and they walked out of the transference chamber, where they were greeted with a recorded notification that Acting Commissioner Orendal had logged a 'request and require' order instructing any and all College personnel to assist Field Op Garron in his search for the computer. Attached to it was a symbed note that it might be worth starting in the storeroom where the effects of the late Commissioner Daiho were kept.

Su told Rico to include a sincere-sounding 'thank you' with his apology.

'Guess what?' said Rico, straightening up from his last pile and wincing as something clicked in his back.

'What?' said Su, still going through a pile of her own.

'It's not here.'

'You're right.' Su straightened up with him. 'That item really is not located in the Home Time.'

They stood side by side and gazed at the junk.

'This computer's more trouble than it's worth,' said Rico. The storeroom was full of the remaining unclaimed worldly goods of the late Commissioner Li Daiho. There wasn't much, he thought without enthusiasm, and he had better things to do than rummage through the remains of a man's life. Daiho had been in his seventies and a patrician: he had lived long and well, and this was all that was left. Bits and pieces, odds and ends. But Marje Orendal had been right – if the field computer, College property, was still in Daiho's possession at the time of death, this was where it would be.

'So what's the big deal about it, anyway?' Su said. Before he could answer she added: 'I think we've taken long enough.'

'No, wouldn't want the supervisor to complain about us wasting College time.' Rico grinned at the thought of Supervisor Marlici's plump, pompous visage quivering yet again with indignation. All that quivering and the man still couldn't lose weight.

Su groaned suddenly. 'I can't believe we're so stupid.' She shut her eyes.

'What are you doing?' Rico said.

'Symbing . . . got it. Have a look.'

Puzzled, Rico symbed in to see what she had found. 'You can't look at his personal records!' he exclaimed.

'Why not? They count as his property and we've got Marje's permission to go through his property.

106

Let's see . . .' Another pause. 'None of them mention it,' she said.

'They wouldn't, would they?' Rico said.

'I suppose not.' The whole point of a field computer was that it worked in isolation from the networks of the present; it had to work upstream as well as in the Home Time. 'None of them were prepared on it, either.'

'Still,' Rico said with a grin, 'it's compulsive reading.' He set up a symb search of his own.

'What are you doing?' Now it was Su's turn to be shocked.

'Reading them anyway. Seeing what they do mention.'

'Now, that is going too far . . .'

'One's dated after he died.'

'Junk mail . . .' Su was plucking at his sleeve to pull him away.

'No.' Rico could see the official seal on it. Naturally it resisted his attempts to read it and for the sheer thrill he flung Orendal's authorization at it. It opened. 'It's . . . a statement of account. He'd made a number of personal transferences . . . and payment has been debited from his account in accordance with instructions previously set up.'

'Fascinating.' Su grabbed his arm and led him to the door. 'The computer's not here, let's just accept you're not going to get it, and stop poking through private correspondence.'

'You started it.' Rico couldn't help making the

point with a broad smile. 'But you're right. We've both got to get ready for the ball.'

Su groaned. 'Oh, no! I hate balls. And so do you.'

'I go to observe.' They were at the door, stepping out of the storeroom. 'Anyway, you want me to keep out of trouble, and what can go wrong at a ball?'

The door shut behind them.

Eight

Union Day! The day the world finally became as one under the World Executive, a composite consensus mind drawn from the governing minds of the ecopoloi. Thousands of years of disunity, war, nationalism, religious differences, all officially done away with, and even if there were still people who would as soon kill each other as look at each other, they could be kept safely apart. So in that regard, planet Earth was united, and it was an achievement worth celebrating.

The College always excelled itself in its choice of venue and this year's was no different: a plateau on what would one day be the Costa del Sol with a stunning view of the Gibraltar waterfall. Another twenty years and the place would be submerged forever by the rising Mediterranean, but for the time being it was the perfect place for a party. The air was soft and warm and delicately laced with spicy scents drifting in from the Spanish mainland. Soft grass underfoot; carefully planned clusters of trees and bushes around which groups of guests could congregate; a stream, fed by sparkling clear water straight from the Sierra Morena and warmed by the College, in which the more adventurous party-goers could take a dip.

Marje Orendal had chosen a period costume at random from the catalogue. Apparently she was a 1920s New York flapper, though what she was meant to flap she wasn't sure and the catalogue hadn't said. As she stepped out of the transference area, she was just glad the venue was warm.

Guests arrived and departed from a terrace that overlooked the proceedings. A page – dressed in powdered white wig, heavy jacket and tight breeches; surely one of history's less comfortable fashions – took her name at the top of the wide marble steps that led down to the party ground. 'Acting Commissioner Marje Orendal,' he declared, and Marje descended into the crowd and headed for the nearest bar.

'Marje! Good to see you!' Commissioner Thomas Enrepil, the chubby head of Social Studies, was beaming at her over a glass of something. He was surrounded by a small circle of people who Marje didn't know. 'Marje, have you met . . .'

No, she hadn't, and she forgot their names with immediate ease, but still she nodded and said 'hello' as each one was introduced to her.

'I was just telling them . . .' said Enrepil, and carried on with his anecdote. The words blurred into the background noise and Marje remained with a half smile on her face, which she extended to full strength whenever the others laughed.

'Commissioner?'

Glad of the excuse to look away, Marje turned. Hossein Asaldra, apparently dressed as a penguin, was standing behind her. She blinked: no, not a penguin, it was . . . what was the expression . . . a morning suit, nineteenth or twentieth century. His arm was crooked through the arm of a smiling woman dressed as an armoured trooper, Five Bomb War era. The helmet and the armour made actually seeing what she looked like difficult, but strands of red hair crept from under the rim.

'Commissioner,' Asaldra said, 'this is my wife . . .'

'Ekat Hoon,' the woman said, holding out a hand. 'How very pleasant to meet you at last, Commissioner. Oh, of course, my condolences on the loss of Commissioner Daiho.'

'Why, thank you. Did you know him well?' Hoon's condolences had sounded more routine than heartfelt, so Marje put the question casually.

'I knew him, of course. Did Hossein mention I'm on the Oversight Committee? I often met him through work, just as I'm sure we two will from now on. I thought we should meet socially.'

Hoon gestured at someone behind Marje. 'Drink, Commissioner?'

Marje looked round and was taken aback to see a Neanderthal standing there. The shape and form were unmistakable. The stocky body radiated a strength that could have snapped Marje in half. The face was strong and stern, framed by ridges of solid bone under the dark tan skin. Incongruously, he wore a one-piece suit tailored to his powerful form and was carrying a silver tray and a range of full glasses.

'Dr'nk, madam?' he said politely.

Marje absently took one of the smaller, more innocuous glasses, and Hoon and Asaldra served themselves. The 'tal wandered off into the crowd.

'Francis is on his toes, I see,' Hoon said. She took a sip and pulled a face. 'Unlike whoever poured the drinks in the first place.'

'Francis?' Marje said. Hoon nodded in the direction taken by the 'tal.

'We loaned him out,' she said. 'There's a lot of them around tonight.'

Ekat Hoon was a patrician: Marje suddenly remembered Asaldra telling her so. He had also said something about getting his own rewards.

'One of my first jobs in the College,' she said casually, 'was working on the 'tal psyche. Fieldwork had just brought back the first tribe. I found them a fascinating challenge.'

'Yes, I remember the reports,' Hoon said with a smile. 'Their languages, their religions, their cultures – just as diverse as we are. They could be just like us.'

'They are just like us,' Marje said. Another 'tal moved close, saw that they already had glasses, and moved off again. Marje took a closer look at the clothes he was wearing and tried to believe she was only imagining their resemblance to a kind of household livery. 'With all the rights that we have,' she couldn't resist adding. 'I think that was when I realized just how much bygoners need protecting. We have far too much power for our own good.' She wasn't being particularly civil, but she knew full well that 'tals were barred from paid labour in the ecopoloi, and she needed to know if Francis and the others were being used essentially as slaves. Bygoners were bygoners, whether they were human or Neanderthal, and they had rights.

'They also serve, who only stand and wait,' Hoon said. 'A pun,' she added, seeing Marje's questioning look. 'Wait, stand around, wait, serve drinks . . . we fully believe in making recompense for labour, Commissioner. Of course Francis isn't able to have a bank account but we pay him in kind.'

Marje realized how tense she had become and made herself relax. Perhaps she was too used to standing on formality, obeying Morbern's Code and all that. If you weren't careful you could get to the point where everything was ideologically suspect.

'What do you look like?'

At last! Rico Garron thought. He had been craning his neck, studying the crowd for ten minutes now. He deliberately put on an air of innocent enquiry and turned round, eyebrows raised. Su was coming towards him on the arm of her husband, Tong. Rico recognized Louis XVI and Marie Antoinette.

'Cinderella and Buttons, how nice,' he said. 'Hello, Tong.'

'Hi, Rico,' Tong said cheerfully.

Rico looked back at Su. 'I don't know,' he said. 'What do I look like?'

'Like . . .' Su looked closely at the thick jacket and baggy trousers. 'Like . . .'

'A man sculpted out of hairy orange peel?' Tong said. Su burst out laughing and Rico gave a polite 'a-ha-ha'.

'English shooting party, 1910,' he said. 'The material's called tweed.'

'Interesting.' Tong looked more closely at the alternating diagonal stripes of the weave. 'Is it modelled on fish skeletons deliberately?'

'Oh, yes, they were heavily into that sort of thing in the twentieth century,' said Rico. 'Fish-bone suits, kipper ties, they just couldn't get enough sea life.'

'Drinks first, talk later,' Su said, with a glance at Tong.

'Bar's that way, but let me,' Rico said. He hogged Su during working hours: it was only right to let the two of them have some time together. He took their orders and pushed off into the crowd.

'*Garron!*'

He paused as he was shouldering his way between a gorilla and a Roman centurion. Had someone . . .

'*Still interested in that computer?*' The words were symbed into his mind: anonymous, impersonal, impossible to say who was speaking.

Rico's eyebrows shot up. Of course there was a

114

symb node here, purely for emergencies, but using it for covert activities was another matter.

'*Yes . . . ?*' he symbed. Nothing had been further from his mind at the party, but if he was going to be approached in this highly intriguing manner . . .

Directions appeared in his mind. '*This way.*'

Acutely conscious that nothing looks more suspicious in a crowd than someone sidling cautiously, Rico stepped out boldly. The symbed directions led him away from the crowd, and the music dwindled to a gentle background melody. Out of the circle of lights, the plateau suddenly became very dark.

Through some bushes, then onto the edge of a small ravine. A stream ran through it, gurgling over boulders with its rippled waters reflecting silver in the moonlight. Idyllic, Rico mused: better watch out for snogging couples.

A bush rustled behind him and Rico turned.

A powerful fist smashed into his stomach, and he whooped and doubled over. Patterns of light flashed in his eyes as a pair of strong hands picked him up and set him on his feet, pinning him upright in a powerful grasp.

The sturdy form of his attacker stood before him, wrist pulled back for another blow, and Rico lashed out with his feet, catching the man on his jaw. Rico yelped as shock ran up his leg – it had been like kicking a wall and the man barely flinched. Someone standing in Rico's peripheral vision stepped forward and caught hold of Rico's leg at the knee. Another equally powerful hand seized his upper leg. Still dazed, Rico vaguely recognized what was about to happen, and rather than struggle he went limp. The hands twisted and Rico bellowed as agony exploded in his thigh. If he had tried to resist it might have snapped. As it was, he felt the wrench in his socket and knew he wouldn't be able to walk on it without attention.

But he had other worries right now. The hands still held him, his chief aggressor still stood in front of him. Rico braced his muscles, clenched his teeth and tried to put his mind into neutral for what was about to come.

Blow after blow sank into Rico's solar plexus. First they knocked the breath back out of him all over again, then even the pain seemed to recede into the darkness and it was just shock, shock, shock.

'Look up,' said a harsh voice. Rico tried, but couldn't. Strong fingers twined in his hair and pulled his head up to look at the beater, and his eyes widened as he got his first clear look at the man's face in a sudden burst of moonlight. The man carefully put his hands together as if praying, then folded the fingers together, and Rico just had time to think, *But it does make sense*, before the man swatted the side of Rico's head with his bunched hands as if with a club.

The supporting hands let go and Rico collapsed in a heap, a man-shaped mass of bruises and pain. His breath sobbed as he drew in vast gulps of air and fireworks exploded in his head.

Someone grabbed his hair again and yanked his head up. He looked into the large, dark eyes of the 'tal who had led the attackers.

'Forget 'ompu'er,' it said. 'Forget.'

It let go and Rico let his head drop back to the ground. He watched as the 'tal walked over to a tree, reached up, snapped off a branch and walked purposefully back to Rico.

Oh, great, Rico thought. But the 'tal just dropped it on him.

''Ou need it,' he said. He turned round and walked away without any further comment, followed by his two companions. Rico watched them go, then with the last of his strength tried to push himself up.

He couldn't do it. He fell back, buried his face in the grass and the smells of the Earth and let himself succumb to the roaring dark inside his head.

'Of course, Hossein was in Fieldwork but it wasn't really for him,' Ekat Hoon said. They had wandered to the edge of the plateau, where the gentle shimmer of a forcefield kept them from plunging down to what would be the floor of the Mediterranean, and the waterfall's roar was oddly muted into a pleasant background thunder. The drinks served by Francis had been judged unpalatable and Hossein Asaldra had been dispatched to find replacements. Marje was amused at the fairly apparent overtones in their relationship: as far as she could see, formal, stand-offish Hossein

Asaldra was – what was the Fossil Age term she had heard once? – chicken-bitten, or something like that. Hoon was happy to do the talking for both of them. 'So, have you ever been upstream, Commissioner?' Hoon said. 'Apart from occasions like this?'

'Not me,' said Marje. 'And do call me Marje, Ekat.'

Hoon acknowledged the permission with a gracious nod. 'I'd be there like a shot, given the chance,' she said. 'There's so much I'd like to see.'

'Whatever you want to see, there's probably a correspondent's report listed for it,' Marje said.

'Not the same as first-hand experience, though, is it?'

'Not in the least,' Marje agreed. From the slight nod of Hoon's head she wondered if she had just passed some kind of test in the woman's mind. 'But perhaps I'm just boring and have no spirit of adventure. My field is psychology and we have all the information we're likely to need on that here in the present.'

'That's not just your preparation talking, then,' Hoon said. Part of the social preparation that every child had was to make people comfortable with living in the modern world, and that meant disinclining them to live anywhere else. The higher up the ladder one rose, the less preparation was required and the more one's thoughts could roam.

'No. I'd know if it was.' Hoon raised a sceptic eyebrow. 'I would,' Marje insisted. 'You have to know your own mind if you're going to study other people's.'

'Good point.'

'So what in our history would you like to see?' Marje said.

Hoon looked thoughtful. 'Where to start?' she said. 'Let's see. I'd like to visit the Neanderthals and learn about their civilization. I'd like to watch the first humans arrive in North America. I'd like to talk to Jesus and Mohammed and Buddha and clear up a couple of points. I'd like to witness the building of Stonehenge and the Nazca Lines, find out what they're for—'

'We know all that. I've seen the correspondents' reports.'

'I know, I know.' Hoon gave a wry smile. 'And you don't want the past overrun with romantics like me. But that's what I'd like. And maybe—'

'Maybe?'

'No.' Hoon shook her head. 'You wouldn't approve.'

'No, go on,' Marje said, intrigued. 'Please.'

'Marje, there is such potential in the Home Time and we don't use it. Instead we let the space nations crowd us in on Earth when there's room for us all out there. Why not send ships back hundreds, thousands of years? Colonize space before the space nations get there?'

Marje knew how rude it would be to express her immediate reaction and so she kept quiet, and Hoon carried on regardless. 'And maybe . . .

correct a few things. This and that. It wouldn't affect us here, would it? This is the Home Time. All the streams lead here. But if you could prevent all the wars, all the plagues, all the famines of history, think how many lives you would be saving.'

Marje sighed. This woman was on the Oversight Committee: she was one of the people responsible for keeping College and World Executive in touch. 'And all the people who lived instead never would,' she said. 'We don't play God, Ekat. Have you heard of Jean Morbern?'

'Of course I have.'

'He left us with a set of ethics—' said Marje.

'And an artificial intelligence that makes damn sure you keep to them. AIs can be overridden, Marje. Do you want a fancified computer telling you what to do?'

'If I disagreed with it, no, I wouldn't. But the Register isn't a fancified computer and I agree with every detail of Morbern's Code.' Marje heard her voice growing cold but made no effort to change it. 'It's not just that all College personnel are sworn to follow it. You have to realize, Jean Morbern was hor-rified when he realized what . . . what godlike things he had done. Creating the timestreams meant creating millions, billions more people, all individuals, all with rights. He didn't mean to create the streams – they just . . . happened when he made his first visits upstream, before he'd got the hang of probability shielding. He felt he had no

120

right to create them and therefore no right to uncreate either.'

'And you're with him, Marje?' Hoon said quietly.

'I'm afraid I am,' Marje said. 'I'm surprised Hossein didn't tell you all this before,' she added.

Hoon paused, then smiled and bowed. 'I was out of order and I apologize. Can we start again?'

If Hoon was offering an olive branch, that was fine by Marje. 'Let's do that,' she said with a smile.

'Ah, here comes Hossein . . .'

Marje turned to look, and winced at a sudden crash. All heads turned in that direction. Asaldra had been worming his way towards them with a tray in one hand. Someone had stepped backwards at the wrong moment and the tray had gone flying. The man who had bumped into the tray staggered, arms flailing about. His foot came down on one of the fallen glasses and it broke into several fragments.

'Don't touch it!' the man shouted, panicked. He stared down at the fragments and from the way his eyes were fixed on the broken glass, Marje knew that his symb was pumping in screaming, lurid images of blood in front of his eyes whenever he thought of picking it up. Antipathy to sharp edges was something that everyone had in their preparation, but lower classifications like this man had it more than most. 'I–I'll call a drone . . .' he said.

'Oh, please,' said Asaldra. He knelt down and carefully picked up the fragments, placing them in his cupped left hand. The man recoiled as he

121

straightened up. Asaldra looked over at the two women, shrugged and pulled a face, and turned to go back to the bar with his unwelcome cargo. The crowd parted in front of him.

Conversation gradually picked up once more, now that the crisis was over and the unpleasant reality of sharp edges that could hurt someone had been removed.

'Social preparation,' said Hoon dryly. 'Where would we be without it?'

Marje took a breath. 'It enables twenty billion human beings to live together without harming each other, and to me that justifies a lot.' She wondered who had had the bright idea of using real glass in the glasses. It was taking the love of anachronism too far.

'Even to the point of not being able to stand the thought of broken glass? Come on, Marje! Our race evolved using sharp edges. Why do we force-feed our children from birth onwards with the idea that that sharp edges are bad?'

'What's your point?'

'My point is that any other society in history would have called social preparation brainwashing, a tool to keep the people down. Can you imagine the Directorate with social preparation?'

This was going too far. Comparing the Home Time to the twenty-second century's most un-pleasant regime was too much.

'But we're not the Directorate,' Marje said with a brittle smile.

'No, but we might very well become that, when the Home Time ends in twenty-seven years' time and the World Executive realizes it has twenty billion people to keep happy and nothing to do it with. Oh, we'll keep cruising on momentum for a century or so, living off the memories which the College gave us . . .'

'Social Studies is working on that,' Marje said. 'The end of the Home Time won't take anyone by surprise, Ekat.'

'It certainly won't,' Hoon agreed. 'You can depend on that.'

'Rico?' Su paused on the edge of the ravine, judged that Rico wasn't down there, and looked around. 'Where are you?'

'Over here,' Rico said faintly. He had dragged himself to a tree and was sitting on the ground with his back to it. He had tried to use the symb channel to get help but it had shut down. Presumably it had been open just long enough to entice him.

Su gasped. The massive bruise on one side of his face was clear in the moonlight.

'What happened to you?'

'Walked into a door.' He held up a hand. 'Help me up, Su.'

'There aren't any doors here.'

'I didn't think so either, but it's –' Rico hissed in pain as he slowly rose to the vertical, Su taking his weight on one side and the crutch on the other – 'amazing what you find if you look hard enough.'

'Rico, you went off for drinks, and that was the last we saw of you, and now . . .'

'I'll be OK after half an hour in a healer,' Rico said. 'Just help me get to the recall area.' Slowly, they began to hobble off, and Rico shut his ears to Su's protests while his mind worked over what he had been through.

Yes, it made sense. Low classification: might be able to do it, but social preparation would prevent it. High classification: less social preparation, but no idea how to do it.

But high classification, and control over a group of very strong 'tals with no social preparation at all: all of a sudden, all sorts of things were possible. And the only high classifications like that . . .

. . . worked for the College.

'By the way,' he said through his teeth, interrupting whatever Su had been saying, 'my theory makes sense now.'

'What theory?' Su demanded angrily.

'The one I tested at Daiho's place, remember? I worked out that if a body was thrown far enough then the agravs wouldn't pick it up. But I couldn't work out how the body could be thrown that far.'

'And?'

'I've just realized what could have done it.' He gasped as his injured leg banged into a rock. 'Still don't know who, though. They tried to put me off, Su.'

'And did they?' Su said, though there was no hope in her tone.

124

'In your dreams.'

They were through the trees, now. Tong came towards them, stopped, gaped, then hurried forward to lend his assistance, cautioned only with a stern 'don't ask' from his wife.

They tried to skirt the crowd to get to the terrace where the recall area was, but at least one member of the crowd saw them and came forward. Rico's heart sank as the familiar and very unwanted toad-like figure of Supervisor Marlici approached, silhouetted against the lights.

'Op Garron!' he said, with a smile like a shark greeting someone else's long-lost relative. 'How glad I am I found you.'

Nine

Matthew Carradine, the founder, Managing Director and President of BioCarr, had started pacing around his office for the third time.

The office was a beautifully decorated room in the magnificent seventeenth-century mansion that he had bought when he inherited his parents' fortune, at the end of the first decade of the millennium. It had a breathtaking view of the park outside. It was decorated with exquisite taste, product of the best interior designers his considerable money could buy. The perfect base from which to put all that money to even better use and build up a fortune of his own.

As he had done. He loved this building, but today it just bored him.

His PA, a quiet and inoffensive man called Alan, was turning into an irritating nag and had been snapped at the last time he put his head around the door to offer some tea. And when a call had finally come through two minutes ago, it hadn't been *the* call – it had been Alan again, with a mundane, routine matter that couldn't wait. The poor man had barely escaped with his life.

'Where are they?' Carradine muttered. 'Where *are* they?'

It was the moment he had been waiting for ever since the visitor, the stranger, had appeared and stood in front of him – just *there*, between the table and the drinks cabinet – and outlined his plans. And then he had put down what he called 'a deposit'. And what a deposit! Information decades, maybe centuries ahead of what BioCarr – or, more importantly, BioCarr's rivals – could offer. No doubt it was passé in – what had he called it? – the Home Time, which lay who knew how far in the future; but here and now in good old 2022, the stuff was so hot it was molten.

A day later, once the information had been verified and Carradine was still coming to terms with the reality of the gold seam he had struck, the man had come back and made the deal. All this in return for certain facilities and a bit of privacy.

Carradine stopped pacing and glanced at his watch. It was 16:07, and the arranged time had been 16.00. Had something gone wrong? Had the Home Timers changed their mind? Had they all been taken – he swallowed, it was a distinct possibility – for a ride?

The call tone sounded and he threw himself at his desk. Then he checked himself and carefully sat down, ran his hands back through his hair and pulled the display towards him. Alan looked out at him, any resentment from his previous tongue-lashing well hidden. Alan was like that. Quiet, reserved, unbelievably discreet, almost ageless. Carradine had suspicions about the reasons for his singleness which he kept to himself.

This once, Alan was indulging in a small smile.

'I've got Holliss at the hotel for you, Matthew,' he said. 'They've arrived.'

'Thank God! I mean, good. Good.' Carradine had to keep his arms flat on the desk in front of him, rather than hug himself with glee, which was his instinct. It was working. It could work. 'Put her through.'

Edith Holliss looked out at him, large glasses taking up most of the image. They irritated him, as they always did. Why did an employee of BioCarr, which stood for progress and technology, insist on such anachronisms when perfectly good vision correction was available to all for a small fee?

'Mr Carradine,' she gushed, 'I'm delighted to say . . .'

'Show me,' Carradine said. Holliss let a brief flash of irritation show around the edges of her polished smile but she nodded slightly and her picture moved to the left of the display. A group shot appeared on the other side. Four people, and a pile of boxes stacked behind them. 'It was quite eerie, sir,' she said. 'We were expecting them and we'd kept the area clear, as instructed, but even so, they just . . . appeared. No noise, no flash, no special effects – it just seemed so natural that suddenly they were there.'

Carradine remembered his own dealings with

128

the Home Timer. There hadn't even been any air displacement, which would surely be expected if a substantial body were to appear and disappear at will. 'I know.' He zoomed in on the picture. A young woman and three men covering a range of ages. None of them was the man he had dealt with. He peered more closely, with interest. Their clothes were strange – nothing to distinguish gender, and impossible to tell if they were wearing separate tops and bottoms or strangely designed one-pieces, though there was plenty of variation within that theme – but otherwise they could be the people next door. 'Any indication of how long they plan to stay?'

'None at all, sir. The booking's open-ended, as instructed.'

'Well, their rent's good for it,' Carradine said.

Holliss looked puzzled. 'Well, of course, sir, BioCarr is footing the bill . . .'

'That wasn't what I meant,' Carradine snapped, thinking that though Holliss was technically a Grade 7 BioCarr employee, at heart she would always be a hotel manager. A very good hotel manager, whose establishment was frequented by senior BioCarr officials and therefore had the best staff and the tightest security BioCarr could buy . . . but still a hotel manager.

She looked offended and he was immediately angry with himself. She couldn't be expected to know about the information the go-between had offered. 'Please tell me the surveillance is in place?' he said.

Holliss hadn't been well pleased to have bugs planted all over her establishment and she dared to look slightly put out. 'It is, sir, only they have some device which we haven't been able to locate, and it jams our local bugs.'

'Naturally,' Carradine said. 'What are you doing about it?'

'The surveillance people,' Holliss said, emphasizing that it wasn't her problem, 'say they're going to have to make do with lasers on the windows, lip reading via telescope, that sort of thing. What you've just seen was the last good shot we had of the guests before the cameras were affected.'

'Very interesting. What did they bring with them?'

'A lot of boxes, sir. I can't tell what they're made of, and it's difficult to say what's in them. As for personal luggage – nothing but the clothes they're wearing.'

'Give them whatever they want.'

'Of course, sir.'

'And now, introduce us.'

The image of two youngsters – Carradine would have said sixteen or so, maybe older but certainly not by much – filled the display. The boy's skin and features looked vaguely Hispanic with sallow skin and dark hair. The girl too was basically white but otherwise impossible to classify straight off. Carradine had no idea what racial intermixings might be the norm in the Home Time.

Holliss was going from left to right. 'These two

seem to be dogsbodies, sir. The boy is . . . it's difficult to say since of course they haven't filled in registration cards or anything. As far as I can tell his name is something like Bayzhay. The girl is something like Killin. They don't seem to speak our language at all.'

The display changed to one of the other men, bearded and in his late thirties or early forties. 'This one appears to be in charge, sir. His name is Phenuel Scott. The two young ones jump when he says.

'And last of all, this one.' The image was of an Asian man of indefinable age. His hair was greying but his face wasn't particularly wrinkled, yet he looked old. Perhaps it was his expression, or his eyes, or both. 'He speaks our language but doesn't say much. I said Scott was in charge but it seems to be because this one lets him be. Scott treats him with honour and respect – that is, his tone changes when they talk together.'

'I see,' Carradine said. 'Name?'

'Again, difficult to tell, sir. It sounds Chinese or Japanese . . .'

'There is a difference, Ms Holliss, as any Chinese or Japanese will tell you.'

Holliss flushed. 'Yes, sir. His name sounds like Daiho. Scott called him "the Commissioner", but I don't know what he's a Commissioner of.'

Ten

London, 1620

The Correspondent lifted his head gingerly and winced as pain stabbed through it. He quickly turned his pain receptors off and cast his senses down into the rest of his body, where his healing powers were working flat out. The bruises had almost cleared up, the cuts had mended and the most serious injury – the broken rib that had pierced a lung – was all but whole again. As was the lung.

He tried to open his eyes. The swelling had gone down but the lid of his right eye was glued shut by encrusted blood. He spat on a finger and rubbed it on the blood to dissolve it. The eye opened slowly and he looked around, carefully so as not to set off another explosion inside his skull.

It was a cell; something he had always tried to avoid, usually with success, in his six hundred years as a correspondent. He lay on a plank bed set into the wall. Straw covered the floor, the only light was moonlight shining through a grill high in the wall, and the whole place stank to high heaven of unwashed humans and the stuff that came out of them.

Luxury, he thought with only a slight sense of irony. Planks, cells, straw; these things all cost money in the England of 1620. It was not unusual to see prisoners who couldn't afford the cost of their imprisonment begging on the streets of London, under guard. No doubt there would be an accounting for this, too; his captors would have seen he was clearly a man of means, so they must have thrown his unconscious form in here first and intended to settle the bill later.

Later. His internal clock told him it was shortly after one in the morning. The sun would rise at about 4:00: he had three hours of darkness. He hoped that being hanged at dawn wasn't *literally* dawn but he didn't intend to find out.

He sat up and only then realized that his hands and feet were manacled – with iron, of course, allegedly proof against witchcraft. Another incidental expense. He looked at his bonds with irritation. They didn't present a problem in the long run, but he had better get started now.

He sat on the plank, feet on the floor, hands motionless on his lap, and began to channel energy into the muscles concerned. And while he was doing that he began to sort the facts out in his mind, prior to preparing a report.

The trial was in a large, gloomy room lined with oak panelling, and was crowded. People nowadays tended not to wash as much as the Correspondent would have liked and the finery of their clothes couldn't hide the stench.

The main witness for the prosecution was a terrified individual named Mr Marks, steward for the household of Francis Bacon – Lord Chancellor of England, Baron Verulam and soon to be created Viscount Saint Albans. Marks' story bore no resemblance to facts as the Correspondent remembered them. A lot of things weren't making sense, but the Correspondent put the matter on hold while he gave the testimony his full attention.

'Tell us,' said the prosecuting council, a tall and balding man named Whitrow, 'in your own words, the events of that evening.'

The witness spoke, with constant fearful glances at the prisoner in the dock. 'Well, sir, on that evening – that is, the sixth of June, sir – I was bringing food for my lord and his, um, visitor.'

'Is this visitor present here?'

Marks was struck dumb, and the look of sheer terror he gave the Correspondent was unfeigned. Whitrow followed the man's gaze and smiled without humour. 'He is bound with iron and surrounded by good, God-fearing men. He can do you no harm. Answer the question.'

'The visitor was the man in the dock, sir,' Marks said, almost in a whisper.

'The man who calls himself Sir Stephen Hawking?'

'Yes, sir.'

'Carry on.'

Yes, carry on, the Correspondent thought. This was interesting.

At first, the steward's testimony bore out his own recollection perfectly. The familiar inner promptings had led him to seek an interview with Bacon, using as an excuse a desire to discuss the recently published *Novum Organum.* In the book, Bacon exhorted for the abandonment of prejudice and preconception, and for observation and experimentation in science. The principles of the book influenced the whole direction that science was to take in subsequent centuries. Naturally, the Correspondent had to interview him.

And then came that baffling point where the recollections of the Correspondent and Marks diverged. The Correspondent remembered that they had discussed empiricism, politics and the transition of the monarchy from the Tudors to the Stuarts – Bacon had served the last Tudor monarch and the first Stuart, and was a rich fund of anecdotes about court life under the two regimes. It had been a pleasant time, with food and drink duly brought by Marks to Bacon's panelled and book-lined study. Then the Correspondent had retired to his own lodgings.

To be woken by the sheriff's men. He could have fought, yes, but they had come for him by surprise, and in large quantities, and they were armed. There were some things even he couldn't do – not all at once. Swords, spears, arrows he could handle, preferably if he was facing them. Bullets, from any direction, were quite another matter; the bygoners' discovery of gunpowder, in his estimation, had been a major step backwards and had made his life significantly harder.

He frowned as Marks gave his damning evidence.

'My lord and that man were talking and laughing, sir. I could hear them through the door. I put the tray down on the floor so that I could open the door, and then I heard a third voice.'

'Go on,' said Whitrow. The room was silent.

' 'Twas a man's voice, sir, and it spoke . . . I don't know what it spoke, sir. It was not English. It was a babble.'

'Who spoke?'

'Sir, it was neither my lord nor this man here who spoke. I looked through the crack in the door and I saw it was a third man, and I heard the man in the dock shout something, then speak in kind . . .'

Debate ensued between the counsels as to the significance of this: Marks argued that there was only one way into his lord's room, and that was through the door, and he swore no other man had entered the house – yet alone that room – that evening. This the Correspondent was prepared to agree with. But, a third man? And he himself had apparently spoken with the stranger, in this strange tongue . . .

Something was nagging at the back of his mind,

like the sudden reminder in the daytime of a dream some nights back. A strange sense of familiarity . . .

'And why did you look through the crack?' Whitrow asked.

'I feared for my lord, sir. I heard such anger in the visitor's shout.'

'Hawking shouted?'

'Yes, sir. The, um, third man spoke, and this man shouted, and . . .'

'Very well. And what else did you see?'

'My lord was as if frozen, sir. He seemed to see without seeing, like this.' The steward gave an impression of a glassy-eyed stare. 'This man had his back to me – I could not see what he was doing. It was blue, sir.'

'What was blue?' Whitrow didn't sound surprised at the sudden change of tack; he had no doubt gone through this thoroughly with Marks beforehand.

'The thing he—'

'The stranger . . .' Whitrow prompted.

'—the stranger held in his hand, sir. He held it to my lord's head. And then . . . then . . .' Marks was on the verge of collapsing in tears.

'Go on,' said Whitrow, with surprising gentleness. The Correspondent heard the eagerness that lay beneath the words – the anticipation of the trap.

'The newcomer vanished, sir. Just . . . vanished. And I fled, sir. I was that scared. I fled.'

*   *   *

137

He had done a lot for his Home Time masters in six hundred years, but letting himself be captured, beaten to a near pulp and sentenced to death on a charge of witchery was surely the most devoted.

After meeting Avicenna in Isfahan, he had found he had no desire to stay there any longer. At first he had wandered here and there with no real sense of purpose, reporting on what he saw, helped by the scraps of foreknowledge that would suddenly pop into his mind. He had soon learned to rely on their guidance. For instance, he had known that Isfahan and the whole area were about to be overrun by Turks, and at the same time he had suddenly found within himself the urge to head for Constantinople and, hence, Europe. He had spent some years wandering in France, then suddenly received the knowledge that the Normans were about to invade England. So he had headed there, and witnessed the landings, but not felt an urge to report them. Rather, another item of foreknowledge told him to head for Canterbury in 1094 to interview the archbishop there, one Anselm: a man who didn't know it but whose work, like Avicenna's, was to shape the future of science.

And so on. After that, it wasn't hard to work out what his mission was: to interview philosophers, thinkers, sages. Those promptings had brought him here and, for the first time, things were going wrong. Still, there was no doubt that the Home Time would appreciate this on-the-spot report of a witch's trial, even if he had no intention of providing an on-the-spot report of a witch's execution, so he had let things get this far. But now it was far enough.

He now had enough energy stored for the first phase of the escape. He pulled his wrists away from each other with a sharp jerk, and the manacles snapped with a satisfactory *crack*. He began to concentrate on phase two, the feet, and as he did so he again thought back.

'Do you speak any other language?' It was the turn of the Correspondent's own counsel, Saxton. Neat, prim, fussy. 'French? Latin? Greek? Would you recognize any of them if I spoke them now?'

'No, sir, I speak none of those,' Marks said.

'Then what is the significance of a man speaking a language you do not know? It is surely unremarkable.'

Marks' mouth moved silently. Eventually he said: 'On its own it is of no significance, but taken in conjunction with other events, it acquires meaning.'

An eloquent little speech for an uneducated serving man, the Correspondent thought with a wry smile, and no doubt quoted verbatim from his prior briefing by Whitrow. Yet, somehow the Correspondent didn't doubt that Marks believed every word he was saying. Whitrow might prime a witness, maybe even bribe a fictitious testimony into existence, but he couldn't force that witness to act as well as Marks must have been acting.

And there was the rub. Surely the most telling

witness for either side would be Bacon himself, yet the Lord Chancellor was conspicuously absent. There was more than a witchcraft trial going on here. The next year, the Correspondent knew, Bacon would be tried by his peers for the less supernatural, more straightforward offence of taking bribes. He would confess and be fined, imprisoned at the king's pleasure and banished from court and Parliament. Would that have happened so easily, the Correspondent wondered, if he had not already been tarnished by association with a witch trial? A small fact left out of the history books. Not that there could be any reasonable suspicion aimed at the man himself – he was Lord Chancellor, after all, and even under James Stuart's witch-hating regime, stronger evidence than a single deranged steward would be needed to bring down a peer of the realm – but this trial could be used simply to chip away at the man's integrity. All that was needed was a conviction. The steward's testimony must have been a godsend to the anti-Bacon brigade, and the verdict was known in advance.

The chains that bound his feet went the same way as those that had been on his wrists. The Correspondent stood up to face the door to the cell, and began to concentrate for a final focus of energy.

When he was ready, he stood facing the door, barefoot. He put his hands together and began a measured pattern of breathing. He closed his eyes and visualized the lock of the door. Then he visualized the energy that flowed through his body. Door and body were the only items in the universe. His body was completely relaxed, there was no tension or effort in it, and it was as if in a dream that he pivoted on one foot and spun and brought his heel against the lock of the door. The wood shattered and the lock flew out into the passage.

He smiled grimly and swung the door open. Pausing only to render the gibbering jailer unconscious and put his boots back on, he left the building.

By the time Whitrow began his summing up, the Correspondent was so caught up with that nagging feeling that he could only give half his mind to the proceedings.

First, Whitrow said, there was no Sir Stephen Hawking. This had been verified by the College of Heralds. Whoever he was, the defendant had gained entry to the house of the Lord Chancellor by deception.

Second, he had spoken in the same tongue as the mysterious apparition. He had not vanished, as the spectre had, which probably showed that . . . third, while the 'third man' was clearly some kind of ghost, perhaps demon, the false Sir Stephen was very real and solid and therefore a necromancer, a medium, a warlock and probably any number of other kinds of undesirable magical practitioner.

Saxton made a half-hearted attempt at defence but it was clear the court had made up its mind and Saxton wasn't going to fly in the face of opinion, apart from covering his own reputation by drawing the court's attention to the fact that there was only one witness and that all evidence was circumstantial.

The verdict and the sentence came very soon after, and while the Correspondent could have broken free, he chose not to. Too many people, a major hue and cry if he got away, more likely a pistol ball in the back. And then came that crack to the head that caught even him by surprise, and he woke up in the cell.

Robert Marks stirred in his sleep, looked up and convulsed. The Correspondent reached down and hauled him out of bed. The woman next to Marks opened her mouth to scream, and the Correspondent squeezed her throat with his free hand just long enough to make her pass out harmlessly. Then he looked back at Marks, and smiled.

'Wh–who are you?' Marks whispered, and only then did it occur to the Correspondent that all the bygoner could see with his normal, unaugmented vision was a shadow.

'Don't you remember me, Mr Marks?' he said pleasantly. He had had no idea where Marks might live; it had seemed a reasonable guess to look up in the attic of Bacon's own residence, and it had paid off.

'You!' There was total despair in the man's

moan. The witch he had sent to the gallows had come for him. 'I am dead.'

'That's a point of view.' The Correspondent looked around him. The room was not large and the bed took up most of it. 'We'll sit here, Mr Marks, and at the slightest hint of resistance on your part, the tiniest thought of raising a hue and cry, I will kill you and drag your soul down to be feasted upon by my lord the master of darkness and chaos. I make myself clear?'

They sat facing each other on the edge of the bed. Marks was bolt upright, rigid in the moonlight.

'Mr Marks, you have compromised my mission. My masters were most definite that I should remain undetected,' the Correspondent said truthfully. 'However, I will let you live if you answer some questions. Tell me about the third man you saw in your lord's room with us.'

Marks' eyes bulged. 'Sir?'

'A simple enough question. Tell me about him. What did he look like?'

'Look like, sir?'

'For God's sake answer the question, man, it's simple enough!' the Correspondent snapped. He used the language of the Home Time, and to Marks it was the unearthly gabble of Hades. The steward almost fainted. 'Do not provoke me, Mr Marks,' the Correspondent said more quietly, in English. 'Now, what was this man wearing?'

'He was – he was dressed like . . . like you, sir. A doublet, a tunic, a sword . . .'

'He was unremarkable? You would walk past him in the street and not notice?'

'Why, yes, sir.'

The Correspondent had to remember that Marks had only seen the man through a crack in the door. A perfect description was unlikely. 'You said at the trial that I shouted,' he said.

'Yes, sir . . .'

'In this strange language.'

'Yes, sir.' Marks' voice trembled.

The Correspondent shut his eyes as he tried, desperately tried, to remember. There was the ring of conviction in Marks' tone: the steward still believed everything he was saying. And the Correspondent, who had been perhaps one tenth convinced when he gained entry to the Marks' room that evening, was now nine tenths convinced.

He tried for another five minutes, but could get nothing more out of the man that had not already been said in court.

'I am leaving now, Mr Marks,' he said. 'I'm bored of this world and I am returning to the nether regions of fire and damnation, where the demons play with their pitchforks and the souls of men who betray them. Do not mention to anyone that I was here.'

He reached out and sent Marks the same way as his wife. Then he walked to the window and looked up at the moon. He made contact and the familiar tone rang out between his ears.

'RC/1029,' he said, 'requesting assistance.'

'*State nature of problem, RC/1029,*' said the neutral voice in his head. It was as uninterested as ever. The Correspondent had thought that for this, his first ever contact that wasn't just to file a report, it might be different. Clearly not.

'I have a problem with my memory,' he said. 'I am having difficulty remembering an individual.'

'*Diagnostic solutions are available for downloading,*' said the voice of the lunar station.

'Please download them. How do I run them?'

'*They are self-executing. Downloading and running now.*' There was a pause, and then it was as if the blood was roaring in his ears. The noise grew louder and louder. He winced, and gritted his teeth, and put his hands over his ears but to no avail. Now the noise seemed to be vibrating his entire cranium from the inside.

Suddenly it stopped.

'*Existence of short and long term memory block confirmed,*' said the lunar station. '*Cause of blockage unknown.*'

'Can you remove it?'

'*It is possible blockage may be self-induced due to previous psychic trauma,*' said the station. '*A defence mechanism exists in all correspondents for such an eventuality.*'

In other words, he might have flipped and the block was the only thing keeping him sane. The Correspondent shut his eyes. 'Do it,' he said.

'*It is done.*'

'I don't feel any different.'

'*Effects will become noticeable over a short period of time. Diagnostic solutions are now removed.*'

'Thank you,' the Correspondent said. 'RC/1029 signing off.'

He turned from the window to look at the two still forms on the bed, then left the house. By sunrise he was out of London, heading north into Hertfordshire.

And by sunrise he had remembered. It had all come back. He remembered the man appearing, and he remembered it hadn't been the first time. For six centuries he had been roaming this Earth, obeying the promptings at the back of his mind to seek out certain people of a philosophical bent and interview them; and every time he had interviewed a philosopher, the man had appeared with his mind-jamming device and his blue crystal. The Middle East, France, Germany, Spain, Africa, England – the man had always been there. Avicenna, Anselm, Abelard, Maimonides, Albertus Magnus, Roger Bacon, Siger, Scotus . . . and others, most lately Francis Bacon.

This time-travelling Home Timer. This lying time-travelling Home Timer, because one of the things that had kept the Correspondent going when times got hard had been the promise that if he made it to the twenty-first century, he would return to the Home Time, and there was no other way home. But now it seemed he could be brought back at any time.

He still had no idea what the man's mission was.

146

Did every correspondent get this treatment? Were the messages he had been sending to the lunar station a waste of time?

No, because the stranger had done nothing to him, the Correspondent, except take his memory of each event. It had always been the philosopher who received his fuller attentions – a blue crystal, which turned red when applied to the head.

So the stranger's purpose was a mystery, but the Correspondent remembered him now. He remembered, and he was already planning what to do next time, because now he had seen the pattern he had a pretty good idea when the next time might be.

Eleven

The air that gusted past Jontan's face was heavy with moisture and laced with salt that kept his mouth permanently dry. It roared in his ears. In his experience, air moved at a sedate pace at the whims of the weather monitoring stations: it was horrible to imagine it rushing by like this naturally.

Everything was grey: the clouds overhead, the sea to his left and the coarse, scrubby grass he was walking on along the cliff path. The one consolation – no, two consolations were that Sarai was there too, and she was walking slightly ahead of him, which meant he could indulge in his usual favourite pastime of looking at her. Like him, she was wearing a borrowed thick, wind- and waterproof jacket. It did her no justice, but he knew the outline within well enough to let his imagination do the rest.

She stopped and looked back along the cliff path. They both had caps on with flaps pulled down over the ears and she peered at him from under the peak of hers. 'Come on, Jon,' she said. He trotted the next couple of steps to catch her up, and together they followed after Mr – 'I doubt I'm a Commissioner any more' – Daiho, who strolled thirty feet ahead.

It was he who had insisted they come for a walk with him before their evening meal – 'before we all go stir crazy'. Mr Daiho's patrician instincts seemed to be taking over and with no one else to sponsor here in the Dark Ages, he had naturally adopted them, even though Mr Scott was their actual employer. Patricians, Jontan thought vaguely, could probably sponsor whom they liked. He had never thought it might be an issue in his own life.

And Mr Daiho had a point. He had been spending fifteen, twenty hours a day for the last month symbed up to the kit they had brought with them, taxing their one symb junction to its limits, while the two journeymen did their best in these primitive conditions to keep the gear going and the cultures in the tank alive. (As opposed to Mr Scott, Jontan thought as darkly as he dared, who as far as Jontan could see had come along to this benighted time purely for the fun of it.) Perhaps they indeed needed the break.

But going on a walk in this storm was another matter, though Mr Daiho said it was a perfectly normal May day. Maybe they were going stir crazy, but at least back in the hotel they were indoors and protected from the elements and supplied with such creature comforts as this whenever-it-was time could provide. But when a patrician suggested something . . .

A stone pillar loomed on the cliff top ahead, and he wondered if this was their destination. Jontan fixed his mind on the pillar and carefully put everything else out of his mind: the men who walked a discreet distance behind them on the coast path; the flying machine – telihop— . . . helit— . . . helicopter, that was it – that hovered to their left over the sea; the precipitous drop over the edge of the cliffs next to them, without any form of agrav for public safety . . . why, he just had to wander some twenty feet off course and he would fall horribly to his death on the rocks below.

'Look at this!' Mr Daiho had, indeed, stopped at the pillar and was waiting for them to catch up. It was twice his height and four-sided, and it sat on a stone base by the edge of the cliff. 'I brought you two here for a reason.'

They looked politely at the pillar. The escort and the helicopter had both stopped as well, still keeping their relative distances. There was a plaque on each side of the pillar, engraved metal lettering which Jontan couldn't read.

'We were all born in the Home Time,' Mr Daiho said, 'and we're used to being able to symb any item of information from any part of the world. Can you imagine a world where that isn't possible?'

Yes, because we're in one, Jontan thought. He was getting used to it but it was like losing one of his natural senses. He still caught himself trying to symb a simple command to the lighting, or put a message through to Sarai. The kit they had brought with them only had a few frequencies available, supported by the symb junction. It wasn't intended for idle chit-chat.

'But our world was without anything like that for thousands of years,' Mr Daiho went on. 'At the end of the century before this one the bygoners finally got the hang of global networking and they owed it all to a man named Marconi, who arranged for the first radio signal to be sent across the Atlantic Ocean to Newfoundland.' They both looked blank. 'Designated wilderness area north of Appalachia,' he said. He pointed out to sea. 'Keep going west, and you'll get there eventually. The signal was sent from this point. Remember, no satellites in those days. No cabling. No signal boosters every ten feet. This was literally just an electromagnetic wave, no words, no images, no text. It went up into the atmosphere, and it bounced off the ionosphere, and it came down to Earth two thousand miles away. It was sent and received by machinery that weighed a ton and was powered by generators which burnt fossil fuel. And it was a technical triumph, an unprecedented application of technology, every bit as significant as Morbern's work or the work we're doing here. I thought you should see this because it's part of the heritage of every human being who has lived since.'

He looked fondly at the monument for a while, then reached out to touch it. He stood in silent reverie for a moment longer while the journeymen shuffled their feet, then turned back the way they had come. 'Back we go,' he said. He threw a glance at the escort and the helicopter. 'We don't want to inconvenience our hosts, do we?' He set off back down the cliff path without a backwards glance. Jontan and Sarai looked at each other, then turned to follow.

The path dipped down into a sandy bay and rose up on the other side. The white bulk of the hotel stood at the end of it, at the top of the cliff. As they started on the downward leg to the beach, Jontan finally grew tired of the fact that his elbow was constantly rubbing Sarai's as they walked, so he pulled his hand from his pocket and took hold of hers. She seemed surprised but then she smiled at him and they continued walking like that in silence, while suddenly the day seemed less grey than before.

Over the tinkle of glasses, the gentle background violins and the soft hum of chatting, laughing voices there was something else. Phenuel Scott sneaked a glimpse past the guard who stood at the entrance of the alcove and took in his fellow diners.

Yes, there was something else, and that something was power. These bygoners were the patricians of the day. There was a casual authority about them all, shown in the calm way they could deal with the waiters that fussed and served around them. It showed in the sheer lack of ostentation: at this point in the twenty-first century, flummery had gone out of fashion and both sexes wore variations on the theme of dinner jackets. No one here had to impress or flaunt themselves. These people were the rulers, and Scott felt that he had come home.

'Mr Scott?' Two men had come into the alcove and the lead one fairly reeked of power. Scott recognized him from his pictures. A square, broad-shouldered man, holding out his hand. 'Matthew Carradine. It's a pleasure to meet you at last.'

He turned briefly to the man at his side – the same height but managing to look smaller, non-descript – and murmured something. The other nodded and withdrew to a nearby table while Carradine turned his attention to his guest.

A waiter materialized to pull Carradine's chair out for him and one of the richest men on Earth, whose corporation would soon dominate half of what the bygoners called the western world, sat down opposite Scott.

'And how was the flight from Cornwall?' Carradine said.

'Very pleasant,' said Scott. 'A bit longer than I'm used to.' A Home Time taxi could have done the trip from Cornwall to Paris in a couple of minutes, far more quietly and in a lot more comfort.

'I'm sorry.' Carradine gestured for the crew of waiters lurking in the background to begin. One of them poured the drinks, others laid out cutlery and plates and served the aperitifs. Carradine raised his glass. 'To you and your work, Mr Scott, whatever that is.'

Scott returned the toast and, since Carradine was

so openly appraising him, trying to assess him, he returned the favour.

'We must seem very primitive,' Carradine said, eyebrow raised and a slight smile on his face.

'BioCarr? The height of sophistication for this time,' said Scott.

Carradine seemed to sense he was being very gently mocked. 'We're very proud of what we've accomplished but there's still a lot of work to be done,' he said.

Scott looked up at the ceiling, hamming the look of concentration on his face. 'Let's see,' he said. 'Phase One – take the governments of the western world out of the world economy and create your own. An amazing application of economics and information technology. Of course, it will ruin several economies of countries not in the club, but they will only have to apply for entry.'

Carradine's smile was more fixed. 'Go on,' he said.

'Ah-hum. Work still to be done,' Scott said. 'If I remember correctly, your present strategy is outlined in the document *Tactical advance into the burgeoning economies of South America, eyes Grade fifteen-plus only.* The first wave will be in the form of artificial intelligences to be released into the net on—' He looked down; Carradine was almost choking on his wine. 'Did I get it right?'

'You know you did.' Carradine dabbed his napkin to his lips. 'That's top secret. I suppose you saw it in a museum somewhere?'

'Something like that.' Scott kept his gaze steady.

Carradine would know the importance of power-play. He would understand what was going on.

Sure enough, Carradine was half smiling back, and with genuine amusement. 'This is fascinating,' he said. 'You know the full history of BioCarr before it's even happened. You know if the next phase will work. You know how long BioCarr will last. You probably know when and how I die.'

'Not how, but otherwise, all of the above,' Scott said.

'And you're not going to tell me.'

'It would make no difference if I did, but no, I'm not.'

'Your emissary did lay down a few conditions,' Carradine said, thoughtful. 'If we lay one hand on you – for example to torture the information I want out of you, though we'd use something far more sophisticated and reliable – you call down legions of angels to smite us. You probably could. On the other hand, it could be bluff. I do get the feeling your Home Time doesn't know you're here.'

'I'm sure you have the need-to-know principle in this century too,' Scott said calmly, and Carradine leaned back in his seat and shouted with laughter. Any hint of tension evaporated.

'Mr Scott, we understand each other perfectly. You've paid us, we provide a service, we don't have to understand or like it. Pure capitalism.'

The first course arrived; bowls containing a brown, translucent liquid with a fragrance that was to die for.

'Beef consommé,' Carradine said. 'I took the liberty of ordering in advance because I wasn't sure how familiar you would be with our menus.'

'Thank you,' Scott said, and cautiously dipped his spoon in. He was an instant convert to bygoner cuisine after just a few drops on his tongue. The flavour was suspended with such delicacy that he felt the liquid in the bowl would flip over into another state of matter if he touched it. They drank it in silence.

'Time travel. It's fascinating. It's truly fascinating.' Carradine shook his head as he put down his spoon and the waiters rematerialized. 'And I've had sleepless nights wondering why you came here, of all the times available to you.'

'You've probably had teams of experts working on the problem,' Scott said.

'I certainly have. The consensus is that you wanted to go as far away from your Home Time as you could, while keeping to a certain technological minimum –' he looked hopefully at Scott, who kept his expression deliberately bland – 'but that still doesn't explain what you want.'

'No, it doesn't,' Scott said.

Carradine changed the subject. 'I was wondering if your colleagues would be coming this evening, too.'

Colleagues? For a moment Scott was confused by the plural, until he realized Carradine was including Killin and Baiget. They would be fish out of water here.

'No,' he said, 'they all have work to do.' And Daiho, the one whom Scott did regard as a colleague, had made it quite clear that he disapproved of Scott going off on this trip. The problem with some College people was that they couldn't imagine transference actually being any fun.

'But you don't?'

'The youngsters are our technicians, Mr Daiho is our . . .' Scott paused for thought. What exactly was Daiho in the set-up? 'Our philosopher. I'm management and this is by way of getting to know our hosts. Good relations.'

'Naturally.'

The second course came. 'This is steak of ostrich,' Carradine said. 'That's a large bird . . .'

'I do know what an ostrich is,' Scott said, twisting his mouth in a smile to take any sting out of his words.

'I'd thought they might be extinct by your time.'

'Nothing's extinct in the Home Time,' Scott said, and let Carradine work it out for himself. After a couple of moments the man groaned.

'*Duh*, of course,' he said. 'I wasn't thinking. Presumably you regularly tuck into filet au brontosaurus and woolly mammoth steak?'

'Saurians are too oily for my taste,' Scott said.

'Mr Scott, you have a lovely way with one-liners,' said Carradine. 'I suppose I never really got rid of my childhood idea that the people of the future would dine out on a single pill that could last for a week. Lousy science, of course, but it caught my imagination.'

'Why on Earth would they do that?' Scott laughed in genuine disbelief. Carradine chuckled too, and they commenced their attack on the ostrich.

Carradine's former companion appeared by Carradine's side with a small, rectangular plastic box in his hand. Scott looked at him curiously. The man had been at a neighbouring table all the time they had been there but he had vanished from Scott's perception the moment Carradine asked him about the flight. It was hard to notice him – he was discretion personified. The perfect assistant.

The man whispered into Carradine's ear and handed him the device.

'Thank you, Alan,' Carradine said, and held the box to the side of his face. He spoke into its lower end.

'Carradine.' His eyes widened and his jaw dropped; then he looked up at the ceiling. 'Oh, Christ. Right. Yes, I'll see to it.'

Scott was waiting, knife and fork poised. Carradine looked at him, annoyance and amusement competing with each other in his expression. 'Trouble up't'mill,' he said.

'I'm sorry?'

'Trouble back at the hotel.'

'Back to work,' said Mr Daiho. He stood up, took a final swig from his glass of water and left the dining room. From their journeyman's table at the other end of the room – just eating in the same room as the other two had been a mental wrench that none of them had enjoyed, and Mr Scott had made his displeasure quite obvious – Sarai and Jontan looked at each other. Then they silently pushed back their chairs and stood too.

They hadn't had much time to talk since the walk, but just before they went through the door Sarai's hand sought his and gave it a squeeze. He risked a quick squeeze and a smile in return, before they left the room a chaste two feet apart and the model of journeyman propriety.

The kit was of course as they had left it, since it was surrounded by a forcefield that could only be symbed off. Mr Daiho had already done this and was settling on to his couch.

'Take your places,' he said. They sat down in their respective chairs and symbed into the systems, with the usual mental jostle for a symb frequency not being used by the others. Representations of nutrient levels and energy flows filled Jontan's mind. Then Mr Daiho activated his field computer to make some fine adjustments, shut his eyes and settled back on the couch. The evening session had begun.

Jontan stole a glance to his right: Sarai's eyes were half shut as she symbed. He reached out and laid a gentle hand on her knee. She covered it with her own hand, but didn't make any effort to remove it. Nor did she look at him.

So Jontan let his gaze roam over the kit, while

half his mind continued to monitor the signals it was sending. One of the popular entertainment shows displayed in that box in the lounge, he had gathered, was meant to be set in the future and the kit there was covered with flashing lights. The reality that they had brought with them was a collection of abstract boxes with not a flashing light to be seen, except for the row of seventeen red crystals that glowed with an inner light. Unlike Mr Daiho and his symb connection, they were physically connected to the main culture tank – a large flattened oval as long as an adult. What was going on in there was anyone's guess. Jontan only knew that it was some form of biological activity, co-ordinated by Mr Daiho, and it was his and Sarai's job to keep the culture alive and healthy.

'Watch it,' said Sarai.

'Got it,' he said. Levels of Filler-A were dropping in the tank. He had to get a bottle from one of the crates they had brought with them and physically top up the contents.

'What's it for?' he murmured as he sat back down again.

Sarai spoke but didn't answer the question. 'I'll check that valve when he's done with this session. The field's out of sync.'

'Oh, yeah.' A symb image of the set-up showed Jontan what Sarai meant. He glanced again at Sarai and, with Mr Scott absent and Mr Daiho under the hood, decided that at last he would say what he had been thinking for so long. 'Sa?'

'Yes?'

'The College doesn't know we're here, does it?'

Now she actually looked at him, and he felt a paradoxical relief to see his own anxiety mirrored in her eyes and in her heavy sigh. 'A College man sent us here,' she said, which he suspected was her way of saying she knew exactly what he was getting at but wasn't going to admit it.

'Yeah, but at school they said every trip should be accompanied by Field Ops, and I don't see any, and that chamber was all hidden away, and the man said something about setting charges, and I think he was going to blow up the equipment after we went.'

'Maybe.'

'Sa?'

'Yes?'

'I think this is illegal.'

'It might be, in the Home Time.'

'Sa?'

'Yes?'

'How do we get back if he blew it up?'

Sarai held her hands up in a shrug. 'The College has got plenty more transference chambers.'

'But—'

'Jon, I don't *know*!' Jontan recoiled from the sharp rise in her voice as if she had hit him. His instinct was to take umbrage, but one sideways glance at her – she was biting her lip – made him change his mind. He thought of something like, *you're upset, aren't you?* He tried it out in his own mind and rejected it. There was someone in the

161

journeyman's barracks back on the plantation who was always coming out with blindingly obvious statements like that and everyone, Jontan included, thought he was an idiot.

So, he gently put his hand back on her knee. When it was obvious she wasn't going to throw it off again, he said, 'Sorry.' She nodded and clasped his hand firmly with both of hers.

'Filler-A's dropping again,' she said. 'That valve's had it.'

The end of the session came surprisingly soon. It was still before midnight. Mr Daiho sat up, stretching and flexing his back. 'We're getting somewhere,' he said, beaming at them. 'We're really getting somewhere. Well done. I couldn't have done it without you.'

Praise from a patrician, even one possibly engaged in illegal activity, was a balm to their souls. It felt like the sun coming out from behind a cloud.

'We need to change a valve, sir,' Sarai said.

'Then you'd better do it, and get some sleep. We'll start again the usual time in the morning. Is Mr Scott back yet?'

'Um, not yet, sir,' Jontan said.

'Hmph.' Mr Daiho rumbled something that sounded very like anger, and stood with his back to them to gaze out of the windows down at the cliffs and the sea. Jontan and Sarai glanced at each other, then Sarai ducked beneath the main tank to check the valve. It was a one-person job, phasing the forcefield that held it in place and the forcefield that actually did the work within it so that they didn't interfere with each other and cause a leak. Jontan wondered what he should do next.

'Give us a hand, Jon?' Sarai popped up briefly to ask the question, then vanished again. Jontan grabbed a spare phase adjuster and crouched down to see what she wanted.

'See up there, I think it's loose . . .' she said. He moved his head in closer to see, and then she kissed him, full on the mouth. He almost dropped the adjuster. It seemed to last forever and it made praise from Mr Daiho a very secondary pleasure. Jontan's heart pounded and he couldn't believe she had kissed him with a patrician standing only a few feet away, when everyone knew journeymen didn't, but he was very glad these two just had.

'I do need you,' she said. 'Symb into the system and tell me how this works.'

'Right,' he said, still in a daze. Again he had to tune his thoughts to the symb junction, and to his surprise he found his frequency of choice already occupied.

'*LD/1919, stand by,*' said a voice he hadn't heard before. It was flat and toneless; he was sure it was artificial, not human. Then, '*LD/1919, transmit.*'

Another voice, and Jontan did recognize this one. It was Mr Daiho. 'LD/1919, nothing to report,' was all he said. Jontan lifted his head up and sneaked a look over the tank. Mr Daiho still hadn't moved from the window. He seemed to be looking up at the moon.

163

'*Report received, LD/1919,*' said the voice. Then contact broke and the frequency cleared. Mr Daiho turned away, but Jontan had already ducked back down.

'That's a correspondent's code,' said Sarai later. They had the lounge to themselves now and were talking about it in whispers, sitting in one corner of the room.

'How do you know?'

'I saw a zine. They're all called something like that, XY/1234. That's how they do it, Jon!'

'Do what?'

'That's how they talk to the Home Time. I bet LD/1919 got killed and Mr Daiho uses the same code, and the Register back in the Home Time doesn't know it, so it stores the messages and releases them one by one, like always, and . . .'

She trailed off and gazed unfocused into space, still working it out.

'And?' he prompted.

'And, someone at that end sees the reports and knows we're OK, and that's how Mr Daiho will ask them to recall us.' She grinned in sheer delight. 'See? So we're safe and it's all right. We're going to be all right!'

Then she kissed him again, and this time he was better able to respond, sliding his arms around her and holding her close, and for the time being that was that, except that both occasionally cocked an eye at the door in case Mr Daiho returned.

Eventually she tightened her grasp around him and just hugged him tight. She rested her head on his shoulder.

'I'm glad you're here, Jon,' she said.

Jontan started another mental search for something un-trite to say. She spared him the trouble. 'Want to go for a walk?'

'A walk?' Romance evaporated as he glanced out of the window. 'It's dark!'

'I know.' She wiggled her eyebrows up and down. 'But the moon's full.'

'We might . . . we might fall off the cliff . . .' he said, feeling pathetic.

'Then we'll walk away from the cliff,' she said. 'Coming?'

Outside there was enough light not to bump into anything, with the moon and the lights of the hotel behind them. The wind had died down since that afternoon and it no longer put Jontan in mind of pressure leaks and field failures; besides, they were in the garden, sheltered by tall conifers that took the bite out of the gale. In fact, the gentle motion of the air past his face, soft and warm, was almost pleasant if he tried not to remember that it had never been anywhere near an atmospheric scrubber and was probably laden with prehistoric pathogens. They strolled down the garden, hand in hand, away from the hotel. The path curved so that before long the hotel was out of view. Then they stopped, and she turned to him, and they kissed again.

After a while they sat down, arms round each other, and looked out at the valley that stretched away from the hotel inland. It was bathed in moonlight.

'It's gorgeous,' she said. 'I hate this time but the view's good.'

'Sa?'

'Yes?'

'When did you decide this was a good idea?'

'Oh, a while ago.'

'How long?'

'How long?' She turned and kissed his ear. 'Maybe when Lano Chon pushed me over, and you helped me up, and then you hit him.'

'When . . .' He frowned. He had no memory of the incident, but he remembered Lano Chon, from a long time before social preparation had settled into them, back when . . .

'We were seven!' he said.

'Like I said, a while ago.'

It was coming back. 'He hit me, too,' he said.

She giggled. 'He said, look over there! And you looked, and he hit you. I couldn't believe it.'

'So . . .' he said, wounded.

'So,' she said, and kissed him on the mouth. 'So, I decided you were never going to be Jean Morbern, but you were all right.'

'Huh.' He tried to think of a way to get the initiative again. He felt the ground behind him, as a possible prelude to inviting her to lie down. Ugh. The air they breathed might be warm but the ground they sat on was cold and damp and totally uninviting. 'All right, let's— what's this?' His fingers had closed on something like wire. He looked closer. It was indeed wire, but not shiny and very difficult to see in the dark. He pulled at it.

Flares blazed up into the sky, bright light burst around them and a screaming electronic howl filled the air. The racket of a helicopter thudded overheard and men in dark clothes burst out of the bushes, brandishing guns.

Twelve

Utrecht, 1646

Cornelius van Crink's heart leaped when he saw
the gentleman come into the foundry. The
man peered in through the door, then stepped into
the main workshop, an island of calm amid the
noise and heat of Utrecht's finest gunsmiths going
about their work. Van Crink's practised eyes
reviewed the newcomer – embroidered cloak,
polished sword, velvet hat, general air of prosperity
and well-to-do – and he stepped smartly forward
before any of his underlings could reach the
gentleman first. Such a prospective customer
deserved nothing but the best.

The man saw him approaching. 'Are you the
master gunsmith?' he called over the racket.

'Cornelius van Crink, at your service, sir,' van
Crink acknowledged with a bow. 'How may I help
you, sir?'

A master merchant, perhaps? he thought with glee.
He looked rich enough. It was fifty years since the
Dutch had thrown off their Spanish masters, back

in the last decade of the sixteenth century. Now the Dutch trading empire was wrapping itself around the world and the merchant class had come into its own. If he was looking to fit out a ship for a trip to the Indies . . . van Crink's heart sang.

'I'm looking for a brace of pistols,' the man said. Van Crink carefully refused to let his disappointment show.

'And will that be all, sir?' He had to strain his ears to catch the man's reply, delivered with a smile:

'I choose to start small, Mr van Crink, but if I am happy with them – who knows?'

Who indeed? Van Crink's spirits were quite restored. 'Then let us go somewhere more conducive to polite conversation, sir,' he said.

Van Crink personally escorted the gentleman to the warehouse, where an underling opened the door for them. He stood for a moment in quiet reverence before entering. It was better even than entering a house of worship: rows and rows of shiny steel and hand-worked wood, the sublime smell of wrought metal and polish.

'My warehouse, sir,' he said quietly. 'I know we will have something to suit you. I have to ask, what does sir have in mind for these pistols? Are they for a duel? For hunting? For display?'

'I want something that is accurate at a range of no more than fifteen feet. More likely ten.' The man's eyes were also ranging along the rows of weapons and van Crink couldn't but notice that there seemed to be a certain casual familiarity there.

'I understand, sir.' Van Crink didn't, but he got the gist of what the man was after. Fifteen feet? More likely ten? Obviously a duel. Unless, of course, it wasn't intended that the other man should be armed at all . . . But van Crink simply sold the weapons.

He turned to a nearby shelf. 'I have here something that might be of interest.' He held up a single example and lovingly presented it to his customer, grip first. An elegant, slim barrel two feet long resting in a beautiful walnut stock. Magnificent carvings in both metal and wood; ornate but not fussy. A weapon of quality.

The customer took it in, and dismissed it, at a glance.

'No wheel-locks,' he said. 'Too unreliable.'

'Unreliable?' van Crink exclaimed. He was too stung for a moment even to remember that the customer's wishes were sacrosanct. His gaze caressed the weapon's priming mechanism, and silently he apologized to it. To fire the gun after it had been loaded with ball and powder, the gun's owner would use a key to wind up a steel wheel connected to a strong spring. Pressing the trigger caused the wheel to spin rapidly, which made it emit sparks, which ignited the powder. A graceful, elegant and above all *modern* device.

'I'll take a pair of match-locks,' said the customer. 'These, perhaps.' He picked up one of the pistols to have caught his eye and held it up, squinting along the barrel.

170

'Then sir will also want some slow-match?' van Crink said, trying not to sound sarcastic.

'It would help.' A length of permanently burning slow-match was fixed to the gun's spring mechanism. When the trigger was pressed, it sprang forward and ignited the powder. An assured spark and hence a reliable weapon – on a sunny day.

Van Crink made one last try. 'My father fought the Spanish, sir. The tales he told me of how his guns were made unserviceable by the rain! "If only I had had a decent wheel-lock in those days, Cornelius," he would say . . .'

He came to realize that the customer was looking speculatively down the barrel of the match-lock, directly at him. For all that he knew the weapon wasn't primed, and had no match attached to it, lit or otherwise, the look in the customer's eyes meant he suddenly felt very nervous.

'I'm sure your father fought nobly for the Netherlands,' the customer said calmly, 'but I also expect he fought outdoors.' Abruptly he brought the gun up to his face, barrel pointing to the ceiling. 'Now, about that match . . .'

The Correspondent checked the brace of pistols for the tenth time. Both were charged and primed, both were ready. He had owned them from new and he had practised with them for months. He could hit anything he chose at up to thirty feet. It was an accuracy that would have astonished

171

that van Crink man, but then the Correspondent had access to thought processes and powers of mental computation that would also have astonished the fat gunsmith. And in the very unlikely event of his missing with one barrel, he doubted his target could move fast enough to avoid the other.

The sounds of busy Utrecht – horses, street cries, the constant murmur of a large population – drifted in through the window. He ignored them. He had planned for this for so long, and the visitor would appear if his plan worked.

It was obvious that the visitor, the man who had appeared at every interview the Correspondent had given in his career, was taking the co-ordinates for his trips from the Correspondent's reports. Well, tonight, if all went well, the Correspondent would file a report with the lunar station to the effect that he had interviewed René Descartes – father of modern science; first mathematician to classify curves according to the equations that produced them; significant contributor to the theory of equations; devisor of the use of indices to express the powers of numbers; formulator of the rule of signs for finding the numbers of positive and negative roots for any algebraic equation – at 10 o'clock in the morning on 30 June, 1646, here in an upper room in this modest house of timber in Utrecht. Descartes lived in a house, bought with his own money, and so it was in a house that the Correspondent had had to set his trap. Any other location might have aroused suspicion in *their* minds. He had bought the place he was in now twenty years ago, back in 1626; time enough for a steady succession of tenants, time enough for any connection that the Home Time might have been able to make with him to blur. Then he had carefully left Utrecht. He had made no mention in his reports of the house purchase and given the impression he had just been passing through. He had continued on his travels around Europe.

To return a month ago. To evict the current tenants. To wait.

And there he was. With that strange sense of no transition, as if he had always been there and it was only the Correspondent's memory at fault, there stood the man, dressed like a prosperous Dutch merchant, raising his right hand.

As did the Correspondent, much more quickly, bringing one of the match-locks to bear on a direct line between the Correspondent's eyes and the man's forehead. 'Don't,' he said, in the language of the Home Time. The pistol was pointing exactly between the visitor's eyes. 'I've seen what these can do to a man's head, which I doubt you have.'

Realization and horror flashed across the visitor's face. 'My god, you remembered me,' he said, and his hand twitched upwards.

The Correspondent fired, moving his hand slightly before he did. The crash of the gun was deafening and smoke filled the room. When it had cleared, the visitor was doubled over, moaning and clutching his ear, and the Correspondent's other gun was raised.

'I've just nicked your left ear exactly an inch above the lowest point of the lobe,' said the Correspondent. His one main worry was unfounded: the man's pain showed that he wasn't another correspondent. 'So don't doubt that I can hit any part of you that I choose. Now, stand up and drop the thing in your right hand.'

The visitor did so, slowly, and the small crystal sphere that the Correspondent had glimpsed so often in the past dropped onto the wooden floor with a clatter. The Correspondent stooped to pick it up.

'Now strip,' he said. The visitor's eyes widened. 'Strip completely.'

Five minutes later they were in another room, the visitor wrapped in a robe that the Correspondent had supplied. If he had had any further Home Time gadgets about him that could have helped him, they were lying in the abandoned pile of clothing in the upper front room.

'I don't know your name,' the Correspondent said. The visitor glared at him but said nothing. 'Herbert, I think,' said the Correspondent, 'until you tell me otherwise. Herbert the time traveller.'

'H–how did you remember?' the visitor asked. They sat facing each other in comfortable chairs. The Correspondent had thought it only hospitable to set some wine aside in readiness, and Herbert's teeth clattered against his cup. The Correspondent held his own cup in one hand and the second match-lock in the other, and the barrel pointed without wavering at Herbert's heart.

'Not important,' said the Correspondent. With the Bacon incident in mind, he had taken the precaution of giving the servants the day off. 'Incidentally, I've stored a written account of everything I remember in several locations around town and elsewhere. Even if you somehow make me forget everything again, I'll remember again. And again, and again, and again.'

Herbert grimaced. 'I was careless.'

'Yes,' the Correspondent agreed. 'And now you can make up for it by taking me back to the Home Time.' Herbert looked at him with blank surprise. 'Back to the Home Time,' the Correspondent repeated, with more emphasis. 'When I first arrived I was keen, fired with enthusiasm to report, a loyal servant of my masters in the glorious, glowing future. I knew I had a purpose, a valuable function, and I was eager to serve. The Home Time was waiting for my reports. They needed them. The twenty-first century seemed a long time to wait, but I could handle it, and of course there was no way home, was there? You couldn't send anyone back to get me because the equipment to do so wouldn't exist before the twenty-first century. I had to wait, I had no choice.

'And then, *then*, I learned the Home Time were a bunch of lying bastards and they could come and go as they pleased. Somehow my motivation just evaporated. And now, you can take me back.'

Herbert slowly put down his cup and sat back in his chair, cold amusement doing battle on his face with natural caution deriving from the fact that the Correspondent still held a gun pointing at him. 'Supposing I said it was impossible?' he said.

'I wouldn't believe you. Everything else has been a lie, hasn't it?'

'Transference doesn't need—'

'Transference?'

'Travel through time,' Herbert snapped. 'Transference doesn't need equipment for the return journey. The Home Time sends a recall field. But it wouldn't work on you. It's a matter of probability frequency, which changes every time a transference is made. The recall has to be the same frequency as the send. We don't want to pick up any Ops—'

'Any what?'

'Time travellers from another point in the Home Time, you see. Now, the probability resonance of objects can be changed, that's how we bring back samples from other times, but that needs special tagging equipment which I don't have on me.' He looked the Correspondent in the eyes. 'That's why I can't take you back. Not won't, can't.'

The Correspondent said nothing for a moment. Then: 'You have one of these recall fields planned, then?'

'I set it to cover the immediate area around the original co-ordinates,' Herbert said, after a pause during which he was plainly wondering how much to reveal. 'If I'd had the foresight to set it to cover a wider area, we wouldn't be having this conversation now. I'd have just vanished.'

'It's already come on?'

'Been and gone by now. It came on two minutes after arrival. But if I miss it it's set to come on every hour at the same point until I do make it.' He scowled. 'I've never missed it before.'

'Supposing I grab hold of you and hold you tight when the field does come on?'

Herbert shook his head. 'Probability masking. You'd get two conflicting probability resonances in the same area, the field would be confused and neither of us would be recalled at all.'

Another pause. 'You've lied to me about the one main tenet of being a correspondent,' said the Correspondent. 'No home journey until the twenty-first century. So why should I believe you now?'

'That bit is true,' said Herbert. 'Recall Day will be the last thing the Home Time does while transference is still possible, and the whole world will be bathed in every transference frequency ever used. You'll be recalled if you live that long.'

'Why that day? And what's this about the last thing the Home Time does?'

The visitor ticked the points off on his fingers. 'That day, because that's when a bygoner scientist will invent equipment that could detect transference. And soon after that, the bygoners will get back to the moon, maybe find the lunar station.

177

The past becomes untenable for us after that date. We call it the Fallow Age.'

'And the Home Time?' the Correspondent prompted.

'The Home Time is a period of set probability flux. There's a singularity beneath the College – our, um, centre of operations – that makes transference possible because it vibrates at a fixed, unchanging probability frequency. It's a permanent referent. An, ah, anchor that will always drag us back home again. But it won't last forever, it's decaying, and the day will come when it ends and transference won't be possible any more. But we keep our word, and you will be recalled before then.'

'How long does it have to run? From your point of view?'

'Is that relevant? Let's just say, not long enough.'

'You've been very forthcoming,' the Correspondent said. 'I could still just kill you now.'

'You could,' said Herbert. 'But this is an imperfect situation, so let's make the best of it.' His earlier shock was all gone now and he sounded almost in charge. 'I can't take you back with me, just now. You've remembered me. Inconvenient, but it's happened. Now—'

'I'm not going to carry on as a correspondent,' said the Correspondent. 'I might have to stay here but I'm damned if I'm going to lift a finger for you again.'

Herbert shrugged. 'It's not unusual for correspondents to take a break, go off-line for a century or two, maybe forever. It's your decision.' He smiled a cold, lop-sided smile. 'Maybe we can discuss things?'

Thirteen

'Marje?' Marje jumped: Su Zo must have been waiting for her just outside the canteen. 'You did say you'd see me around,' Su said with an embarrassed smile.

'Su! Um, I, ah, yes, yes, I did,' Marje agreed. 'Good to see you. How's things?'

'Um . . . can we walk?' Su said.

'Why not? I've got to get back to the office. This way.' They started walking towards the nearest carry-field, side by side.

'Thanks for letting us look through the Commissioner's things,' Su said.

'It was my pleasure.' Su was plainly ill at ease, so Marje cast around in her mind for a way to continue the conversation. 'Did Op Garron find his computer?'

Su shook her head. 'No. We found all kinds of interesting things, I mean, he did a lot more transferring than we ever thought he would have, but not that. Marje . . .' Suddenly it all came out in a rush. 'Rico's been suspended and there's to be an enquiry into his conduct.'

'Oh,' said Marje, nonplussed. 'I'm, ah, sorry.'

'Supervisor Marlici cornered us at the party last night and delivered a reprimand. Rico's third. And suspension is automatic for an Op with three reprimands.'

Marje shrugged. There were only so many times she could say she was sorry, and she wasn't sure she was. Su carried on talking.

'One of those reprimands was yours, Marje, and I know for a fact it was, um . . .'

'Unjustified,' said Marje. 'I know, and I apologized for it.' Now she did feel something, and it was anger. It was just what she had been afraid of at the time – that ass Asaldra getting Garron into trouble. She had let it pass because surely one reprimand wasn't career-threatening. It hadn't occurred to her that Garron might already have had some on his record. But if he was the kind of man who attracted reprimands, perhaps he deserved suspension. 'Which one was mine?' she said.

'The second. The third . . . we had to do a routine courier job in gamma-Vienna. Pick up the superintendent's report, nothing special. Except that the superintendent there was abusing his position with the bygoners. Rico took him to task for it . . . he must have symbed a complaint into the report crystal I was carrying and we brought it back without even knowing it. I reported my version as well, but it doesn't seem to have done any good.'

181

If Su had just come to beg, Marje would have dismissed her. If Su had asked her to use her influence, such as it was, with Fieldwork's Commissioner Ario, the result would have been similar. But Su was simply stating facts, and whether by design or accident, that was the approach that captured Marje's attention.

'Op Garron has a lot to learn about tact if he's to make progress in Fieldwork,' she said.

'Rico used to be senior to me, Marje. He was a Senior Field Op in Specific Operations.'

'Really?' Marje stopped walking. Now, that did surprise her. The Specifics were the elite of Fieldwork. 'I see,' she said, to give herself time to think. 'Thank you for telling me, Su, I'll . . . I'll look into it.'

Su still didn't smile: she bowed her head slightly. 'Thank you,' she said, and turned to walk away.

'Wait,' Marje said. With the matter of Garron out of the way, something else that Su had said finally sank in. 'What did you mean when you said Li did more transferring than you thought?'

Ten minutes later an even more pre-occupied Marje Orendal entered her office and sat down at her desk. Li had gone transferring? *Li* had gone *transferring?*

Su had told her about the list of transferences they had found in Daiho's effects. She and Garron hadn't thought twice about them; but then they hadn't known the man. Marje had, and if ever

182

a man was born to be a stay-at-home stick-in-the-mud it had been Li Daiho.

One transference here and now, well, maybe. But a spate of seventeen was . . . odd. Where could he have gone?

Well, that was easily settled. Marje called up the list herself, on her authority as Commissioner. *'Compare against list of approved transference sites,'* she symbed, and the answer came back: they weren't approved sites.

'Not approved?' Marje exclaimed out loud, in sheer surprise. But Li must have got those co-ordinates from somewhere. Co-ordinates were assembled from historical records, or simple deduction, or on-the-spot Field Ops, and in all cases were entered into the database of approved sites . . . assuming they were found to be safe. But there was another source of information, as she of all people should know.

'Compare against all co-ordinates returned by correspondents,' she symbed cautiously.

And there it was. Marje gazed in awe at the two lists displayed side by side across her vision. Every site chosen had been reported by the same correspondent, RC/1029. (Where had she seen that correspondent's designation before? She pushed the question away, to come back to later.) None had subsequently been entered into the approved general list, which could only mean one thing. Li didn't want anyone following him.

And that would be fair enough: if a Field Op

transferred to co-ordinates that were found to be unsuitable – for instance, they were in the middle of a crowded room, or something – then that site would be put on the banned list and, if bygoners had become aware of the Home Time as a result, the Specifics would be sent in to clear things up. Not unusual.

But to go unerringly to seventeen unsuitable sites? And – it took a second to check – the Specifics had *not* been sent in. Li had kept all this secret. And that itself was illegal.

Another thought . . .

'*Summarize the reports in which these co-ordinates were delivered.*' Another heartbeat's pause, and then the bald summaries were laid out before her. Each time the correspondent had been interviewing a philosopher.

I really did not know this man, Marje thought. But she remembered where she had heard of RC/1029: Li had been getting regular reports from him. And then, apparently, going along to see for himself.

Having a hobby was one thing – but this? What had he been doing?

Well, she was going to find out. If her predecessor had been engaged in illegal activity then she had to find out; and if there was an innocent explanation that was simply escaping her right now . . . well, she should find it. She really should.

And she knew just the man for the job.

* * *

'Op Garron. Come in.'

It had taken over an hour in a healer, but Rico's wrenched thigh had been unwrenched, his bruised tissues regenerated and the damage from the beating was just a memory, so he was able to enter the office without difficulty. It was only the second time he had seen Acting Commissioner Orendal face to face, and it seemed there was a momentary warmth there before she froze over and became appropriately formal. She was one of those people, Rico decided, who for some reason felt that different personae were needed for their private and their public lives.

She stood up as he entered her office and held out a hand; he hesitated for just a fraction, then walked across the glowing carpet (Twenty-first century? Hideous, anyway) to shake it. He had resolved, to himself and to Su, that he would behave himself. He was suspended and she might – *might* – be able to do something about it, so there was no point in antagonizing her.

'Please, sit down,' she said. He sat in the chair indicated, across the desk from her. It was more modern than the rest of the office, an empty frame with a forcefield for the seat. Perhaps, he thought, Orendal was imposing her more contemporary tastes on her predecessor's room with a wave of modernity that emanated outwards from the desk but hadn't yet reached the rest of the office. She rested her elbows on the desk top, steepled her fingers. The lines on her face showed she was perfectly capable of smiling, if she chose.

'Thank you for coming,' she said. 'I want to make you a proposition.'

'Please do,' Rico said.

'You've been suspended, pending a tribunal, and that's partly my fault.'

'One of the reprimands was because of a complaint from your office, yes,' Rico said without expression.

'One of them,' she said pointedly. 'Of three.' Rico said nothing. 'I've no doubt that the matter will be cleared up at the tribunal and you'll be put back on the active list.'

'Will you be speaking on my behalf?' Rico said innocently.

'No,' she said. She paused a beat, while Rico thought, *typical,* then: 'the individual who made the complaint will be speaking instead.'

'I see.' *Nice touch,* he thought. 'May I ask what this proposition is, Commissioner?'

'You may, but first I'd like to know about the other reprimands.'

'They're on my record, which I expect you've read by now,' he said.

'I just finished, yes, but I'd still like to hear about them. The most recent one – I gather you gave a supervisor some lip, or something like that?'

'Something like that,' Rico said, thinking, *what the hell.* He still had no idea what she wanted with him and his reprimands were none of her business, but . . . 'He was a superintendent, who . . . aw, let's name names. Superintendent Adigun is in charge of sixteenth-century gamma-Vienna and he's shacked up with one of the bygoner women. I . . . well, I took exception to his using his position to that purpose.'

Any remaining hint of humour or goodwill in Orendal's expression had vanished. 'Go on,' she said.

'I drew attention to the matter and he construed my words as insulting. He made a complaint.'

'Was his conduct mentioned in your report?'

'I'm not the senior partner, so it wasn't my report. But no, it wasn't. There are firmly defined areas, Commissioner. If he had been beating her, we could have reported him. If he had told her anything about the Home Time, we could have reported him. But as it was, he wasn't doing anything illegal.'

'Morbern's Code—'

'Isn't law,' Rico said. 'Not all of it. Physical abuse, yes. Emotional, no.'

Orendal still held his gaze, but her eyes were blank and he guessed she was symbing. 'Edigun?' she said.

'Adigun.'

'Superintendent Adigun, Vienna, sixteenth century, gamma stream. Thank you.' She seemed to collect herself and put the matter to one side. 'The second reprimand I know about. What about the first?'

The first was the one Rico was both least and

most proud of. 'That one was a supervisor, also in the field,' he said. 'Beta-Rome, C minus three. He was cheating on two women – he had a wife here in the Home Time and at the field site. The bygoner already had a child. Both women suspected another woman. The pressure was on him and he took it out on his bygoner wife's little girl.'

'A child beater?' Rico hadn't thought Orendal's expression could get colder, but it did.

'A child beater. I confronted him and . . . well, I lost control. As I recall, I told him that for every bruise I found on her, he'd get five. And I demonstrated how. Field Ops are taught to fight unarmed, to kill if necessary, so I was able to rough him up quite a bit.'

'You should have reported him. They'd have busted him.'

'I did and they did. They also kicked me out of Specific Operations, knocked me down from Senior Field Op and partnered me with Op Zo to keep an eye on me.'

'Yes, I heard you were in Specific Operations,' Orendal said. Rico could tell she was impressed.

'I certainly was,' he said. 'I didn't always have a career escorting snotty students and collecting reports, Commissioner. It used to be a bit more exciting than that.'

'You were lucky not to be sacked,' Orendal said bluntly, and while he could tell she was angry he couldn't tell if it was at what he had done, or what his victim had done, or both. Field Ops necessarily spent time out of the Home Time's symb network and hence social preparation had no way of enforcing itself on them. A very great trust was placed on them not to use their skills to abuse that privilege, and while Rico's victim had betrayed that trust, so had Rico. 'You should have gone straight to his superiors, not taken the law into your own hands. They'd have moved in at once, replaced him, given him therapy . . .'

'With respect,' Rico said shortly, 'you're not telling me anything I don't already know, and you don't need therapy not to beat children.'

'No?'

'No. You just don't do it, it's very easy. I'm not doing it now and I'm not even trying.'

Orendal glared at him for a few seconds in silence, and he thought, *I've blown it.* Then, obviously with an effort, she said, 'I suppose you've got good reason to care about bygoner children?'

Was she trying to wind him up? 'Being one myself, you mean?' Rico said, as mildly as he could. But it showed she had done her homework and gone through his records. 'No, not really. Children are children and you don't abuse them. End of.'

To his surprise, Orendal was flushing. 'I'm sorry,' she said. 'I said a very stupid thing. You're quite right.'

'Why, thank you, Commissioner.'

'Purely out of interest, do you think of yourself as a bygoner? That's a personal question which you don't have to answer.'

'Oh, I'll answer,' Rico said. He shook his head. 'No, I don't think of myself as a bygoner. I just happen to have been born in an accidental timestream that the Specifics were forced to close down. In the main stream I hadn't been born, so they had to take my parents' memory of me from their minds. But they couldn't just rub me out, so they brought me here at the age of two months. No, I belong to the Home Time.'

'Do you think that's why you wanted to work for the College? I notice you started training at sixteen. That's quite young.'

'You mean, I owe my whole existence to the College – and believe it or not, I am grateful – so naturally I want to give something back to them?' Rico shrugged. 'Maybe. Or maybe I just like the adventure and the challenge.'

'But you don't like everything the College does. Your file mentions a certain antipathy towards correspondents.' Orendal sat back and studied him with one eyebrow raised.

Rico paused a moment to gauge the level of frankness he should use in his reply. *What the heck*, he thought, *set it all to max.* 'I loathe the whole correspondents programme,' he said bluntly. 'I think it's a big stain on what otherwise could be a quite fair and just society.'

'They're contributing to that society,' Orendal pointed out.

'And how many volunteers do you get?' Rico demanded. He didn't give her the opportunity to answer. 'The correspondents are our way of sweeping our failures under the carpet. Heaven forbid we should try and do anything as useful as help them.'

'The percentage of correspondents . . .' Orendal said.

'Oh, of course, percentages.' Rico sat back and flung his hands in the air. 'That makes it OK. There's, what, twenty billion here on Earth? Say a quarter of one per cent of them go wrong each year, and conveniently none of them has friends or families who'll miss them. So, that's a mere fifty million people whose lives are torn apart. A pinprick.'

'It's considerably less than that,' Orendal said quietly. 'Mistakes were made in the past, yes. Psychopathic failures were sent through on the nod. Nowadays, everyone gets at least one try at help and rehabilitation. They enter the programme if all other means have failed. Making them correspondents actually increases their chances of survival.'

'Maybe you should try harder,' Rico said. 'Out of interest, what are the figures? Do as many patricians enter the programme as, say, level fives?'

A hit, he thought with satisfaction, because he could see Orendal control her expression and change the subject.

'Op Garron, you lost control once in the field,' she said. 'Can you be trusted not to do it again, without the restraining influence of Op Zo?'

191

Rico was taken aback. 'I hope so. Yes. It depends on the circumstances. Why?'

'Because you're on suspension and off the active list, but that doesn't preclude you doing private work for a sponsor. Now –' she held up a hand to ward off any comments he might have been about to make, but truth to tell, he was too surprised to make any – 'I offered to sponsor you once and you turned it down. This needn't be a permanent arrangement, just while you're suspended. You'll still be putting in your hours pending the tribunal, and at the tribunal, it won't do you any harm to say you've been contracted by one of the Commissioners. Are you interested?'

'Can I ask what work you have in mind?' he said, if only to play for time while he tried to work out her game.

'Looking at you, I imagine you're rated for Europe, tenth to twentieth century?'

'Sure.' There were combinations of geographical area and time period that certain Ops couldn't work in because their ethnic background would make them stand out, but Rico was essentially Caucasian and good for Europe in any period.

'Commissioner Daiho,' Orendal said. 'I want to find out about him.'

'Find out what?'

'You know that he made some transferences quite recently – you learned that when you and your partner were going through his things. Op Zo made a report to me.'

'I remember.'

'We have co-ordinates for those transferences. I want you to be there too, to observe. Not to interact, you understand.'

'Of course,' Rico said. Interacting would mean bringing Home Timers from two different periods together, and Morbern's Code had definite views on that. But incognito observing was quite in order.

Orendal kept talking. 'For reasons of my own, I want to find out more about him, and I want reasons for any and all unusual behaviour. Can you manage that?'

This was a lifeline! The same woman who had inadvertently contributed to his suspension was giving him a chance to make good. She had pitched it just right: it would keep him active, it would keep up his hours, it would impress the tribunal – and there was just the slightest hint of mystery, though no doubt Daiho had had perfectly good reasons for his transferences, which were frankly neither his business nor hers.

'I can manage that,' he said.

Now there was no mistaking her smile, or its warmth. 'I'm glad,' she said. She stood up and held out a hand. 'I'd like you to get started as soon as you can. You'll need to prepare, so I'll give you authorization for all the records you need . . .' She stopped and glanced behind him. 'Yes, Hossein?'

Rico turned round. He hadn't heard anyone else come in – the thick carpet had hidden the footsteps. The newcomer had the slightest hint of a sneer and large, cool eyes which now widened in surprise.

'I, um, I'm sorry, Commissioner, I didn't know you were busy,' he said. He looked curiously at Rico, as if trying to place him.

'We've met before,' Rico said.

'Of course you have. At Li's place. This is Op Garron,' Orendal said. 'You might remember him. He's going to do some fieldwork for me. Op Garron, Hossein Asaldra. Can I help you, Hossein?'

'It was nothing, Commissioner. I'll come back.' Asaldra nodded to them both and backed out.

'Mr Asaldra,' said Orendal, one corner of her mouth turned up, 'will be speaking at your tribunal.'

'I'll look forward to it,' Rico said. He almost returned her almost-smile, before he remembered who she was. Not just the one in charge of the correspondents but the one who sent them out. 'Show me these co-ordinates of yours.'

Orendal symbed the list at him. 'Would you be able to start at the beginning?'

'Um . . .' Rico studied the list, then shook his head. 'No. Nothing like it. They're all enclosed spaces. Rooms in houses. There might be other people about and I won't be able to hide any-where.' He frowned at her. 'Presumably he knew that?'

'Presumably,' Orendal said neutrally. Rico shook his head and turned his attention back to the list.

'Look. From number thirteen onwards, it gets

194

better. He started transferring to outside co-ordinates, and that means I'll be able to turn up early and hide somewhere.'

'So you'll start at number thirteen?' she said eagerly.

'It looks like it,' Rico agreed. 'France, 1657. I'll go and get ready.'

Fourteen

'I have never known anything like it!' Scott raged. 'What were you thinking? How dare you? You're meant to be journeymen! You were brought here to do a job, not go wandering off on moonlit walks . . .'

'They were off duty,' Daiho murmured, just loud enough for Scott to hear.

'That's not important!' Scott glared at the two recalcitrants, pictures of misery. Some bygoner guards still milled about in the background, making no effort to conceal their smirks. This, this was what he had been brought back from Paris for. Two of his idiot employees showing him up, neglecting their duties and . . .

His imagination filled in some extra details. No, probably not. The guards seemed to have found them fully dressed.

'Do you know,' he said, 'do you have any idea how badly you endangered this project? Supposing one of the guards had shot you, eh?'

'They've only got stunners,' Daiho murmured again. 'Nothing lethal.'

Scott swung round. 'That is completely missing the point,' he snapped. He turned back to the other two. 'You're confined indoors for the duration of our stay,' he said, 'and when we get back to the Home Time you will each be fined a week's pay. That's all. Now get to your rooms.'

They shuffled out and Scott turned to Daiho. 'What were you doing, letting them go off like that?'

'They're not my staff,' Daiho said mildly. 'Perhaps they just need proper leadership.'

'Is that supposed to mean something?'

'I think the mating season's begun all round,' Daiho said with a sweet smile, his eyes on someone behind Scott. He walked off and Scott turned round with a sinking feeling to face Ms Holliss, the manager of the hotel.

'Good evening, Ms Holliss,' he said, switching to twenty-first-century English. 'I apologize for this upset . . .'

'Please call me Edith, Mr Scott. And I should apologize.' Ms Holliss was standing far too close to him, as she usually did, her head tilted right back to look at him. Her eyes looked deformed behind her anachronistic glasses, but from the way she batted her eyelashes that was probably not the idea. 'I had no idea Internal Security had wired this place quite so closely. It was a breakdown in communication, you see.'

'Was it.'

'Of course, I've had to discipline staff too, sometimes . . .'

'How interesting,' Scott said. 'Excuse me, it is late and I need my sleep. Good night.'

The gentle sound of the waves was like a lullaby. On previous nights Jontan Baiget had fallen asleep listening to them. They reminded him of the pump mechanism in a hydroponics plant, and with every surge it was like another wave of lassitude sweeping over him until eventually sleep took him completely.

But not tonight. He had rather been hoping not to be alone, but apparently it wasn't to be.

Their rooms were on the very top floor of the hotel and they had walked up the stairs to Sarai's door. And she had flung herself into his arms.

'I've never been so afraid.' Her voice was a desperate whisper. 'They'd have killed us. They would!'

'Um . . .' he had said.

'Jon, they've never had social preparation. They would have! Think of Lano Chon. They're all Lano Chon, only he had preparation like us when he grew up, and they never did, no one in this world has, they could all kill us . . .'

'And they don't have basic hygiene . . .' he agreed.

'Guns and those flying things . . .'

'No symbing . . .'

'We could be killed tomorrow . . .'

And they had looked at each other, and Jontan had felt his heart pounding, *this is it, this is surely it,* but then she had given him one last kiss – a very pleasant, lingering one, he had to admit – and gone into her room. And, just as he was plucking up his courage to follow her, shut the door firmly.

He had banged his head deliberately against the doorpost – which hurt – and gone into his own adjoining room. Where, now, slumber seemed as far away as ever.

Then, to his surprise, drowsiness came quite suddenly, and he was actually aware of it. His thoughts began to disassociate and his eyes grew heavy, even while a small and rational part of his mind thought how unusual this was. There was a faint smell in the air, a sweet and rosy smell getting stronger, and his last waking thought was that maybe Sarai had changed her mind . . .

Matthew Carradine took his place at the end of the table and the members of the investigative team sat down when he nodded. Alan sat at the other end of the table, chairing the meeting of the team he had headed.

A display on the wall showed the four Home Timers, each snapped by a spy camera and blown up, enhanced by computer to remove fuzziness. The same four who had been knocked out by gas in the early hours, letting Alan's investigators pounce. The investigators hadn't even taken them out of their beds, instead performing all their tests on the spot with mobile equipment. The Home Timers had woken up at the normal time and suspected nothing. A beautifully timed and executed operation.

'Hit me with it, Alan,' Carradine said. 'Are they human?'

His assistant nodded. 'They're *Homo sapiens*, yes. Their DNA holds no surprises at all. We can't tell how far in the future they're from, but it's not long enough for our species to have undergone any major changes.'

'So they're just the same as us?'

'I didn't say that, Matthew. Dr Gerard?' Alan nodded at Madeleine Gerard, who was normally Carradine's personal physician, and she consulted her notes.

'All four have perfect teeth – no crowns, fillings, bridge work, whatever,' she said. 'None of them have wisdom teeth but there's no sign of their having been removed. All four have perfect, twenty-twenty vision. Not short-sighted, not long-sighted. All four have the optimum body weight for their metabolism. There isn't a single scar on any of them. If they've ever had broken bones then they've healed perfectly. Scott has a beard but neither of the other two males even produces facial hair, though they have the follicles for it. All four are fertile – they could make babies any time they chose, including the oldest one, this Daiho. He's even more interesting. He shows no real signs of age, yet I gather from overheard conversation that he must be at least in his seventies. No physical or mental deterioration, no wrinkling, no wear and tear on the joints.

'Now, in any one individual, all this would be odd but not unknown. In a group of four, it's statistically very unusual. So, to answer your original question, sir, they're as human as we are but they're not necessarily just the same as us. They've all been well looked after. Their technology can do wonderful things.'

'I think I'd deduced that from the fact that they can time-travel,' Carradine said. He looked back at the pictures. 'And there's no way of telling how far in the future they're from?'

'They never say, Matthew.' Now Alan looked at his notes. 'Scott and Daiho only ever refer to the Home Time. We've no idea if this is a period of history, or a specific date, or a place, or what. They don't give dates and they don't give a timescale. I don't think they're being perverse – I think it's just their way, where, whenever they come from. As for the kids, they don't even mention the Home Time. Between themselves, they speak about "home", "the plantation", "the College", "Appalachia" . . .'

'Well, I know where that is.'

'Likewise, though their accent isn't recognizably American. But even so, we're learning a great deal just from the few facts we know about them.'

'Like?'

'Well, like the social set-up in the Home Time. The kids are journeymen, which suggests a fairly rigid social structure, like a medieval guild of some kind. They're more than mere apprentices, they're qualified in whatever they do, but they're way down the scale from the other two. Scott and Daiho are very reticent about what they say in our presence, whereas Romeo and Juliet can babble away without a word of rebuke from their superiors. I really don't think it's occurred to the men that the kids would be able to say anything of interest to us. They're not stupid, it's just something outside their mindsets. And that alone says interesting things about their world. The lower orders don't think for themselves, or are not perceived to do so by the higher ones.'

'Yes . . .' Carradine said. He shook his head in wonder. 'Those journeymen are at the bottom of their ladder and yet I'll bet they have more proficiency in their subjects than our scientists ever will.'

'That's another point, Matthew. They're clearly good at their job – Scott isn't the kind to tolerate shoddy work – but apart from that their education is abysmal. They can read, write, as far as we know do simple arithmetic but . . . do you know, they still have no idea where they are? The boy thinks this may be the Middle Ages and he doesn't hide his opinion that we're all barbarians. The girl is closer – she knows the steam engine was invented in the eighteenth or nineteenth century, so she thinks that's where we are.'

Gerard spoke again. 'Given that some children born this century have never heard of Adolf Hitler, it could mean they're from no distance in the future at all,' she said.

'Believe me,' Carradine said with feeling, 'they're from far enough ahead for our most guarded secrets to be in their museums.' He recoiled inwardly from the memory of Scott blithely identifying a top secret document. That had been a calculated demonstration of power, and Carradine appreciated it. 'From all this, I take it we don't have difficulty understanding them?'

'In a way,' Alan said. He looked at Visconti, the linguistic specialist, who coughed.

'Scott and Daiho speak English perfectly,' the man said, 'but their natural language – the only one the two youngsters speak – is very different. A layman that they spoke to would have extreme difficulty understanding them. They speak some-thing very like English, but it's as close to modern English as modern English is to Chaucer's version. It's peppered with non-English words and con-structs, some of which I just can't decipher, some of which seem to come from other languages. Mandarin and Spanish are the two main ones. There's scatterings of Latin, Greek . . .'

'So there's linguistic drift,' Carradine said. 'Could that tell us when this Home Time is?'

'No, sir. If the Chaucer analogy holds then we could be talking another thousand years, give or take. But then, they obviously come from a very technologically automated time. If the world's one global village, everyone could be picking up every-one else's language and incorporating it into the lingua franca, and that could be, oh, just a century

203

ahead of us. Or, and this is where my head begins to hurt –' he paused and the others looked at him in expectation – 'perhaps they speak a version of English which has been distorted by time travellers from their own far future, speaking an even more distorted form of English—'

'Stop there, please,' said Carradine. He shook his head to clear it. 'Alan, I want you to learn their language to a passable degree.'

'Already working on it, Matthew,' Alan said simply.

'Of course you are. Carry on.'

Alan smiled and Carradine was happy. Alan only smiled that smile when he was pleased with himself, and in Carradine's experience that only happened when he had pulled off a coup on behalf of BioCarr.

'I've been saving the best till last,' Alan said. 'The aim of all of this, ultimately, has been to see what they could give us that they haven't already. First of all, please look at this recording of the boy getting dressed in the morning.'

Carradine pulled a face. 'Watching young men in states of undress isn't my idea of fun, you know.'

'It's in the interests of science, Matthew. Watch.'

An image appeared of a sleepy Jontan Baiget stumbling from his bathroom. He was wearing what looked like a vest and shorts. He stretched, yawned, then reached out and pulled on his overalls.

'Keep watching,' said Alan, and the image slowed down. With his overalls hanging loosely off his gangly frame, Baiget appeared to walk like an astronaut towards the door. Carradine frowned, blinked and looked closer. His overalls were *moving*. By the time the boy reached the door, what had been a loose and baggy tent slung around him had metamorphosed into a still slightly baggy but much better fitting body-suit.

The image froze.

'They brought no changes of clothes with them,' Alan said, 'and yet, when we checked their clothes after knocking them out, they were as clean and fresh as if they were just back from the cleaners. Both journeymen have these shifting overalls. Scott and Daiho must have the next generation of gear because they appear in a different outfit each morning, even though it appears they also brought this one overall item. Ladies and gentlemen, these clothes are intelligent. No power source, nothing that looks like a central processing unit or any kind of electronics. I think the intelligence, the programming, is in the molecular structure of the fabric.'

'I want one,' Carradine murmured.

'And it gets better.' Alan had obviously been saving the very best until the very last. He beamed at them all before continuing. 'Now, all four of them have, at least once, walked into a dark room and said "lights on". Then they look foolish and fumble for the light switch . . . it took the journeymen longer to grasp this concept than the other two. They all had difficulty with hot and cold taps, too – they kept talking to them. We took this at first as evidence of living in a very automated society.'

'Voice recognition?' said Carradine.

'Precisely. Nothing special there. And Daiho occasionally asks something called Register to record something, or to provide information, then remembers that Register isn't there. The other day, Scott was on his own and he suddenly said –' he scrolled through his notes quickly – ' "journeyman Baiget, could you . . . oh, damn." Then he stood up and walked out of the room to deliver his message to Baiget verbally.'

'A constantly monitoring artificial intelligence?' said Carradine.

'Accessible mentally,' said Alan. Carradine's eyes widened and he continued. 'Our recordings of the kids at work are eerie. They hardly say a word but they work together like a machine. One wants a tool, the other hands it over, just like that. They have to be communicating – it's more than just good teamwork. But – and this is the big one – it's only in the hotel lounge, where all the equipment is. Outside the lounge, they speak out loud.'

'They're telepathic?' said someone. Alan's glance withered him.

'No, or they'd be able to communicate any-where,' he said.

'You conclude?' Carradine said quietly.

'There's clearly some kind of universally avail-able mechanism in the Home Time,' said Alan, 'and a local example is in their equipment, though

I don't know which of the many bits and pieces it is. But it seemed reasonable to assume there's something in their own heads that makes the connection. And so, I asked Dr Gerard to X-ray their skulls.'

'And?' Carradine said. All eyes turned back to Gerard.

'There's something in there,' she said. 'There's a cloudiness in all of their brains that isn't natural. I showed it to a neurosurgeon and he immediately diagnosed widely distributed brain cancer, which is incorrect. As it is, I think it's something implanted, which has since grown inside them. I'd . . .' She coughed. 'I'd need to do a post mortem on one of them to know more.'

'I see.' The silence around the table was absolute. Then Carradine pushed back his chair and stood. 'Thank you, everyone. Alan, that was truly fascinating, and if the opportunity for a post mortem turns up, we can discuss things further. You'll let me have a copy of your report, of course?'

Fifteen

Rico Garron arrived in seventeenth-century France ten minutes before the list said Daiho was scheduled to appear in exactly the same place. The site was a back alley in Port-Royal-des-Champs near Paris in 1657, and the ambience of unwashed humans and plentiful livestock hit him like a slap in the face.

All around him the town was buzzing and – in more ways than one – humming, but here in the alley he was alone. 'Good choice,' he said to himself, looking approvingly around. Yes, it stank and it was gloomy and an open sewer ran down the middle, but it was secluded and it was an excellent transference point. Home Time smart drugs in his system would deal with any diseases. All he had to do was put up with the smell.

The one disadvantage was that when Daiho appeared there was no way Rico could hide somewhere nearby, so he would have to lurk at a discreet distance. He squared his shoulders and walked down the alley and out into the France of 1657. His fieldsuit had tailored itself to make him look as close as the France of the day could come to the middle classes: a bygoner would think he was maybe a factotum for some rich household, maybe slightly seedy. Not rich and dressed out in glowing finery, but not struck down with poverty either. He nodded to a black-robed clergyman who turned into the alley as he turned out of it: the priest bowed slightly back.

Rico cast a glance back at the priest. If Daiho appeared in front of him . . .

Well, one of the advantages of transference was that it cut both ways. Tampering with probability so as to insert the travellers into the timestream disoriented the transferee but it also confused any observer. Still, he steeled himself for any surprised yells and cries of witchcraft. He might have to help out a fellow Home Time citizen, albeit one engaged in dodgy activity.

He leaned against a wall and watched seventeenth-century France go by. Smelly, crawling with germs – he loved it. Yes, the rich were very rich and the poor were very poor; yes, people were starving; yes, children were dying of disease and malnutrition; and if he were somehow to get into the French court then, yes, he knew he would find a level of pomp and formality that made the Home Time's patricians look like children in a nursery. But out here, out on the street, it was all so refreshingly *not* the Home Time that he was prepared to forgive its shortcomings.

Ten minutes later he was back at the entrance to

the alley, just as his field computer told him that the transference he was awaiting was taking place. Daiho was now in there and Rico lurked as only a Specific or a correspondent can lurk, in plain view and completely anonymous.

'How far to the convent?'

'A mile or so.' The voices came out of the alley-way and made Rico frown. He hadn't been expecting two of them. Daiho must have brought a friend. Rico poised himself casually to follow them when they came out.

'Why are we so far from it?'

'So that you need me to guide you there and back, of course. You don't think I trust you, do you?'

'It stinks here.'

'I thought you might like to savour the atmosphere. I have to live in it, remember. And now, *parlez français.*'

And two people appeared at the end of the alley, talking together in seventeenth-century French like old friends. They looked casually around, then set off down the road away from Rico. One was the priest and the other was Hossein Asaldra.

'You?' Rico muttered, eyes wide. He and Marje had assumed that because Daiho authorized the transferences, therefore it was Daiho doing the transferring. But no.

And who was the priest? 'He met up with a bygoner?' Rico murmured. No, the other man was speaking the same language as Rico and Asaldra always spoke. Therefore, the clergyman must be another Home Timer. So why hadn't they transferred together? Why had they met up here?

Radiating indifference, Rico followed the couple.

Following in a straight line would be too obvious: it only worked in the adventure zines. Rico set off on a zig-zag route whose average course took him after the two Home Timers. He would wander across the road; study some livestock; engage total strangers in conversation, actually asking for directions but making it look from a distance like they were old friends.

The disadvantage was that he was seldom near enough to Asaldra and his companion to hear what they were saying, and he really did need to know. They seemed engrossed in one another: maybe they wouldn't notice if he drew nearer. He began to catch up, slowly and without fuss, and came within earshot as they were passing a church. The tower was covered with wooden scaffolding and a gang of workmen swarmed over it.

'The Jansenists are very similar to Calvinists,' the priest was saying, 'but they say they're strictly Catholic—'

A shout of alarm and a snapping *twang* from above made the priest, Asaldra and Rico all look up together. A load of bricks was being hauled up to the top of the tower and the pallet was spinning dangerously while a snapped rope dangled beneath it. Then another twang, another rope gave, and the bricks began to fall. Asaldra and his companion were directly beneath.

Rico's training took over.

'Look out!' he shouted, already halfway to the two others before the words were out of his mouth, arms outstretched to push the two away from the danger. All his senses slowed down, taking in every datum, every aspect of what was happening.

The bricks were halfway to the ground, and suddenly the priest and Asaldra weren't there any more. The priest had grabbed the frozen Asaldra round the waist and spun them both out of the way. Rico couldn't check his momentum and now he was the only one in any danger. The bricks were directly above him.

The priest, who had already moved impossibly fast, moved faster. He let go of Asaldra, turned and leaped back, catching Rico in a flying tackle around the waist that knocked him backwards and jarred the breath out of his body.

And the world returned to its normal speed as the bricks crashed loudly onto the spot where the men had been standing. Rico and the priest lay in the dirt and looked thoughtfully at the heap for a moment.

The priest climbed to his feet, brushing down his gown with one hand and holding the other out to Rico.

'You move quickly, my son,' he said.

'You move quicker, Father,' said Rico. He took the hand and let the priest help him to his feet.

'Yes,' the priest said simply.

'Is your friend hurt?' Rico said. The priest looked calmly at Asaldra, who leaned against the wall, staring at the bricks. His eyes were wild, his hair dishevelled and he was breathing fast.

'No,' the priest said. He walked over to Asaldra and patted him on the back. 'Just a little shaken,' the priest added.

'Father!' It had all happened so quickly that the workmen in the scaffolding had only just got to the ground. The foreman ran up to the priest, twisting his cap between his hands. 'Father, are you hurt? I must apologize for the neglect of my men . . .'

'No harm done,' the priest said mildly.

'But to have interrupted your journey with this . . .'

'You didn't interrupt; we're where we want to be.' The priest put his hands on Asaldra's shoulders and guided him towards a door in the wall. Then he looked back at the foreman and at Rico. 'Thank you for your assistance, my son. Good day.'

The door shut behind them, leaving Rico and the foreman looking at each other blankly. The foreman, determined to apologize to someone, began to apologize to Rico, who wasn't listening. He was running through what he had just seen, and thinking about it.

'Oh my God,' he thought.

'He was a correspondent,' Rico said.

'Nonsense,' Marje said.

'He was a correspondent!' Rico insisted. 'I saw how fast he moved. I couldn't have done it, and I've been trained for Specific Operations. No one could. I tell you, he was a correspondent.'

'So.' Marje pinched the bridge of her nose. 'You are saying Hossein Asaldra has befriended a correspondent? You are saying Hossein has broken every code of conduct in the book? You are saying—'

'You're still not getting it,' Rico said. 'The correspondent saved my life when he thought I was just another bygoner. He got involved, Commissioner. I would say his conditioning has been quite severely compromised, presumably by Mr Asaldra.' He saw the look of irritation sweep across Marje's face and got to his feet. 'What the hell. You wanted me to do a mission, I did it. Use the results as you will.'

'I haven't dismissed you,' Marje said to his back, bringing him up short.

He turned round slowly, and gave an ironic bow. 'I didn't ask you to,' he said.

'You didn't complete your mission, either,' Marje said, and fury swept through Rico. Being treated like a servant was one thing, but attacking his professionalism . . .

'You didn't find out what Li Daiho was doing there because it turned out he didn't appear,' Marje continued, 'but did you bother to find out what Hossein was doing there instead?'

'Actually, yes,' Rico said sweetly, 'but you won't believe it, just as you don't believe my professional opinion that your friend was talking to a correspondent.' He turned to go again and this time reached the door.

'Tell me. Please, tell me,' Marje said. The sudden meekness in her tone made him stop. 'And I apologize for doubting your professional opinion.' He grinned, then carefully wiped the grin off his face before turning round once more.

'Well, now you're talking.' Rico sauntered to a chair. 'And this is why I came to make my report in person, Commissioner, because I really didn't want to say this over symb.'

'Blaise Pascal,' Marje said a bit later. 'No, I haven't heard of him.'

'In 1657 he was living in a Jansenist community in a convent in Port-Royal-des-Champs, France,' Rico said. 'I looked it up. And a convent in Port-Royal-des-Champs was what Mr Asaldra and the correspondent were visiting.'

'And he was some kind of philosopher?'

'He was all sorts of things, according to the records. A mathematician, a physicist . . . He invented the first mechanical adding machine, he showed how a barometer worked, and starting at the age of sixteen he formulated mathematical theories – including a theory of probability – that we still use today. Some of his work even shows up in Morbern's mathematics. Not bad for a pre-industrial bygoner, eh?'

Marje was pinching the bridge of her nose again. 'And Hossein went to see him. Why? I could understand Li using his privileges to go and visit all his heroes. It's illegal, but I can understand it. But Hossein?' Marje took a breath. 'We're going to go to the source.'

Rico looked alarmed. 'Um, is that wise?'

'Hossein Asaldra, please report to me at once,' Marje said, glaring him into silence. A pause, and then she frowned.

'Symb says he's not available,' she said.

Rico tried the same request and sure enough, his own symb told him: '*Hossein Asaldra is not in the Home Time.*' Which meant Hossein Asaldra was either off Earth or dead.

'He remembered me,' Rico said suddenly. 'Remember when I was in the Commissioner's apartment? He asked me if we'd met before. And, for him, we had. He'd just escaped having a load of bricks fall on him, so I probably wasn't the first thing on his mind, but he remembered me . . .'

'And I told him you were going to do some work for me,' Marje said.

Rico felt the thrill of the chase run through him. 'He must have remembered properly,' he said.

'He last saw you three hours ago, before you transferred . . . three hours! He could be anywhere.'

'But that's not long enough to get off-planet.'

'He's transferred somewhere,' Marje said. 'It's the only answer.'

Another symb query: 'He isn't on the transference log,' said Rico. 'So, unless you know of any unofficial transference chambers . . .'

'It was meant to be a joke,' Rico muttered. Smoke filled the cavern and wrapped itself around the single transference chamber, this time from another freshly slagged bank of equipment. He looked around him with appreciation. 'Quite a find,' he added.

'Hossein showed it to me,' said Marje. 'He said a power surge was detected, they followed it and found this.' She pointed out at the original fused, blackened console. 'That was the one that melted down that time.'

Again, they were projecting; again, Security Ops and technicians were there in the flesh, inspecting the scene.

'When was this?'

'Two days ago.'

'So this stuff has been ticking over for centuries, then we suddenly get two meltdowns in two days?' Rico moved his projection over to the remains of the consoles; first one, then the other. 'You know, it wouldn't be difficult to make this happen. Charges could be set that would be undetectable, but enough to make this unusable.'

'For what reason?'

'So no one could tell where you'd been. Look, Commissioner. The consoles are almost identical. Mr Asaldra knew the transference would be detected, so he set charges to make sure no one could know where he was going and he transferred out of the Home Time. He has a seriously guilty conscience.'

'But . . . but the first one? Why did that catch fire?'

Rico pursed his lips thoughtfully. 'I imagine,' he said quietly, 'because someone else transferred out through this chamber a couple of days ago.'

'He told me he didn't think anyone had transferred. He said setting co-ordinates without the Register was too complicated.'

Rico blew a raspberry. 'He had field training? He knew how to do it. We all do.'

'This is getting ridiculous,' Marje said. 'Cease projection.' Rico blinked as suddenly they were back in her office. Marje dropped down into a chair. 'We have personal contact with a correspondent. We have unauthorized transferences. I want this answered and I want it answered now. Is there any way, any way at all, of establishing exactly where he went?'

'Let's see those transferences again,' Rico said, and the list symbed into their minds. The transferences they had thought were made by Daiho had all been through a regular transference chamber. 'Mr Asaldra,' Rico said. 'Fond of home comforts, is he?'

'Why do you ask?'

'Transferences from the eleventh to the seventeenth centuries,' Rico said, 'and then this'. He jabbed at the last item on the list. 'Twenty-first century. Almost the start of the Fallow Age. I'd guess that's where he went, but it's pure guesswork.'

'So what is—' Marje said.

'I'm already there,' Rico said, symbing into the database. 'It's . . .' His jaw dropped. 'Oh my god, it's Matthew Carradine's headquarters!'

'Who?' Marje said.

'Matt Carradine.' Rico stood up and paced the. office. 'The first great biotech giant. He's on the Specifics' list of secondaries – one of us drops in on him, incognito, every couple of years to see how he's doing. Not a primary like Einstein, under constant surveillance, but—'

'Getting back to the point?' Marje said, breaking Rico's flow.

'Ah. Getting back to the point, in the twentieth century they discovered penicillin and other powerful antibiotics. And they overdosed on them so badly that by our boy's time, most of the lethal bugs were immune to them. Tuberculosis, small-pox, measles and all sorts of things with strange Latin names . . .'

'The plague years,' Marje said.

'Exactly. Carradine's company, BioCarr, devel-oped the next generation of antibiotics that attacked the bugs at the genetic level. He was already rich and powerful through BioCarr at the time – he fed the world and he helped cure SuperAIDS – but after that he was one of the most powerful men in the world. That's all in the Fallow Age, of course. Mr Asaldra went to see him when he was just starting to flex his muscles.'

'Perhaps he went to observe?' Marje said.

'Hardly. The database says these are the

co-ordinates for his actual office. Unless he was out taking a whiz, your friend must have appeared right in front of him.'

'You're being frivolous.'

'I am not.' Rico's face was cold and thoughtful. This, Marje thought suddenly, was the other Garron. Not the boy in a man's body that she had been becoming used to. Give him something worth taking seriously and this was what happened.

'So what is it?' she said, almost afraid of the answer.

'The main BioCarr site was excavated a few years ago. They found . . . well, things. By the end of his career, Carradine wasn't bothering with smart viruses and super crops. His clients wanted people who can breathe underwater, or live in a vacuum. He never provided successful models but it didn't stop him trying. I can't help wondering where he got his technology from . . .'

'Oh, God,' Marje said. She saw from his face that there was more. 'And?'

'Just a feeling,' Rico said, 'but remember, I was a Specific. I'm trained to be suspicious.'

'Suspicious about . . . ?'

'Commissioner Daiho.'

'Oh, for goodness' sake!' Marje exclaimed. She threw up her hands. 'You're going too far. The Commissioner died of an aneurysm, that's been established.'

'They can be induced, and there wasn't much of him left to conduct an autopsy on.' Marje opened her mouth to object: Rico interrupted. 'No! Listen!' More quietly: 'I'm dealing with facts, that's all. An aneurysm can kill you on the spot. What it can't do is lift you up and chuck you twenty feet through the air, because that's what must have happened for the agravs not to catch the body.'

Marje opened her mouth again. Her mind had simply been cruising on the assumption that Daiho's death had been an accident and anything that said otherwise was nonsense. But she knew conviction when she saw it, and that was what was on Rico's face.

'Social preparation would prevent anyone from doing that,' she said, 'assuming they were strong enough in the first place.'

''Tals could do it, and they don't have social preparation.'

''Tals need to be told what to do, by one of us. Social preparation would prevent that from happening.'

'Not if the person telling them what to do was a former Field Op,' Rico said quietly. 'Especially not one who still works for the College and therefore has access to the 'tals in the first place.'

Marje had gone pale. 'Hossein has a tame 'tal as a servant . . .'

'There you are,' Rico said, as if that solved everything. 'Perhaps Commissioner Daiho learned your friend was using his name in vain, or—'

'That's enough!' Marje said. 'I'm sorry, this is suspicion and circumstantial evidence. I'm not going to convict Hossein Asaldra on a charge of murder in his absence. We stick with what we know, and that's already got him into enough trouble.'

'There's an easy way to find out,' Rico said.

'Damn straight.' Marje Orendal was a woman whose world had collapsed around her. She had taken a new job upon the death of a friend and had thought herself surrounded by like-minded professionals, serving the College and the Home Time. And now she discovered that at least one of those like-minded professionals was casually engaged in activities that blew the code by which she ran her life to pieces. She had reached her decision: no more meekly sitting back and letting the others run her life for her. 'I'm hiring you full-time,' she said. 'I want you to locate Hossein Asaldra, bring him back here and find out just what the hell is happening.'

Sixteen

Jontan, grinning, crept up behind Sarai, who was crouched next to one of the culture regulators, peering into its innards. He pounced forward and covered her eyes.

'Guess who?'

She shrugged him off. 'Leave it, Jon.' She didn't even look round.

He retreated, wounded. 'I thought . . .'

'Jon, I know. I just . . . I just need time to think, OK?' She snapped her fingers at the toolkit. 'Pass me a joiner.'

He mutely obeyed and crouched down a few feet away; close enough to enjoy her presence and make himself useful when required, far enough to be only on the fringes of the zone of hostility. And he could think happy thoughts of when they had been closer. Still not as close as he might have liked, but closer than ever before. Just a few hours ago.

But not today. It had started with the silence at breakfast, which he had put down to the continuing frostiness from Mr Scott, but even during the day when Mr Scott wasn't present there had been a growing chill between them.

He had just been happy that they seemed to be getting it right at last. It was all so straightforward for him – why couldn't it be for her? Why did she need this 'time to think'? He shook his head. He would never understand.

Waking up with limbs like lead and a clogged head hadn't helped. At breakfast, to his surprise, Mr Scott and Mr Daiho had looked fairly hungover too. Maybe some antediluvian germ had got into the food, but he had had the strange sense that the night had been full of activity which he just couldn't remember.

Something shimmered in the corner of his eye and he blinked as something seemed to cloud his concentration for a moment. What was . . . where was . . .

He shook his head to clear it, glanced up, then quickly jumped to his feet.

'Sa . . .'

Sarai looked up over the top of the regulator, then shot to her feet herself. The man standing in the middle of the lounge was in College dress, and the College was the last place they had seen him; or rather, deep beneath the College, as the doors of the transference chamber closed. He looked at them.

'Get me Mr Scott or Mr Daiho, now,' he said.

* * *

224

'What the hell are you doing here?' Mr Scott shouted.

'I couldn't help it.' The newcomer, Mr Asaldra, was flushed and ran a finger round his collar as he spoke. 'Marje Orendal was on the point of finding out about us.'

'Who's she, and how?'

'She was my designated successor,' Mr Daiho said calmly. 'But the how, Hossein?'

'I don't know what alerted her but she's got a Field Op working for her. I saw him on one of my trips but I didn't recognize him until now.'

(Their personal differences forgotten, Sarai and Jontan were working side by side on the regulator with only half their minds on the task. Listening to their betters falling out was much more interesting. Jontan tightened the last valve, and they glanced at each other. Then he untightened it again, and they began methodically to undo all the work they had been putting in.)

'Yul Ario was meant to be keeping an eye on that sort of thing,' said Daiho.

'This is a private arrangement.'

'Oh, great!' Scott exploded. 'And by running, you've proved her suspicions!'

'If they'd taken me in,' Asaldra said, 'they'd have got the plans out of my mind and this place would be swarming with Specifics come to take us home. Ario couldn't sit on that. As it is – yes, they know something's going on but, no, they don't know where I am or what it is.'

'I suppose you used the duplicate controls to come here?' Daiho said.

'And destroyed them. That's right. We can't go back that way, but then they can't come for us either.'

'You said Ario knew,' Scott said. 'They could get it from him.'

'He knows the gist of it. Not the details. Not where we are.'

Scott was beginning to sound desperate. 'So when it comes to getting back to the Home Time . . .'

'We use the fallback plan,' said Asaldra. 'Inconvenient, but that's life. Why do you think I came here now, not when you first arrived?'

'You're joking!' Scott sounded aghast. 'That's—'

'We all knew there might be costs.' For the first time, Asaldra looked as if he were standing up to Scott. 'This is one of them.'

'That's easy for you to say, when all you have to go back to is that woman . . .' Scott began.

Asaldra bridled. 'Don't speak about my wife that way, Scott.'

'That will do, Phenuel,' Daiho said. 'Hossein is right. Sacrifices were to be expected.'

And Jontan and Sarai glanced at each other. Sacrifices?

Matthew Carradine nodded his head slowly as he studied the picture.

'Well, well, well,' he murmured. 'My old friend.'

'He's the one you made the arrangements with?' said Alan.

'He's the one. When did he turn up?'

'Oh-nine thirty-three.' Alan handed him a dataslate. 'And we have a transcript of their conversation.'

'You've broken through the bug jammers?' Carradine said hopefully.

'Still using the lip readers with binos.'

'Oh well.' Carradine read the slate and his eyebrows rose higher. 'We have dissent in the ranks,' he said. He read further . . .

'Yes!' He slammed the slate down on his desk and jumped to his feet. He paced about the room in his excitement. 'I knew it! I knew it!'

'Matthew?'

'They *are* doing something illegal! I got the vibes, I had my suspicions, but I couldn't prove anything and they weren't saying. But now! Look! This man, Asaldra, he was responsible for bringing them back but now something's gone wrong at his end and the Home Time don't know where he is, Alan. *They don't know where he is.*'

'There's this fallback plan of theirs,' Alan said quietly.

'That's how they plan to return. But look at this! This line here!' He picked the slate up again and jabbed a finger at a line of text. 'Oh-nine thirty-seven, fifty-two seconds. Asaldra, quote, *we can't go back that way, but then they can't come for us either,* unquote.'

'That is interesting,' Alan said, even more quietly but now with a very faint smile.

'And if we keep a suitably close eye on them then they won't be able to implement this fallback plan,' said Carradine. 'I take it you have something set up for this contingency?'

'It just needs your say-so, Matthew.'

'You have it.' Carradine thumped a control pad on his desk. 'Get me the Security chief and Holliss from the hotel. Priority one.'

Jontan was leaning over the mixture regulators when the doors flew open and armed men poured into the lounge.

'Move away from the equipment!' Jontan was too surprised to notice that the man was shouting in badly-accented Home Time. 'Stand up! Move away from the equipment!'

They shoved him against a wall and held him there at gunpoint. Two of the others grabbed hold of Mr Daiho and lifted him off his couch. He shouted angrily but a second later he too was pinned against a wall.

Another thug thrust Sarai into the room. Jontan took a step forward and a gun barrel jabbed into him just below the ribs. Mr Scott and Mr Asaldra were herded in after her. The five Home Timers were spaced around the room, each with their own personal bygoner thug pointing a gun at them.

The kit chose that moment to symb an alarm signal at Jontan. A valve needed closing or the whole mixture would be rendered non-viable. Sarai heard it too and they both instinctively took a step towards the regulator. They collapsed, wheezing, as two fists caught them hard in the stomachs.

'Move away from the equipment!'

'Please,' Jontan gasped, 'the mixture's going critical.'

'Move away from the equipment!'

'I think you've exhausted their grasp of our language,' said Mr Daiho from across the room. The man guarding him raised his gun. Mr Daiho looked calmly back at him.

'Sir,' Jontan pleaded, 'you can talk like them. Tell them I've got to adjust the mixture . . .'

'I don't think they care.'

'We care.' Two more bygoners had come into the room. The speaker was small and slight; his accent was imperfect and he spoke slowly, but he could be understood. 'What is the problem?'

'I have to adjust a valve,' Jontan said. The small man spoke to his companion, a broader man with confident, appraising eyes. This other man nodded and said something; Jontan's guard stepped back.

'Mr Carradine says you can do what you have to do,' said the small man. Jontan gratefully hurried over to the regulator, picked up a phase adjuster and switched the flow over to a backup valve.

'Can you shut all this down?' the small man asked.

'Not without ruining the mixtures and killing the cultures,' said Jontan.

'What do you do at night? When you go to bed?'

'Well, we put it on standby.'

'Then do that now.'

'I . . .' said Jontan, with a glance at Mr Daiho. Yes, these people were now in control; yes, they had guns; and yes, they didn't have social preparation and would no doubt use them if necessary. But sheer instinct made Jontan seek Mr Daiho's approval for any course of action.

'Do it,' Mr Daiho said, and Jontan symbed the appropriate commands to the control module. The action also had the automatic effect of activating the forcefield that protected the gear from the wandering hands of bygoners.

The other man, the one who seemed to be in charge, walked into the centre of the room and gazed longingly at the gear. Then he spoke again.

'Mr Carradine says that you two journeymen are to be put under guard for the time being,' said the interpreter. The guards shouldered their weapons; hands like vices grabbed hold of the journeymen's arms; and Sarai and Jontan were frog-marched from the room.

Scott, Daiho and Asaldra were shown into one of the hotel's meeting rooms and, finally, things were a little more civilized. They were allowed to sit down and drinks were served. Guards still stood around the room.

Matthew Carradine sat facing the three Home Timers as if they were an interview panel.

'We've played around enough,' he said.

'This wasn't the agreement,' Asaldra protested. 'We arranged—'

'Oh, shut up,' Scott murmured in their own language. Carradine speared him with a glance and Scott interpreted his comment into twenty-first-century English.

'And kindly keep it that way,' Carradine said. 'Mr . . . Asaldra, wasn't it? Yes, of course. No, it wasn't the agreement. However, as things have obviously changed at your end, I don't see why they shouldn't change at this end too. Tell me, gentlemen, what should I do with you?'

It wasn't the question they had expected.

'I thought you already had ideas along those lines,' Daiho said. Carradine chuckled.

'Interrogate you, get the secret of time travel, perhaps?' He shook his head. 'No. We might pump you for everything you know, yes, but we'd be very selective about what we used and time travel wouldn't be part of it. It would be wonderful to be able to travel back and forth like you do, but your people are obviously far more advanced than we are and I can imagine what I would do in their place, if a bunch of primitives started monkeying about with my prize technology. They'd be on me like a ton of bricks. No, what I'm after is your more elementary tech. Your mind-to-mind communi-cation. Those clothes you wear. Your amazing state of health. And anything else our surveillance hasn't picked up yet.'

'I'm not sure there's so much we can tell you,' said Scott.

'Of course not!' Carradine pointed up at one of the ceiling lights. 'Any more than I could describe how the power grid works. I have a pretty good idea, but actually communicating it to a savage so that the savage can make it work . . . no, I'm just a layman. As are you and Mr Daiho.' He took a swig of coffee. 'Your journeymen, on the other hand, must be wonderfully well-informed.'

'They work for me!' Scott sounded outraged.

'Back in the Home Time,' Carradine said calmly. He grinned. 'Where I expect they're the lowest of the low. Here, I can give them a level of luxury and freedom they've never known in their lives. They're young and they're only human. I think I can get through to them.'

Until now he had only been looking at Daiho and Scott when he spoke. Now he looked pointedly at the third Home Timer present. 'And then there's you, Mr Asaldra. You're obviously a trained agent of your organization. You travel through time routinely. You must know a few useful things, and from those few useful things, who knows what might spin off?'

The sudden change of subject caught Asaldra by surprise and his mouth worked a couple of times before he answered.

'Yes, I was a Field – an, um, trained agent, but that was a long time ago,' he said.

'And I was a Boy Scout a long time ago but

232

I can still remember my knots,' said Carradine.

Asaldra laughed, disbelieving, almost desperate.

'I'm not telling you anything, Mr Carradine, so please get used to it.'

'Whatever.' Carradine nodded to one of the guards at the back of the room. There was the buzz of a stunner and Asaldra crumpled in a heap on the floor.

Daiho and Scott just watched, not daring to move, as two of the guards lifted their stunned colleague up and carried him from the room.

Carradine calmly watched them go, then stood up. 'And that just leaves you two,' he said as he turned to leave. 'A philosopher, and management. I don't have any vacancies for philosophers and in this century we have managers coming out of our ears. However, one of my staff did tell me she'd welcome the opportunity to do a post mortem of a Home Timer, should the opportunity arise. I'll leave you to think up ways of convincing me you're more valuable than just dead meat.'

'Come in, come in.' The barbarian who spoke their language smiled with an almost convincing display of friendliness as Sarai and Jontan were nudged at gunpoint back into the lounge. The chief barbarian was there: he snapped at someone behind them and Jontan felt the muzzle of the gun – they *said* they were just stunners – removed from the small of his back. 'Let's have some introductions,' said the interpreter. 'This is Mr Carradine, we all work for him. You can call me Alan. I already know that you are Sarai and Jontan.'

They just looked back at him. He shrugged and turned to the Carradine man. More gabbling. The worst of it was, so much of what these savages said to each other sounded almost familiar. The words bounced and skimmed off the top of Jontan's understanding.

One of the guards came forward and approached the kit, which still sat in one corner of the room, completely untouched. Jontan bit back a smile. He knew what was coming and it would be fun to watch.

Sarai was smiling too. She reached out and took his hand.

A zap and a bang, and the guard was thrown back across the room. Carradine was grinning too, and several of the guards were unnaturally poker-faced as their colleague picked himself up off the floor. Watching and enjoying someone else's mis-fortune was a brief moment of shared humanity between civilized Home Timers and bygoner primitives.

'I want you to turn off the forcefield,' Alan said.

'We can't,' Sarai said. A brief exchange between the two bygoners.

'Can't or won't?' said Alan.

'We're not allowed to,' Jontan said. 'Mr Scott—'

'You don't work for Mr Scott any more,' Alan said patiently. He gestured at the man standing next to him. 'You work for Mr Carradine.'

Jontan and Sarai were shocked. 'Mr Scott is from the Holmberg-Chabani-Scott combine,' Jontan said.

'I doubt that will mean anything to him, Jon,' Sarai said with forced patience. The point had occurred to Jontan as the words left his mouth, but it seemed so *right*. If only this Carradine person knew what it meant, there would be no more of this 'you work for me' nonsense.

'Does he?' Alan pursed his lips and nodded. 'Well, well. The Holmberg-Chabani-Scott combine. We'll all certainly have to tread carefully with them, if we live long enough for them to be around, which I doubt.' He nodded at one of the guards behind them.

Jontan yelled as a strong hand grabbed his wrist, and the yell turned to a howl as his arm was pulled behind his back to make his wrist touch his shoulder. And then a powerful shove sent him flying forward towards the kit, and he just had time to symb a turn-off command at the forcefield before he thumped into the culture tank. He lay across it for a moment and drew a couple of deep breaths, before he slowly stood up, rubbing his arm.

Carradine was chuckling and even Sarai, he was mortified to see, looked as if she might have been amused.

'You see? You can,' said Alan. 'And if that forcefield goes up again, we'll simply repeat the process.'

Carradine strolled over to stand next to Jontan,

hands in his pockets, surveying the kit. He said something that was obviously a question.

'Matthew, that is, Mr Carradine wonders which of these bits and bobs controls it, anyway?'

Carradine was standing right next to the control module but Jontan had no intention of telling him that.

'Well, never mind,' Alan said. 'Our people will do a preliminary examination of this lot and in the meantime I want you two to relax a bit, spend some time together, think things over. You see, your Home Time doesn't know you're here. This is Mr Carradine's offer. We want to learn from you. You won't be journeymen any longer, you'll be world experts and we'll hang onto your every word. In return, you'll have every want supplied and you can be as close together as you want. Do what we ask and you'll be free. Do think about it.'

He paused for a moment.

'Well,' he said, 'free-*ish*.'

Night fell. The engineering team still pored over the equipment from the Home Time. Some of Carradine's team wanted to drag the journeymen out and interrogate them on the spot. Carradine reasoned that two relaxed, well-fed journeymen with a good night's sleep behind them would be more useful than two physical and mental wrecks, and he vetoed the idea.

Despite his promises of their being free together, he kept the two apart for the time being, each with a guard on their door. Promises could always be kept later. Neither slept much anyway.

The entire end of the room where Asaldra had appeared – and the others, three weeks beforehand – was cordoned off. Motion detectors were set up, cued to powerful stunners. If any other Home Timers appeared there, they would be detected and shot down in a moment.

Guards patrolled. Motion sensors cast their electronic net over the entire area. Helicopters with infra-red cameras patrolled the skies. The detectors and stunners set up around the arrival point in the lounge were checked and double-checked, and an armed guard was stationed there too.

Rico Garron arrived in the twenty-first century.

Seventeen

'Marje? Do you have a moment?'

Marje looked up in surprise to see Yul Ario, Commissioner for Fieldwork, standing in the entrance to her office with a friendly smile on his face. Not a projected eidolon but the real thing.

'Yul? What can I do for you?'

'If you'd like to come with me, I'll show you.' His smile turned into a grin, and there was something infectious about it. Whatever it was, it seemed it could only be good. 'It's a surprise.'

'I'm a bit old and a bit busy for surprises, Yul.'

'You're never too old and you'll love this one.'

And so she went with him.

The carryfield whisked them away to the transference hall. A minute later they stepped out into what had been Daiho's Himalayan apartment. Without Security Ops crawling all over it and the knowledge of its occupant's recent death, Marje at last began to savour it for what it should have been. Tranquil, quiet, isolated: somewhere Daiho could come to get away from it all, to immerse himself in ancient philosophies and meditation.

They stepped out into the courtyard. The fountain still chuckled, the sun still shone, the mountains still ringed the view with immense grandeur. Ario filled his lungs with the crisp, clean air, then turned to face her. For some reason, the smile was less intense, as if to emphasize an underlying solemnity.

'Marje Orendal,' he said, 'it is my pleasant duty to inform you that your appointment as Commissioner is confirmed, and the Patrician's Guild has accepted you as a member. You're one of us in every way, Marje. Congratulations.'

'I . . . ?' said Marje.

'And that means, this place is yours,' Ario went on. He handed her a crystal. 'Your credentials. We're all entitled to an upstream residence, if we want one, and do forgive the morbidity but this is the only one available at the moment. If prehistoric Himalayas aren't your thing then of course you can apply for a residence to be constructed somewhere else, but in the meantime, you are mistress of all you see.'

'I . . .' Marje said again. She was finally able to frame the only words that could actually describe what she was feeling. 'I'm overwhelmed.'

Ario nodded, his mouth quirked on one side in an ironic half smile. 'I know.' He led her to the patio edge. One part of her mind protested at the thought of celebrating at the point where her predecessor had fallen, but otherwise she was still too awhirl with the news. 'Take a seat. I know where Li kept his drinks: I'll be back in a moment.'

Patrician! Marje lounged back in a recliner and looked at the great skyscraping peaks the other side of the balustrade. She had made it. She was, as Ario had said, one of *them.*

Everything she could want was hers. Oh, there were responsibilities, yes. She could expect to be worked into the ground. No more of this tentative offering of provisional sponsorship to errant Field Ops. She would have to cultivate a whole new crop of sponsorees, use her power and privilege to their advantage . . .

It was what she had always wanted. To do good, to help others and at the same time – she glanced around appreciatively – reap the rewards. A private, secluded lodge far away from the hustle and bustle of the Home Time was only the beginning. It was only scratching the surface of what was now available.

Ario was back with the drinks. He handed her one and settled back into a recliner facing her. He held up his glass.

'To you,' he said, and they drank.

'It's sudden,' Marje said.

Ario cocked an eyebrow. 'Is it?'

'The patrician thing, anyway. I mean . . .' She remembered how she had abruptly put off the interview with the Patrician's Guild the first day on the job. 'I wasn't aware my name was in the system anyway.'

'Of course it was,' Ario said. 'You can't do a

patrician's job and not be a patrician, Marje. And the full works – you know, interview, assessment, probation period – we only give that to people we don't really like anyway.' He paused a beat. 'Well, maybe we have to keep the probation period, that's the law, but everything else in an application we can push through on the nod. You have powerful friends, Marje. You were one of Li's sponsorees. We knew we wanted you.'

'So I'm on probation?' Marje said. Ario's face clouded.

'Hmm. Yes,' he said, and he stood up to lean against the waist-high balustrade, palms flat against the smooth stone as he gazed out into the abyss. 'The people don't understand us, Marje. To them, things appear so black and white, so right or wrong. They can't see the pressures we're under. They can't see that sometimes we have to delve into the realms of moral ambiguity for the greater good. Do you know the Christian scriptures? "It is better for one man to die for the sake of the nation." The people can't understand that. We can.'

Marje looked up at him, baffled. He continued to look straight ahead.

'What I'm getting at, Marje, is that many new patricians find that they have some on-going project, some work in progress left over from their previous life that they started for all the right motives . . . but then they find that their motives were based on a distorted perspective. It turns out things weren't all they seemed. And why should they be? How can children understand the world of adults? And it turns out that their grand scheme is not only embarrassing and annoying for the rest of us but it's actively counter-productive, because they've inadvertently stuck their nose into something of great benefit to everyone, patrician and non-patrician alike. Marje, I won't go into specifics, but I will say that if there's anything in your life or your work that could conceivably rock the boat, show the patricians up in some way . . . I'd drop it. Quietly, without fuss, without fanfare.'

Now he did look at her, and the friendly smile was back. 'And the best thing is, you don't have to explain or apologize to anyone! Look, Marje, I've got to get back to the College. I'll leave you here to look around your new home, take things in, all that.'

Marje stayed in her seat as he left. If she had got up, she might not have trusted herself to speak. What Ario had just said sounded badly like a very heavy hint. And there was only one on-going project she could think of that came remotely near the kind of thing he had described.

But it involved breaking Morbern's Code and every tenet of College life! Or did it . . . *How can children understand the world of adults?* If she had really believed the worst straight away then surely she would have reported it straight away, rather than hire a Field Op to find out.

That was it. She was still *finding out.* She had just wanted the facts. Ario was a Commissioner too – he wouldn't connive at something that struck at the heart of the College. Would he? She felt cautiously relieved . . .

Marje realized she could argue this in circles for hours, and she had work to do. She would look round the house later. For the time being, she was needed back at the College. Without an assistant, work was piling up.

She stood to go and the blue-outlined eidolon of the house's intelligence appeared in front of her. It was an old man with a white beard and robe: Plato or Aristotle or Socrates, one of that lot, anyway. She smiled – what else would Daiho have used?

'Yes?' she said.

'A message for you, Commissioner Orendal. The sender was anonymous.'

'Show me.'

The image was replaced by a simple field of text hovering in front of her. Whichever line Marje looked at, the field scrolled so that the text stayed in front of her. She started at the top.

A few lines down, she frowned.

A bit further and she gasped.

'No!' she said when she was halfway down. She took a step back and the text vanished. Socrates was standing there again.

'Have you finished, Commissioner?' he said.

'Bring it back!' Marje snapped, and the text reappeared. Marje steeled herself and finished reading.

She looked at it for a long time, then re-read it. Slowly.

'Did Commissioner Ario leave this?' she said.

'I have no record of who sent it,' said the eidolon. This time it was taking no chances and left the text showing.

Marje glanced quickly through the message a third time, but she knew what it was. The first line said it all:

'What follows shows how you could conceivably be implicated in the murder of Commissioner Daiho, were such to have taken place.'

And from then on, the message showed precisely that. It used assorted facts and circumstantial evidence to weave together a case for the prosecution – any prosecution that wanted to show how she connived in Daiho's alleged murder so as to reach her new, exalted position. The logic was inescapable, just the facts were wrong.

But it could wound her. It might not get her sent to Reconditioning or the correspondents programme, but it would be the end to her career.

And then there was the last line:

'This need not happen.'

Murder? Marje had forgotten Rico Garron's strange theories. She had certainly never believed them. But was Li Daiho's death connected with whatever Hossein Asaldra was mixed up in? Surely not!

And again, surely Ario wouldn't be party to any murder . . .

But if something was going on that could conceivably make it look like murder, however circumstantially . . .

Not only embarrassing and annoying for the rest of us but actively counter-productive, he had said. Marje didn't need it spelled out. Ario had presented the carrot, this was the stick, and the end of both was the same: drop the investigation.

'Erase it,' she said, and slowly made her way to the recall area.

She thought hard as she waited for the next scheduled recall field, and then as she took the carryfield back to her office. She wanted to get this exactly right. She wanted to reassure Ario (*that smug bastard with his smooth talk . . .*), let him know everything was OK . . . and at the same time, make it clear there were some things she just would not tolerate.

She symbed Ario back in her office and he appeared before her in full image. He was affable as ever, as if he hadn't just dropped a hint that could ruin her life if she didn't take it.

'How can I help you, Marje?'

'I've been thinking over our conversation,' she said slowly. 'I just want to let you know that I'm examining all my projects, as you suggested, and if I find anything that matches your description, I'll certainly cancel it at once.'

See? I can talk patrician just like you.

'Wonderful!' Ario beamed. 'That's a good idea, Marje. Welcome on board.'

'But there is something that might upset you, personally, and I have to say it.'

Ario's smile suddenly turned into a good-humoured mask over a very wary face.

'Yes?'

'It's my assistant, Hossein Asaldra. I know you're his sponsor and all that . . .'

'Yes?' Now Ario sounded both wary and dangerous.

'I'm sorry to say his performance has been far from satisfactory. I have reason to believe he has kept things from me, deceived me, misled me. I can't have him working for me any longer and I can't endorse his record for further promotion.'

'He might,' Ario said very mildly, 'have been following orders.'

'As my assistant, his first duty was to me,' Marje said. 'And this only reinforces my point. Perhaps he was working for some greater good. Perhaps it was one of those things you told me about that non-patricians simply can't understand, in which case, he should have done it a lot better. He acted in such an unbelievably sloppy manner that I actually suspected, for a while, that he might be involved in something illegal. If he's that sloppy working for others, I don't want him for myself.'

Ario's eyes were cold. 'I can see your point. And meanwhile . . .'

'Meanwhile,' Marje said, 'I will continue to act

in the best possible interest of the Patrician's Guild.'

'Thank you for that assurance, Marje. Goodbye.'

One small victory, Marje thought. *One very small victory.* Not in the least looking forward to it, Marje symbed Field Op Rico Garron.

'*Op Garron is not in the Home Time,*' was the automatic response.

'What?' Marje actually spoke out loud. Garron had gone already? She propped her elbows on her desk and massaged the bridge of her nose with her index fingers. Damn, damn, *damn.* When you had just mustered all your courage to sell out, it was extremely annoying to be thwarted.

She symbed Op Zo.

'Su, I gather your partner left sooner than I expected.'

'Yes, a vacant slot came up in the transference schedules. I've just seen him off.' Su sounded pleased with herself. 'Is there a problem?'

'There—' Marje stopped. If this was as sensitive as she suspected, it probably shouldn't be talked about on the networks. 'Can you come to my office, please?'

Besides, she owed it to Su not to shelter behind a symb but to deliver this face to face.

Su's face when she heard what Marje wanted was expressionless.

'This comes as a surprise,' she said.

'I have my reasons,' said Marje, hating herself

but finding patrician confidentiality a surprisingly easy thing to slip into.

'Can I ask why?'

Marje ignored the question. 'I know you're not trained for Specific Operations,' she said. 'All you need to do is go to the arrival point, stay there and symb Op Garron to return for recall immediately.'

'I won't be able to get there for at least an hour after he arrived,' Su said. 'That's how long he's been gone.' The Register would insist on an hour's interval.

'I know, I know. We'll have to hope he stays out of trouble,' Marje agreed.

'And he might have done everything he needs to do in that hour. He might recall as I transfer.'

'In which case, just come back,' Marje said. 'The point is, can you do it?'

'I can do it,' Su agreed, 'but he won't be happy. He was enjoying this.'

'Do the job, Su,' Marje said, 'and let me worry about your partner's feelings.'

'Whatever you say,' Su said without expression. She stood to go. 'I'll be off, Commissioner.'

If Su could play formal, so could Marje: she kept her professional, patrician face on as Su left the office. Then she winced.

Scratch one friendship? she thought. *God, being a patrician had better be worth it.*

Eighteen

The waves rippled a hundred feet below Rico. The cliffs were a dark outline ahead of him and the white shape of the hotel was striking in the moonlight.

He was grinning with the sheer joy of it. This was more like it. Now to see if his guess was right.

BioCarr played such an important part in twenty-first-century history that as many of its records as possible were archived. A study of the database had turned up a cryptic mention of a senior BioCarr executive and his family having their reservation at the company hotel abruptly cancelled, on their boss's own orders, for some mystery VIP guests who were there for an indefinite stay. The exec had fired off an angry memo to complain. Matthew Carradine had answered personally that this was need-to-know, the guests came first and if this man wanted to keep his pension and position, there was a good way to go about it.

It was a good clue: Rico just hoped it was the one he needed. He had the date of the exec's intended holiday. He had the co-ordinates of the hotel, and while he didn't have records of the building that had stood at that point, he did have records of the local geography. So, he had chosen a new set of co-ordinates, half a mile to the west of the original, and thus he appeared clad in a fieldsuit set to full camouflage and wearing an agrav that held him safely in mid-air above the sea.

The lenses he wore gave him night vision, the sensors in his suit took a 3D reading of the area, and the data from both of them were fed into his fieldsuit's computer and thence directly into his brain. In two seconds, Rico was in complete command of the situation.

The cliffs were ahead. He set the agrav to a mild descent and forward thrust, and began to move towards the hotel on the cliff top. Primitive flying machines were cruising the area slowly but even in the unlikely event of one of them shining a spotlight directly at him, they probably wouldn't see him, black against the night sky. Invisible electromagnetic pulses were sweeping periodically over him and his surroundings, but the suit's camo took care of them and made sure no incriminating echoes bounced back to their source.

The hotel was swarming with bygoners. Armed bygoners: the sensors were picking up clear indications of weapons. But then, he had guessed that from the presence of the helicopters and the other security precautions.

'*Attempting contact.*'

What the . . . ? There had been no mistaking that

mental brush against his awareness, though it was something he hadn't expected to encounter in the field. His computer was networking.

'*We are receiving a signal on the wavelength assigned to correspondents,*' the suit symbed at him. '*Should this unit respond?*'

'Negative! On no account,' Rico said immediately, though his heart sang: *right guess!* Asaldra was here all right. Then: 'There's a correspondent down there?'

'*Incorrect inference. The signal comes from a symb junction in the vicinity that is routinely attempting to make contact.*'

'Scan area for this unit,' Rico ordered.

'*Unit is located in the building immediately ahead.*'

One corner of Rico's vision expanded, showing an infra-red view of one of the larger rooms in the hotel on the ground floor. There was a whole jumble of equipment there and the symb junction was outlined while a crowd of people were gathered about it. It was an innocent item of Home Time equipment, doing what it had no doubt been doing since it got here, which was vainly reaching out to connect with the rest of the world-wide symb network that wouldn't exist for centuries.

'Identify the rest of that,' Rico said, feeling suddenly cold.

'*Unable to determine function of items indicated at this time.*'

'Can you tell where it all comes from?'

'*Provenance of the items indicated is the Home Time.*'

'What is the man doing?' Rico murmured. He drew up a mental list of Hossein Asaldra's misdemeanours. Item: abused correspondent-derived information. Item: possibly (still circumstantial, he reminded himself, and Orendal was having none of it) been somehow involved in the murder of the late Commissioner Daiho. Item: made contact with a correspondent. Item: engaged in unauthorized transferences. And now, item: runs guns to the natives. Dangerous, stupid and very illegal.

'He's not in this alone,' he muttered with a sudden realization. Any one of the above, an aberrant individual of the Home Time might get up to . . . but all of it? There was just too much happening. And that probably meant there were more Home Timers down there too. Maybe they were those people he could see around the equipment. God, he hoped they were Home Timers: the alternative was too horrible to contemplate.

Rico scowled and set the agrav to descend.

He touched down gently in the hotel garden, with the trip wires and security beams clearly outlined in his enhanced vision, and moved silently towards the back door. It was wired, too.

'*Get me in,*' he symbed.

'*Please place your hands accordingly,*' symbed the computer. Outlines of his hands appeared in his vision – one over the door lock, the other at the jamb where the alarm sensor was located. Rico did as he was told and felt power tingle in his fingertips for a moment.

'*You have ten seconds to enter the building.*' Rico did so without fuss or delay.

He was in the staff area of the hotel – a narrow passage, plain white walls – and the lights were on, which for the first time meant the fieldsuit's camo would be compromised. Machines wouldn't be worried that nothing was reflecting back at them; human eyes would. He would be a black, man-shaped hole in their vision and he needed a more visible disguise.

From the first room on his left he heard happy shouts, just beating the roar of ten thousand voices and a bygoner apparently on the verge of a heart attack.

'*Go-al! And what a triumph that was for this young striker in his first league match, with five minutes to go . . .*'

A sporting event being reported on; and that meant bygoners watching it. He peered slowly round the door. Four cheering men, each with an open can in one hand and the other hand waving or pounding a comrade on the back, never moving their eyes more than a couple of degrees from the screen mounted on the wall. Much more of interest to Rico was their dress: white jackets, dark trousers. Hotel staff.

'*Match that,*' he symbed to the fieldsuit.

'*This unit requires a three hundred and sixty degree view of the clothing in question.*'

'*I thought you might.*' He tensed his fingers and a synjammer slid down his sleeve and into his hand.

He stepped into the room, brought the crystal sphere up and beamed it in one smooth movement. The four men froze in mid action, then slowly straightened up and sat still in their chairs. Rico grabbed the nearest one and pulled him to his feet.

'*Do you have a good enough view now?*'

'*Affirmative. This unit is complying with previous instruction.*'

Rico put the bygoner back in his chair and looked down at himself. The suit's hood retracted into its collar as his body seemed to ripple for a moment, and then he was wearing dark trousers and a white jacket identical to those of the other men. Nor was it just an optical illusion: anyone who handled him would have the feel of the bygoner material transmitted into the nerves of their fingertips.

The computer showed him a route through the building, based on his previous scans. He quickly searched the nearest frozen bygoner for some kind of identification and came across a primitive smartcard in the breast pocket. He took it, grabbed hold of a silver tray and stepped briskly out of the pantry. He set the synjammer to revive, held it around the door and discharged it, then walked quickly away as the conversations started in mid-sentence again. Why the sports programme had suddenly skipped thirty seconds, he left to them to work out.

He met his first guards immediately he stepped into the guest area: two of them, either side of the door that led to the staff quarters. His sensors had already told him they were there and he didn't even spare them a look as he walked past. He was in uniform, in a secure area where everyone had been thoroughly vetted already, and the only thing to do was look confident.

The guards wore no attributable uniform, just black jumpsuits that could have belonged anywhere. Rico suspected they were BioCarr's private army, which was actually a slight relief. Officialdom in this era hadn't been alerted as to the Home Time's existence.

Two more guards came down the short passageway that led to the lounge. There wasn't enough room for them all, so he courteously stepped aside.

'Ta, mate.'

Even guards could be human, Rico reflected as he pushed open the door to the lounge.

'You! What do you want?'

Rico put on his best wounded face at the bygoner gorilla approaching. He brandished the tray.

'Just clearing up,' he said, careful to match the accents of the four sports fans. He had spent leave in the best hotels of the nineteenth and twentieth centuries. He knew how good service was done, and that included clearing up at regular intervals.

'It's all cleared up. This is a secure area.'

'Blimey! What's all that?' Rico said, peering past the bygoner. It was what he had come to see: an array of equipment, nothing whose function he recognized but whose design was unmistakable. And the jumble of people was still there – bygoner civilians, whose poking and prodding of the Home Time tech made Rico's heart jump into his mouth.

'Never mind. Now push off.'

'All right, all right,' Rico said, still in his best hurt hotel staff tone of voice, and backed out.

'*Identify,*' he symbed.

'*One symb junction. One field generator. Four fluid regulators. Seven—*'

'*What was the overall purpose of that equipment?*' Rico symbed impatiently. He was back in the main hallway and he couldn't afford to linger under the gaze of the guards there, so as if it was the most natural thing in the world he headed for the stairs.

'*This unit conjectures that the equipment had a biotechnological function.*'

'*Can't you be more specific?*' Rico asked as he took the stairs slowly, one at a time: a humble servant, all too aware that those guards were still down there.

'*Not with this level of data.*'

He was halfway up. '*Scan the floors above. Give me layout and personnel deployment.*'

The computer analysed what lay ahead. Most interesting were the four bedrooms, each with an armed guard outside it. Surely, Rico conjectured, if you wanted to guard important people at a hotel then, OK, you would seal off the area, mount patrols, station sentries, throw up a security blanket . . . everything the bygoners had done. But individual guards on individual rooms? That didn't connect. You only did that if you wanted to keep certain parties apart . . .

Rico began to suspect he knew where the Home Timers were.

Two of the rooms were next-door neighbours on the landing, with their sentries in plain view of each other. Rico walked past them without a glance. Beyond them lay a small staircase, up to what had once been the servants' quarters in the hotel's pre-history. At the top was a narrow and conveniently dog-legged corridor, giving access to the other two guarded rooms.

The inhabitant of one of the top rooms was asleep, or at least in bed; the other was still awake, sitting on his or her bed, head in hands. Rico chose that room. At the top of the stairs he turned left and walked quickly round the bend in the passage, synjammer already up and discharging before the sentry could say a word.

The computer told him of three listening devices and two hidden cameras in the room the other side of the door, and added that it was able to feed them false data. Rico raised the synjammer again and slid past the frozen sentry. He threw the door open and a terrified face looked up at him.

'This one?' said Alan, looking thoughtfully at one of the Home Time modules.

'That's it, sir,' said the scientist who had reported the event. He had been put out to find that an incident he had tried to report to Matthew

257

Carradine had only garnered a visit from Matthew Carradine's assistant, but he was getting over it. 'It suddenly started flashing. Well, lights running over it. Then it went dead again.'

'Did it, now.' Alan looked down at the module, rubbing his chin. 'Right.' He moved suddenly into action, turning quickly to the nearest guard and suddenly sounding far more like someone in authority. 'You. Fetch the two youngsters down, get them to dismantle the equipment and stow it for transport. Give them all the assistance they need and do whatever they say. Don't worry, you'll get Mr Carradine's authority.' He already had his phone out and was jabbing at the buttons.

'Daiho?' Rico exclaimed. 'And when was this?'

'U-Union Day.' The still-shaken biotech journey-man whom Rico had found in the bedroom was obviously convinced he had just compounded his crimes. *Union Day*, Rico thought – two days after Daiho was meant to have taken the final plunge from his apartment.

So who had gone over the side of the mountain instead? Rico shook his head to clear it and said, 'Go on.'

'And then, just this morning, Mr Asaldra arrived, and an hour later, all those thugs came pounding in and rounded us up, sir,' said Jontan. 'They knocked Mr Asaldra out and took him off in one of those flying things.'

'Any idea where to?'

'Um, no, sir.'

'Oh, great.' Rico leaned against the wall and shut his eyes. An unauthorized Home Timer on the loose somewhere in the twenty-first century, probably not even equipped with a fieldsuit. He'd worry about that later; maybe even head back to the Home Time and hand over the job to the Specifics.

Half his mind was working on the problem, the other taking in Jontan's story. 'Holmberg-Chabani-Scott . . .' he said. 'Could they whip up a force-grown clone, if the need arose?'

'Why, yes, sir. Dead easy.'

'Light dawns . . .' Rico murmured, and retreated into his thoughts again. He felt a sudden shock as he remembered the autopsy report back in Daiho's apartment. 'Oh my God. They picked up brain patterns, which means Daiho gave it intelligence, which means it was fully alive and he committed murder. The bastard.'

'Sir?'

'Yes?' Rico registered he was about to be asked something, not told it, and switched more of his attention to his fellow Home Timer.

'It's illegal, what they did, isn't it? I mean, they broke your rules, and when they brought us here they didn't say anything about sacrifices, but now Mr Asaldra says – said – we'd have to make them, and . . . I mean, it's not right, is it, sir?'

'Yeah, you noticed that too.'

'So I . . .' Jontan swallowed. 'I just want you to know that . . . that Sarai had nothing to do with it,

259

she was just doing what she was told by Mr Scott . . .'

'And you weren't?'

Jontan blinked. 'Well, yes, sir, I mean, I didn't have a choice either, but if you're going to arrest anyone . . .'

Rico grinned. This boy was defending his girl, ready to take the flak for her. He was a better man than either of the Home Timers incarcerated a floor below.

'There'll be arrests,' he said, 'but first there'll be a hearing to decide exactly who should be arrested. And for that, I have to get back to the Home Time.'

'Sir?'

Rico sighed. 'I was only expecting Asaldra to be here, Jon-boy. The recall zone is a long way out from the cliffs and a long way up. My agrav could take me and one other, but it couldn't take all four of you.'

He saw the sudden gleam in Jontan's eyes.

'Or just you and your girlfriend,' he said. 'No. I'll report back to the Home Time and we'll send a general recall field to these co-ordinates. That'll get you all back, and I'll testify for you when you're there.'

Jontan almost glowed and a huge grin split his face.

'Thank you, sir!' And then he subsided as he realized the implication: just a little longer here in the Dark Ages. 'When will that be, sir?'

'They can't send the recall while I'm still here – that would be a paradox . . .'

'Sir?'

'They would be recalling me before I get back to request a recall,' Rico translated. 'But I expect they'll time the recall to a second after I go back myself. So, five, ten minutes. Can you wait that long?'

Jontan was aglow again. 'You bet, sir!'

Rico smiled and patted the journeyman's shoulder for a moment. 'I'll see you, then,' he said, and slipped out past the still frozen sentry.

And then, the biggest surprise yet.

'*Rico? Come in please.*'

The words pulsed into his mind via symb and he paused at the top of the stairs down to the landing.

'*Su?*' he symbed back in disbelief. '*What are you doing here?*'

'*Change of orders. Abandon mission.*'

'*WHAT?*'

'*Marje has called you off, Rico. I'm sorry.*'

'No. No way.' Rico started moving again.

'*Rico . . .*' Su's familiar exasperation was warming up in her tone.

'*Su, it's suddenly got a whole lot bigger. There's five Home Timers in this century, four of them here and Asaldra vanished into the great blue yonder. And two of the ones here are kids who've been virtually kidnapped, plus the bygoners want to milk them for their distinctly non-bygoner biotech skills. Does Marje know that?*'

'*Um . . .*'

'*Su, where are you?*'

'*At the recall point.*'

261

So, Rico thought, she had the fieldsuit, the agrav
. . . But it still wasn't enough to take the entire load
of Home Timers back with them. The original plan
would have to stand: get back to the Home Time,
send a general recall field.

'*Wait there for me,*' he symbed. '*We'll go back together
and raise hell.*'

'*Rico, some of us don't like dangling about in mid-air
for open-ended periods.*'

Rico grinned. Personally, he found flying in an
agrav exhilarating. '*Get to the foot of the cliffs and wait
for orders,*' he said.

'*ORDERS?*'

'*Instructions,*' Rico amended hastily. '*I mean, sug-
gestions. Requests! Polite, if-you-please requests from a
junior to a Senior Field Op.*'

'*Just get here, Garron.*'

Rico grinned again as Su broke contact. He took
the first flight of stairs at a quite un-stewardlike trot,
and then adjusted pace and expression before he
came out onto the landing and into the view of the
sentries guarding the other three Home Timers.

When he got to the top of the stairs down the
hall, Rico saw that the scene below was suddenly
less peaceful. It was like a disturbed ant's nest.
People hurried about and a small, slim man standing at the door into the lounge was talking urgently
into his phone.

'Mr Carradine says yes,' the man said. 'You three,
come with me.'

He headed for the stairs and began to bound up

them two at a time. Still in steward role, Rico stood aside to let them pass. He risked a quick glance at the leading man but it was no one famous, no one who had made it into the history books. The man met his eyes briefly and looked away.

The crowd passed and Rico started down the stairs.

'Wait!'

Rico half paused; no, they couldn't mean him . . .

'You on the stairs!'

That narrowed it down too much for Rico's liking. He stopped, turned, looked up. The slim man was at the top of the stairs, hands on his hips, arms askance. He had a 'haven't-we-met' expression similar to Asaldra's on his face.

'You work here?' he said.

'Yes, sir,' said Rico.

'Your name?'

Rico gave the name he had found on his borrowed ID.

The man nodded slowly, not taking his eyes off Rico's face. Then suddenly he snapped his fingers at the sentries down in the hall.

'You two! Stun this man. Stun him now.' The guards brought their guns up before Rico could react.

His last thought, as the stun charges lanced through his body and he felt his body arch and then start its slow, dreamlike tumble down the stairs, was: 'what did I do wrong?'

Nineteen

Berlin, 1700

'You look very sprightly today, Herr Wittgen-stein.' Frau Hug noticed the spring in her lodger's step the moment he came into the room. 'Is it a special day?'

'Today is a perfectly normal day, Frau Hug,' the man said with a broad smile. 'As normal as any other day in the considerable history of our planet. Please, carve me a slice of that delicious bread of yours for breakfast.'

Frau Hug, with only a very slight frown, turned back to the sideboard and started preparing her lodger's morning meal. Herr Ludwig Wittgenstein had been in Berlin for a week and so far had resisted all attempts to be lured into conversation. Quiet, kept himself to himself, almost non-descript. But now . . .

She set the plate before him and sat down in her chair at the head of the table – the place that had been hers for most of her adult life, ever since the smallpox took Herr Hug away and left her with four small children – to watch Herr Wittgenstein eat. None of the other lodgers had come down yet; he was up bright and early. And he was still smiling, even as he ate and . . . she strained her ears to hear . . . was that *humming*? Why, she hadn't seen or heard anything like this since her oldest boy, Elmar, had . . .

She gasped and her hands flew to her mouth. 'Herr Wittgenstein,' she said with a jocular scold, 'you're going to meet someone today, aren't you?'

The bread stopped halfway to Herr Wittgenstein's mouth and he looked at her over it with wide eyes.

'I beg your pardon?'

'A young lady! Don't deny it, Herr Wittgenstein, a woman can see the signs.' Delighted, she rose and carved him another slice. 'Here, take some more. You'll need all your strength, believe me. Women like a man with a bit of meat on his bones.'

'I really . . .'

But there was no stopping Frau Hug now. One by one the other guests came down for their own breakfast; one by one they were greeted with the good news. Even when Herr Wittgenstein made his escape half an hour later, his attire had to pass his landlady's scrutiny and she tutted in despair; hat crumpled, boots not polished, cloak downright dowdy. Well, it would have to do, she said with a sigh. Finally she watched her lodger leave for the day, half her mind already taken up with passing the good news about that nice Herr Wittgenstein around her friends.

Having made his escape from the valkyrie Cupid of the Grunewald, the Correspondent made his way into town. It was summer in the Berlin of 1700, early in the morning. The day was already comfortably warm and dry and the light had a clean, liquid quality. Not many of the future Prussian capital's thirty thousand–odd people were around yet, just those with whom the Correspondent had instinctively identified himself ever since arriving in Isfahan. Butchers. Milk sellers. Servants on their way to work. The tradesmen, the people who did the work that ran the electorate of Brandenburg.

Going to meet someone . . . For the first time in seven centuries, he had almost believed in telepathy. But Frau Hug was a kindly soul under the general bossiness and desire to run the lives of everyone she met, so he had gone along with the charade.

He wondered how disappointed she would be when he didn't come back. Well, the month's extra rent he had left on his bed would help ease her hurt.

His first destination of the day was the shambles behind a butcher's shop in Schmargendorf. He paused in the dim alley and glanced about him. The sounds of a small town coming to life were all around him, but the people themselves were well out of the way. It should be safe. He sat down on a box and ate an apple.

Two minutes later, Herbert appeared.

'Oh, *my God.*' The Home Timer screwed his face up in disgust and put his hand to his nose. 'What is this place?'

'We're behind a butchers,' the Correspondent said. 'Good morning, Herr Herbert.'

'Good morning, Herr . . . ?'

'Wittgenstein. Ludwig Wittgenstein.'

'Your loyal servant.' Herbert gazed around him and it looked as if he were going to be sick. 'You've always been good at locating dirt and grime but this time you've excelled yourself.'

'How kind.' The Correspondent stood abruptly and chucked the apple to one side. 'First, show me you brought it.'

'Of course.' Herbert reached into an inside pocket and produced a thin, hexagonal wafer of dark green crystal that filled his palm. The Correspondent took it reverently between thumb and forefinger, looked at it from both sides, held it up to the sky so that the light shone through it like a lantern at the bottom of a murky pond.

'More crystals,' he said. 'Is everything in the Home Time crystal-based?'

'Most of the technology is. It's an organic, solid-state world.'

'How do I make it work?'

'You don't. Just keep it on you, and when the recall field comes on, it'll pick you up as well.'

The Correspondent pocketed the tag. 'I can't believe I'm going home. I've been looking forward to this for a long time.'

Herbert gestured towards the alleyway entrance. 'Shall we go?'

Berlin had well and truly come to life as the two men entered the city proper, walking up through Schöneberg and into town. Herbert was breathing heavily.

'You're not getting any fitter, are you?' the Correspondent said.

Herbert glared at him. 'It's been fifty years for you,' he said. 'I've been making these trips in quick succession. I haven't had time to get fit. It wasn't meant to be like this.'

'Oh, I was forgetting,' said the Correspondent. 'Of course. I was meant to be an innocent dupe, lied to and used by you so that you can do whatever you do to the people I interview. You should never have had to walk more than ten feet in any given direction. If this weren't the last one, I'd be more considerate in future.'

They walked in silence for a couple more minutes.

'So, where are we going?' said Herbert. They both spoke fluent eighteenth-century German, though it occurred to the Correspondent that while he could easily pass for a native Prussian, Herbert sounded like what he was – a foreigner who had learned the language but not the accent.

'To see Leibnitz, of course.' *The last one!* the Correspondent thought with silent exultation. *Seven centuries, seventeen seminal scientific thinkers, and Baron Gottfried Wilhelm von Leibnitz is the last one!*

268

'I meant, where are we going to see Leibnitz? At his home?'

The Correspondent stopped in his tracks. 'You're joking!'

Herbert rolled his eyes. 'About what?'

'It's July the seventeenth, 1700,' the Correspondent said slowly. 'We are going to see Leibnitz. Can't you put the two facts together?'

'His birthday?' Herbert said with elaborate sarcasm.

The Correspondent started walking again, taking long strides that meant Herbert had to hurry to catch up.

'Leibnitz founded the Academy of Science, and today is the day he's sworn in as life president. There's going to be a ceremony, and that is where we'll meet him.'

'Oh,' said Herbert. The Correspondent looked at him askance and shook his head.

'You didn't know? You really didn't know?'

'I just follow orders,' Herbert said. 'I know the name of the person I've come to see and a few general details. Someone else decides on the itinerary.'

'It doesn't interest you that he worked out the principles of differential calculus at the same time as Isaac Newton?'

'Since I've no idea what differential calculus is, no. But it sounds like something my associate would think is useful. What else did he do?'

The Correspondent shook his head. He was so

primed with every useful detail there was to know about his interviewees that it had never occurred to him Herbert might be ignorant of it all. Didn't the man even read his reports? Do some research? Apparently not: Herbert was just doing a job. So the Correspondent simply answered:

'This and that.'

Herbert wasn't even interested in the answer: he was looking curiously at the Correspondent, his expression thoughtful.

'Besides,' he said, 'when did you start caring?'

They arrived at the ceremony just as it was starting. It was a grand but crowded room full of men standing and jostling as people did on these occasions, chatting idly, catching up with each other, making new acquaintances. It was an era of grand clothes and wigs but the finery was only a visible distraction from the fact that the bygoners still hadn't entirely got the hang of hygiene. Herbert was obviously trying not to pull a face.

Now the men were drifting to their seats and Leibnitz was taking the stage. The philosopher had a long, dark, curly wig, arched eyebrows and a face that was usually calm and placid but, on this occasion, could be excused for more than a hint of smugness.

The Correspondent had timed their arrival so that Herbert would not have to make casual conversation with bygoner German scientists and be revealed as the fraud he was. As they took their seats he mused that it had been a wise precaution;

bearing in mind what he had just learned, Herbert wouldn't have been able to bluff his way for a second. What kind of idiot, the Correspondent wondered, would come back however many centuries, knowing he would have to blend into the population, and not even try to learn something about the time?

But that question was only incidental to the main one bothering him as everyone applauded the man at the front. The main one was: *when did you start caring?*

When indeed? He thought back to his arrival at Isfahan. He hadn't cared then. He had had a desire to get to the city and to meet Avicenna, and lurking at the back of his mind had been enough information about the man's career to be able to make conversation and conduct an interview.

But now?

Now, it *mattered* to him that Leibnitz – mathematician, statesman and philosopher – had founded and presided over the Akademie der Wissenschaften. It was important that Leibnitz saw the universe as composed of what he called monads, centres of spiritual energy that together formed the harmonious and perfect conclusion of a divine plan. And above all – as the Correspondent could see, even if Herbert could not – both men owed everything to people like Leibnitz and all the other interviewees, because they were both the products of a highly advanced technological society, far removed from the on-going Iron Age that was currently all around them in eighteenth-century Berlin. The world would move from this bygoner age to the Home Time through scientific advance, and that scientific advance was made possible because of the theoretical groundwork laid by the men the Correspondent had interviewed.

So, yes, it mattered to the Correspondent. It mattered a great deal.

Leibnitz ended his speech with the hope that great things would come out of the new Academy of Science. The Correspondent applauded quite genuinely while Herbert's applause seemed more out of relief that the speeches were over.

'And now, let's go and meet the man,' the Correspondent said as the assembly rose from their seats.

'I need to be alone with him,' Herbert muttered. 'How am I going to manage that here?' They began to sidle along their row of chairs towards the aisle.

'That thing of yours only works on contact, doesn't it?' The Correspondent had seen it work enough times. Herbert invariably touched a crystal sphere to the subject's temple.

'That's right.'

'Give it to me.'

'What?' Herbert exclaimed.

'Give it to me, and watch.'

Herbert fumed but could see he had no choice, and a moment later the Correspondent felt the sphere press into his hand. It was the size, shape and feel of a golf ball (*A golf ball? How long had he known what one of those was?*) and a deep, translucent blue.

'Herr Leibnitz!' the Correspondent called. They had reached the aisle and Leibnitz was coming towards them. He was talking learnedly with the crowd of men around him but he looked up in polite expectation.

'My master Sir Isaac Newton sent me,' the Correspondent said, pushing his way forward and holding out his hand. 'It's a pleasure.'

'Isaac Newton?' Leibnitz said with polite interest. 'I've heard of him.'

And will continue to hear more, the Correspondent thought, since neither man yet knew that the other had worked out the principles of calculus on his own, and a bitter dispute and accusations of plagiarism were looming in the years to come.

'My master is very interested in your thoughts on monads,' the Correspondent said, 'and he has sent me with a request that might seem odd.' He held up the sphere, and heard Herbert behind him draw in a breath.

'Indeed?' As was obviously expected, Leibnitz took the sphere and rotated it in his fingers. 'It's an interesting ornament.'

'Would you mind, sir, touching it to your temple?'

Leibnitz's eyebrows rose, but he obligingly pushed back the fringe of his wig. 'Like this?' he said, suiting action to words. 'Good lord,' he added, as the sphere abruptly changed colour.

'It's a substance my master has devised in his alchemical studies,' the Correspondent said. 'He believes the human brain is full of currents of energy, similar to the monads you have written about, and that this material reacts to them. Ultimately he hopes to be able to record human thoughts in devices just like this. He wonders if you would be interested in sharing in his researches?'

Leibnitz burst out laughing, followed a moment later by his friends, taking their cue from his reaction. 'Tell your master that I'm flattered by the invitation.' He studied the sphere a moment longer, then passed it back. 'It's a pretty toy, but given that two or three of these could fit inside the human head, it hardly seems likely that the contents of a human head could fit into one of these. Good day, sir.'

He bowed slightly and the Correspondent returned the gesture, letting a look of polite regret flit over his face. Then the Correspondent turned back to Herbert, proud smile on his face.

'Yours, I think,' he said, passing the now red sphere back to its owner.

'Let's get out of here,' Herbert muttered.

And all that was left was the walk back to Schmargendorf. The Correspondent was aware of a feeling he rarely had and he spent some time analysing it. Yes, he was in a supremely good mood. *Supremely* good, yet tinged with regret.

A shrieking, laughing crowd of children burst out of a gate as they walked along the dusty track, squabbling or playing or both but generally making a loud noise and having a good time. He gazed benevolently at them. Children, the future of the human race; long dead by whatever age Herbert came from, but here so full of potential, life, *future.* He cared about them. He wanted them to have only the best.

All these people. He looked around him. Passers by. Men and women; on foot, in carts, on horseback. He cared for them all, bygoners though they might be. Each one unique, each one with their own story to tell; historically of no consequence but each one of infinite value.

He would miss them.

There was that question again: *when did you start caring?* The first thing he had done when he arrived at Isfahan was save the life of his then young, now also long-dead friend Ali, but even that hadn't been motivated by care. He had only got involved because Ali's attackers had turned their attention on him, and after that he had kept Ali's friendship for exactly as long as was needed.

If he assumed that his condition upon arriving in Isfahan, prior to any contact with Herbert and subsequent reordering of his mind, was the Home Time's intended factory setting, then he had changed a great deal. All for the better.

'How will they react when I come back from my mission three hundred years too soon?' he said. Recall Day wasn't officially for another three centuries.

275

'It won't be three hundred years, just twenty-seven.' Herbert really was worn out and was getting more and more irritable with every step.

'Even so,' the Correspondent said. He had meant it as a joke.

'They'll get used to it.'

'How will you explain it?'

Herbert sighed. 'I'll smuggle you in, somehow. Your details will be on file; it shouldn't be hard to reintegrate you.'

'This way,' the Correspondent said, gesturing towards a familiar alleyway.

'Thank God.'

Perhaps Herbert was getting used to this time; he didn't make any expressions of disgust as they picked their way back to the shambles at the end of the passage.

'Good timing,' Herbert said. 'A couple more minutes.'

The Correspondent studied him. 'You always know these things, but I don't see you carrying any kind of watch.'

Herbert plucked at his coat. 'You're not the only one with hidden technology on you. Believe me, this isn't wool. One minute.'

They stood and waited. The Correspondent's heart pounded and his mouth was dry. *Almost there* . . . He picked the tag out of his pocket and held it up. 'You're sure I don't have to do anything?'

'Of course not. Thirty seconds.'

A pause.

'Sure?'

'Sure.'

The Correspondent grasped the tag tightly, like a believer with a crucifix.

'Ten seconds,' Herbert said. 'There's something you should know.'

'What?'

'You didn't volunteer as a correspondent.' Herbert looked him in the eyes and smiled that mirthless smile. 'No one does. You're a criminal, a reject, a psychotic failure, and there's no way you'd be welcome back.' And he vanished.

The Correspondent stared at the spot where he had been. He took slow, shuffling steps forward so that he stood in Herbert's footprints. He stared at the ground beneath him.

'No,' he breathed. He stared at the tag in his hand, willing it to carry him back to the Home Time. Its glow faded before his eyes and it crumbled into dust.

He drew in a breath.

'No!' He hurled the handful of grit at the wall and swung a kick at a nearby crate, shattering it. '*No!*' He seized a length of wood from the fragments and swung it at the other nearby boxes. *Smash!* 'You bastard!' he howled. *Smash!* 'I'll . . . I'll . . .'

Herbert's face seemed to swim in the scraps of wood and he brought his makeshift club down on them again and again. 'I'll . . . I'll . . .' he sobbed.

He didn't know what he would do, and he had

never cried in seven centuries, but his breath heaved and adrenaline poured through his body. Laying waste to the alleyway was the only safe way he could disperse that strength, that emotion.

'Oi!' The shout brought him round. The butcher who owned the place had come out of his shop's back door. His apron was bloodstained and he held a large cleaver in his hand. Nervous customers peered over his shoulder. 'What the hell do you think you're doing?' The man took a step forward, cleaver raised. 'Get out of here!'

The Correspondent glared at him, picturing and in his mind enacting a good twenty ways to get past that cleaver, with the butcher never knowing what had hit him.

But no. *Self control. Discipline.* Something correspondents had in abundance. With a deliberate effort the Correspondent willed his boiling, seething rage away and it was as if ice, hard and cold as iron, flowed into his veins to replace it.

'I'm sorry, sir,' he said calmly. 'I'll pay for the damage.' He took a bag of coins from his pocket and tossed it over. 'Will that cover it?'

It certainly should have; the coins were gold, saved up and amassed for centuries. The butcher's eyes widened when he opened the bag and saw them.

'Why, yes,' he said.

'Then that will be all,' the Correspondent said, and set off on the walk back to the Grunewald.

* * *

'Herr Wittgenstein?' Frau Hug heard her lodger's footsteps as the front door opened and closed, and she bustled out of the front room to greet him. Hope bubbled in her heart. Had he popped the question? Had the young lady said yes? She would be so happy for them, and she had a lovely double room, south-facing, that was perfect for a new young couple.

But Herr Wittgenstein was alone, his shoulders sagged, and he just looked at her silently out of deep, dark, hollow eyes with such an intensity that it was like running into a solid wall. Frau Hug saw the story immediately.

'Oh, Herr Wittgenstein, I am sorry . . .'

But he was already walking up the stairs. She watched his receding back, saw him take the corner, listened to the remaining steps and finally heard his door shut behind him.

She walked back to the front room, where her best friend was waiting with the tea, poised expectantly.

Frau Hug shook her head. 'She must have said no, poor thing,' she said. 'Silly little girl. Herr Wittgenstein was so in love with her, you should have seen his face. And now the poor man doesn't know what to do.'

She sank into a chair and took a bite of her cake.

'Still,' she said brightly, 'he'll get over it.'

Twenty

The whine of powerful turbines starting up. A vibration that ran through him and stabbed into his brain. An unbelievable thirst.

And a whining human voice.

'This wasn't in the agreement. This wasn't how it should have been. This wasn't—'

'Please be quiet, Phenuel,' said another voice wearily. Rico forced his eyes open.

The first speaker was a bearded man whom Rico assumed was the Phenuel Scott that the biotech boy had told him about. The two were sitting opposite each other in a metal cabin of some kind, and next to Scott sat the very well and un-late-looking Commissioner Daiho. Rico was feeling better and stronger by the second as his fieldsuit pumped medication into his system to clear his mind and soothe his jangled nervous system.

Scott was the first to notice Rico's wakefulness. 'You did this!' he said. 'You're a Field Op, aren't you? And obviously not a particularly good one. What did you do to upset the bygoners, hey? And now we're all suffering—'

'Your . . . your friend told you to shut up,' Rico gasped. Something was nagging at the back of his mind, something forgotten, but for now he swallowed and worked his mouth to get a bit more saliva flowing. The next words came more easily. 'I wouldn't be here at all if your pal Asaldra hadn't left a trail a mile wide behind him.'

'And you are?' Daiho said. The man sounded amused and not at all upset.

'Field Op Rico Garron.'

'I suppose you've come to arrest us?'

'Just Asaldra, originally,' Rico said. Now he felt as if he could move his head without it falling off and he looked cautiously round. It was the passenger cabin of a flying machine, probably a helicopter. Though it was dark outside he could see it was still on the ground, but the noise of the engines was getting louder and louder and the cabin was vibrating. There were two rows of three seats, facing each other. He and Scott were at the end of their rows, facing each other. At the other end of each, next to the door, was a bygoner guard. There was an empty seat between Rico and the guard on his side. Daiho sat opposite it next to Scott. The kid he had met earlier – what was his name, Jonjo, something like that, it wouldn't quite come through the mists at the back of his brain – and his girlfriend were nowhere to be seen. Behind Daiho and Scott, Rico could see the backs of the helicopter pilots.

Rico realized two more things. His Field Op's equipment had passed the camo test – he was still in the fieldsuit and he still had his agrav – and his hands and feet were cuffed.

He jerked at the links experimentally. '*Can you get me out of these?*' he symbed at the suit.

'*Negative. The locks are non-magnetic and mechanical in operation.*'

'*Can you just break them for me?*' Rico symbed impatiently.

'*Affirmative . . .*'

Excellent!

'*. . . with an 87.6% probability of operative sustaining fractures to the carpal bones.*'

Less excellent. And he was still sure he had forgotten something: the stun charges had pummelled it out of his brain. It would come to him.

'We were doing fine until you came along, Garron,' Scott said, warming to his theme, 'and you—'

'Of course, it could just be that the stupid, primitive bygoners outsmarted you,' Rico said.

'And all your fancy equip—' Scott said.

Rico jack-knifed his body and lashed out with his feet. The cuffs helped keep his heels together as they pounded into Scott's jaw. This ass, this idiot had been about to mention out loud the fact that Rico had special equipment. Rico didn't know if the helicopter was bugged, or if the guards had been briefed on the Home Time language – the boy had told him some of the bygoners could speak it – but he intended to take no risks.

Scott's head thumped back and blood poured from a split lip.

'Stop that!' the guard next to Daiho shouted, bringing his stunner up. Rico flashed his brightest smile.

'He was annoying me,' he said in English. Scott looked at him through slitted eyes with pure hatred, but kept quiet.

'You know,' Daiho said, 'my colleague did have a point in that we aren't the ones who let themselves be detected by a bygoner.'

I'm working on that, Rico thought: how had that man on the stairs known who or what he was? But out loud he said: 'And I had a point that I wouldn't be here if you'd done it properly. You people are amazing. You have such power, such privilege, and what happens? You –' he nodded at Daiho – 'had the authority to bend the rules, to send your assistant on field trips in complete contravention of every rule the College has. And, I suspect, grew and murdered a sentient clone just to cover your tracks. You –' he nodded at Scott – 'lured those two kids back into the past and broke even more rules. But the one thing none of you can be bothered with is being good at what you do.'

Scott was almost purple. 'How dare you speak to us like that—'

'Mr Scott,' Rico said mildly, 'I know ten ways of killing you, many more of disabling you and causing you a lot of pain, and I'm a long way away from the Home Time and social preparation and I don't like you very much. Why not join the dots and shut up?'

He turned to Daiho. 'You seem to speak the most sense. How long was I unconscious?'

'You were laid out in the hall when they got us from our rooms,' Daiho said. 'They bundled us out here, strapped us in, then brought you along. You woke up about a minute later. So, not long.' He paused. 'Rico Garron. Is that *Ricardo* Garron?'

'Why?' Rico said, suddenly cautious.

'Author of *George Washington and the Crusades*?'

'Of what?' Scott exclaimed, and Rico felt his toes curling. No one was meant to have read that!

'It was, um, a private project, just a hobby . . .' he said.

'I take it it's meant to be satirical?'

'What are you talking about?' Scott demanded to know.

'Op Garron is an aspiring novelist and he left an extract from his latest opus on the computer I appropriated,' Daiho said. 'I imagine you wrote that passage while you were on assignment somewhere? Yes, a rather naïve voice, I felt. Quite a pleasant if undemanding read but rather an over-stated use of imagery . . .'

'You do remember I wanted that computer back,' Rico muttered.

'You mean,' Scott said, incredulous, 'this man became involved in this whole business because he wanted his novel back?'

But Rico wasn't listening. With a flood of relief,

he remembered what had been bothering him.

Orders! Wait for orders!

Su Zo sat on her rock and wrapped her arms round herself. The fieldsuit was keeping her perfectly warm but she felt cold. The rocks were jagged and sharp around her. The solid bulk of the cliff rose straight up behind her into the night and freezing cold waves were breaking just below her – solid masses of water breaking down into seething foam that sucked and gurgled as it ran in fractal shapes back into the sea.

Why does everything involving Garron have to be complicated? she thought. A simple investigation turns into a major crime that needs uncovering. A simple withdrawal turns into sitting at the foot of a cliff and feeling bored. And Rico wasn't talking to her: she had sent several symbs over the last couple of minutes and got nothing but silence. She could take the hint.

With her suit's night vision she looked sardonically at a seagull perched a safe distance away from her.

'What are you looking at?' she said.

'*Su! Get up here now!*' The symb was such a relief she wasn't even bothered by the lack of a 'please'.

'*At last!*' she symbed back. '*I'm on my way.*'

The agrav carried her straight up, the rock of the cliff-face blurring as it scrolled rapidly before her eyes. She came to the top of the rock wall, and a black mass of machinery and howling turbines and lethal whirling blades came straight at her out of the night.

Su cut the climb just in time and yelled as she thumped painfully into the ground.

'*Garron!*' she symbed furiously. '*I just almost got cut in half by a helicopter . . .*'

'*And I'm on it! Follow it before it gets up to full speed.*'

'*Do what?*' But she had already pushed off the cliff top after the flying machine. Rico's point was valid: the agrav's full speed could never match a helicopter going at much more than a crawl. The two were designed for different things.

'*And when you get here, hang on,*' Rico added.

'*I would be so lost without you to explain things,*' Su symbed back, but she was already reaching out for one of the helicopter's struts, a few feet away. The agrav harness around her was growing warm as it fought to keep up and match the buffeting of the helicopter's rotor, and the noise was deafening. Her fingers brushed the metal just as the helicopter tilted slightly further forward and increased speed. Su lurched forward with the last reserves of her agrav's power and her outstretched hand caught hold of the strut. She grabbed it with her other hand and ordered the fieldsuit to lock both gloves, and there she was, being towed by a helicopter at five hundred feet over the open sea.

Did the helicopter swerve slightly? Rico kept an eye on the two pilots. They glanced at each other and said something, but he couldn't hear what.

Through the seat of his pants he felt the machine give a couple of experimental wiggles as they tested the controls. Yes, they had felt something, but hopefully a mid-air interception by a flying woman from the future wouldn't have occurred to them and they would put it down to mechanical causes, to be looked into the next time they landed.

'*I'm here, Garron, and it's bloody uncomfortable,*' Su symbed.

'*Hang on,*' he symbed back, and was taken aback by the sheer, livid fury in her reply.

'*What do you think I'm doing? I'm—*'

'The first thing,' Rico said out loud, 'is to take out these goons. Mr Scott, you sit tight for the time being. Mr Daiho, when I give the word, you take the one next to you. I'll be responsible for the other one – I can get these cuffs off in no time. Count of three: one, two . . .'

The Home Timers were staring at him without even thinking of moving: the guards were looking unconcerned out of the window.

'Take out?' Daiho said, as if Rico had suggested he fly to the moon. Rico smiled.

'Forget it,' he said. 'Just testing.' So, the guards didn't speak their language. That was a start.

'Do you have a plan?' Scott said scornfully, apparently dismissing Rico's earlier advice about silence. Rico just looked at him coolly, silently, just long enough to get Scott thinking that maybe it had been good advice after all.

'*Rico . . .*'

287

'I hear you, Su. It would be lovely if you could join us.'

Su Zo had swung her legs up and wrapped them around the helicopter's skid, locking the suit there for good measure. Now she pulled herself upright, hand over hand, through the freezing gale of black air. Release glove. Move hand, take new grip. Lock glove. Release other glove, take new grip . . . It was slow and uncomfortable but it was sure. She had set her agrav to support only, cancelling forward motion: it would save her if she fell but it could never catch up with the helicopter again. So, don't fall.

'I'm standing,' she symbed. *'With you in a moment.'*

Her feet were planted on the skid and she was leaning against the helicopter's sleek fuselage. Up here there were fewer things to hold on to, which made things more problematic. At least she could see and breathe: the suit had grown a transparent mask across her face to protect her from the rush of air and the burning blast of the engine's exhausts. She inched her way forward until her hand was on the door and peeked through the window. The two bygoner guards Rico had told her about were the nearest passengers to her.

'Playback,' she ordered her suit, and in a corner of her vision it displayed the movements she had just programmed in.

'Instructions confirmed,' she said. *'Rico, I'm coming in . . . now.'*

With one yank she had the door open and the

gale blasted into the interior of the helicopter. Su let her whole body go limp as the fieldsuit took over. She felt her wrists lock on the edge of the door, the suit tightened around her, and her whole body swung round and into the cabin. Her feet together caught the rear-facing guard on the side of the head and knocked him back.

Rico sprang forward between Scott and Daiho and brought his arms over the head of the right-hand pilot, pulling back so that the chain of the cuffs pressed against the man's throat. Momentum had carried Su into the cabin and the other guard was fumbling for his stunner. The suit returned control of her own body and she raised a hand towards him. A stun charge from her fingertips struck him in the chest and he crumpled, sagging in his seat.

Su reached out and pulled the door shut, then turned back. Rico winked at her.

'Great! Now get these cuffs off me.'

First, Su picked up one of the stunners and gave it to the nearest Home Timer. Who, she saw with a sudden shock, was Daiho.

'Long story,' Rico said.

She thrust the stunner into Daiho's hand. 'Just point it at the pilots,' she said. 'Let go, Rico.'

Rico lifted his arms up and released the neck of the pilot. 'Just keep flying,' he ordered in English. 'Keep your hands on the controls and nowhere else. Come round to bearing two hundred and forty degrees, height two hundred feet.' The helicopter began to bank. 'You, guy on the left, put your hands on your head.'

The co-pilot did as he was told. Su was checking the pockets of the two unconscious guards. She found the key and quickly released Rico; then they put the cuffs on the guards, binding them to their seats. Rico took the stunner from Daiho and Su picked the other off the ground. They looked at each other.

'Thanks,' Rico said with a warm, quiet smile.

'Are there any more of you?' Daiho asked. Su looked at him askance.

'You're meant to be dead,' she said.

'But as you can see, I'm not.'

'It was a clone,' Rico said. 'A sentient, self-aware clone,' he added, just to make sure she was getting it.

'Sentient?' Su looked at the man in horror. 'You made it sentient? You . . . you . . .'

'Are an accessory to murder and kidnap,' Rico said, 'and you're going to face the authorities back home.'

'Not with what I have in my head,' Daiho said calmly

'Kidnap?' said Scott. 'What do you mean, kidnap?'

Rico glared at him. 'Those two kids, and thanks for reminding me. Su, get your agrav off. I'm going to need it.'

'*We are now at recall point,*' said their suits together.

'Cut speed and hover,' Rico ordered the pilots. 'Hold this position.'

Su was looking round and doing a head count. 'You said there were five of them.'

'The other two are back at the hotel and Asaldra is God knows where. With two agravs, I can at least get the kids back to the recall point.' The helicopter rocked slightly. 'I said, hold position!' Rico snapped.

'Windy,' the pilot said nervously, glancing back over his shoulder.

'Do what you can.'

'Yes, sir!'

'What will you do with the equipment?' Daiho said. Rico looked blankly at him.

'Destroy it, of course,' he said.

'You can't!'

'Oh, I think I can . . .'

'Rico,' said Su, 'it's not worth it. We'll be home in five minutes, and then we can just send a general recall. It'll get them and the equipment too. They'll be back in the Home Time thirty seconds after we are.'

Su held his gaze, and Rico reluctantly had to admit she was right.

Scott sat back comfortably in his seat, stretched his legs and put his hands behind his head. 'Those two kids, as you call them,' he said, 'work for me. I think you'll find their contracts allow me to take them where I want and do with them what I will. The era in which they work isn't specified. I broke no laws.'

'Unauthorized transferences . . .' Rico said.

'I authorized them,' said Daiho.

'Making contact with bygoners . . .'

'Again, something that someone at Commissioner level can do.'

'Did you order Asaldra—'

'Mr Asaldra,' Scott corrected.

'— to make contact with a correspondent?'

'Of course,' said Daiho.

'And that's not illegal?' Rico was beginning to feel desperate.

'Actually, no. Unusual, but not illegal.'

'By the way,' Scott said, with an enormous smile on his face, 'thank you for getting us out of the bygoners' hands.'

Rico's jaw tensed and he turned back to Daiho.

'Did you order *Mr* Asaldra not just to make contact but to reveal the truth about the Home Time to a correspondent? To let the correspondent know that recall is possible?'

Daiho's smile became fixed. 'No,' he said, 'but that didn't happen, did it? There would be witnesses.'

'I witnessed their conversation,' Rico growled.

'We have your word for that, yes, but that's all.'

'I recorded it on my field computer!' Rico shouted.

'When we get back to the Home Time and this little matter comes to the tribunal you'll no doubt insist on, I think you'll find you didn't.'

'Almost definite, I'd say,' Scott commented.

'After all, Op Garron, you're not very good with field computers, are you?'

'Why, you . . .' Rico took a step forward and Su had to step in his way.

'It's almost time for recall,' she said. 'Will you both please stand up. Remember that we'll arrive home in the same position as we leave this time, so sitting down won't be very comfortable.'

With an insouciant ease which made Rico's teeth stand on edge, the two men undid their buckles and slowly stood up. The helicopter was still rocking and they had to put arms out to balance themselves.

'Please, Op Garron, believe me,' said Daiho. His voice suddenly held quiet, rock-steady conviction. 'It may seem to you that we've stepped outside the law, but what we've been doing has been for the good of the entire Home Time. Everyone will be grateful to us, and that includes you.'

'Somehow I'm not interested in people like you deciding what's good for me,' Rico snapped. 'And there's still the matter of murder, isn't there? That clone might have had the mind of a baby, or maybe you implanted it with just enough of your brainwaves to give the forensics people the idea that it was you, but—'

'I would have been prepared to lay down my life for the Home Time,' said Daiho. 'Therefore, so would that clone. Therefore, what happened was voluntary suicide.'

'You can't be serious,' Rico said in amazement,

but then he saw the look of firm conviction on Daiho's face. 'Good God. You believe that, don't you? You really can use a clever little lawyer's argument to absolve yourself of all moral guilt. So much for the noble patrician.' He shook his head, not in doubt but as if to shake the revulsion of the sudden insight from his memory. 'Well, we'll see what they say when it comes to trial.'

'You keep talking about this trial,' Scott said, 'but let's face it, you really don't have any evidence, do you? For . . . well, anything, really. Unless . . .' He had to grab the back of a seat as the helicopter reeled again, which rather spoilt his superior air. 'Unless you interview the correspondent,' he added with a laugh.

The look on Rico's face wiped the smile from Scott's own.

'Rico!' Su warned him, loudly, but she needn't have worried.

'Mr Scott,' Rico said quietly, almost in awe, 'I could almost kiss you. But I won't.' Instead he grabbed Su's shoulders and gave her a kiss on each cheek. 'Hold the fort,' he said, and pulled the door open. The wind blew into the cabin again.

'Where are you going?'

'To get the evidence,' Rico said, his eyes agleam. He grinned at Scott. 'Thank you so much.'

'For what?' Scott took a step forward. 'This has gone far enough, Garron. Just face the fact that you have bungled . . .'

It seemed to happen in slow motion. The

294

helicopter took another buffeting from the wind; Scott stumbled forward towards the open door and stretched out a hand to catch himself, but with the door open there was nothing to hold on to and with a shriek he fell into the night.

'*Shit!*' Rico bellowed, and dived into the dark after him. His night vision showed a wriggling, screaming Scott plunging down to the waves and he symbed the instructions to his agrav to dive after the man. He plunged head first, hands by his side, down towards the sea, then to his amazement felt his rate of descent suddenly slow.

'No!' he bellowed. 'Keep diving . . .'

It was too late: Phenuel Scott smashed into the freezing water. A few seconds later Rico drifted across the seething mass of bubbles where Scott had splashed down. A man's dark outline showed through the froth, and Rico didn't need his field-suit's sensors to tell him that there was no hope. The shock of impact with the bitterly cold water would have killed him straight off.

'What the hell were you doing?' he shouted.

'*This unit could not permit the operative's intended course of action.*'

'I could have saved him . . .'

'*Incorrect. You could have reached him before he hit the water, but your combined momentum would be too much for this unit to overcome.*'

The fieldsuit was probably right, Rico realized angrily, floating above the waves. No – not *probably*, it was right. He and Scott would have died together.

He swore for a very long time, then looked back up at the helicopter.

'*Too late,*' he symbed.

A pause. '*Are you coming back, then?*' Su said. '*We'll recall any moment . . .*'

'*Pick me up with the general recall,*' Rico said.

'*Do what? Where are you going?*'

'*Mr Scott was exactly right,*' Rico said, and told his agrav to fly back to the cliffs.

Twenty-one

Alan was propped against the lounge window sill
with his arms crossed, idly supervizing the two
Home Time youngsters dismantling their equipment, when he realized he had been hearing a
helicopter hovering nearby for a quite unrea-
sonable time now. He pulled back a curtain and
glanced out of the lounge window. The lights of the
machine hovered over the sea a quarter, perhaps
half a mile away. He frowned, but let the curtain
drop back down again. Internal Security were a law
unto themselves and what they did with their
helicopters was up to them. The helicopter that
counted, the one with the prisoners on it, should be
miles away by now.

He turned back to his main task and his hungry
gaze feasted on the prize from the future. This
could be used. There was real potential for . . .

Then he stood up straight and anyone looking in
his direction would have seen the first look of
surprise to cross his face for a very long time.

He recovered quickly.

'Get out,' he said to the BioCarr guards. None of

them budged. Alan walked up to the nearest one –
a hulking, large man who dwarfed him – and
looked up into his face from a distance of a few
inches.

'I said, get out, if you want a job to come back to
tomorrow morning,' Alan said. The guard looked
stonily at him, then glanced up at his fellows and
shrugged. They filed out, leaving Alan alone with
the two kids. They hadn't understood the words but
they had picked up the tone and were looking at
him nervously.

Alan shut the door and turned to face the
French windows.

'They're gone,' he said.

The French windows opened and a ghost walked
in – a shimmering, rippling outline of a human
being. Then abruptly the distortion vanished and a
man was standing there in a dark grey, one-piece suit
that covered him from his feet to the top of his head.
Even the face was covered with a kind of mask.

The hood and mask pulled back of their own
volition, vanishing into the suit's collar, letting Alan
see the newcomer's face.

'I was right,' he said. 'You're not a hotel steward.'

'No,' Rico said. 'Thank you for saving my life, by
the way.'

'And you are?'

'Field Operative Ricardo Garron. You?'

'Call me Alan.'

The two looked at each other for a moment
longer.

'How did you know?' Alan said.

'I'm good, I'm damn good, but you still spotted me,' Rico said. 'I know I didn't do a thing you could have picked up on. So, you must have recognized me. But even then, Paris was a long time ago for you – something must have tipped you off in the first place.' He indicated the equipment with a nod of his head. 'And, of course, that gear over there broadcasts on the correspondents' frequency. QED.'

'I turned my back on the Home Time a long time ago,' Alan said.

'I don't blame you. Some of us don't have that luxury. Any particular reason?'

'That man Asaldra,' Alan said. 'He used me, he lied to me . . . and I decided I would do everything in my power to frustrate his little plans. I don't know what they are—'

'You and me both.'

'—but I'm going to make sure they don't work.'

'And where is Asaldra now?'

'Somewhere safe, where he's telling us all about everything. The right drugs and it all comes pouring out.'

One more job for the Specifics, Rico thought. 'It won't do you any good,' he said. 'My friend has taken over that machine out there. Another five minutes and everyone in it goes back home. And then my colleagues come in, extract Asaldra and make sure none of this ever happened. But you can still help foil Asaldra's little plans.'

Alan didn't *look* disappointed – he had learned that lesson way back – but by now every ounce of humanity, of emotion, had vanished from his face. 'How?' he said.

'Testify. Tell me everything Asaldra did. I'll broadcast it to my friend and the testimony will go back to the Home Time. They can't cover that up.'

'You're some kind of policeman?'

'Under the circumstances, yes.'

Alan held Rico's gaze for a moment longer. 'You're from the Home Time too. Why should I trust you?'

'Count the options.'

Another pause . . .

'My designation,' Alan said, 'is RC/1029. My mission began on the thirteenth of May, 1029 AD, in the Persian desert ten miles from Isfahan. I was first contacted by the man I now know as Hossein Asaldra that evening . . .'

'You get all that, Su?'

'I got it. Beautiful job.' Su glanced at her fellow passengers, keeping her expression calm and cool. The two guards had woken up and were still dazed. Daiho was gazing into space.

'How much longer?' he asked without looking at her.

'Any moment now,' Su said as the countdown from her fieldsuit entered single figures.

'Your friend had better get back if he's going to make it.'

Su felt the field take hold of them, felt the disorientation at the fringes of her consciousness.

'*This is it, Rico. See you soon.*'

'*See you, Su.*'

And the transference chamber materialized
around them.

'*Zero,*' said the voice in Rico's head. He turned to
look outside. The helicopter, which had all the
while been hovering, speared by searchlights –
someone on the ground had finally had their
curiosity piqued by the machine hovering beyond
the cliffs – suddenly lurched to one side and
banked down towards the hotel.

He turned back to his new friend.

'They've gone,' he said.

Alan was gazing around him in confusion. 'Why
are you still here, then?'

And Rico suddenly realized the former correspondent hadn't quite understood after all.

'I'm sorry. The *helicopter* was at the recall point,'
he said. 'Now they're back, they'll send a field to
these co-ordinates to pick the rest of us up.'

'How long?'

'Could be thirty seconds, could be five minutes . . .'

Alan filled his lungs. 'Guards!' he bellowed.

Rico looked at him in shocked dismay. 'But . . .'

'You and the youngsters can go,' Alan said
quietly as the doors burst open. 'But the equipment
stays.' Then: 'You!' to the cohort of guards that had

301

just come in. 'Get that gear out of here, now. Get it as far away from here as you can. Now! Move!'

Rico leaped to stand between the advancing guards and the cowering Jontan and Sarai.

'I'm sorry,' he said, 'I can't possibly let you do that.'

'Stun that idiot,' Alan said.

'Shut your eyes!' Rico shouted in the Home Time tongue, for the benefit of the kids, and squeezed his own tightly closed as he did. *Full radiance*, he symbed at his fieldsuit, and at once he was transformed into a man-shaped blazing white sun. Men yelled as the white light showed red through his eyelids, and when he opened them again it was to see the guards staggering back, hands covering their faces.

And Alan, looking at him. Either the former correspondent had also obeyed Rico's command or his enhanced eyes had been able to cope with the light, but the effect was the same.

A dropped stunner lay between them.

Rico met Alan's direct, calculating gaze.

A pause.

'There's no need . . .' he said, and Alan moved – fast, a blur, towards the stunner. Rico was too slow to get there first but not to get there before Alan could raise it. He leaped at the correspondent's gun arm; Alan swatted him casually off and sent him flying across the room.

Rico landed in a crouch and raised an arm at Alan. His fieldsuit let loose a full stun charge, and the correspondent's body absorbed it without effort. Rico sprang forward and caught Alan in a tackle around the waist, bringing him to the floor by sheer momentum. Rico sat on top of his prone rival and used the moment of shock to grab both his opponent's wrists and pull them behind his back, before Alan could use his correspondent's strength to pull them apart again. He locked his hands over the crossed wrists and told the fieldsuit to freeze itself in that position. Alan lay face down, not even breathing heavily but straining at his bonds.

'Listen,' Rico said urgently, 'you've got to—'

'Over here,' Alan called. His face was pressed into the floor but he could see across the room with one eye. Rico turned his head to follow the line of sight. A guard – still blinking, tears still streaming down his face – had retrieved his stunner and was waving it about uncertainly.

'More to the right – that's it! – down a bit . . .'

The stunner was pointing directly at them.

'. . . And *fire!*'

And as his body twisted under the stun charges for the second time that day, Rico felt the recall field take hold of him, and this time his closing thoughts were of satisfaction.

But when he awoke some hours later, he was still in the twenty-first century.

Twenty-two

Hossein Asaldra looked up when the door opened, and he knew the time had come. Two guards with stunners levelled, and a third with a pair of cuffs.

This was where his Field Op's training should have come flooding back. A couple of swipes and kicks to render the guards unconscious and with one bound he would have been free. But he hadn't trained for a long time, he wasn't wearing a fieldsuit – he wasn't even wearing his gelfabric day-to-day clothes, which had been taken away from him and replaced with a simple one-piece boiler suit – and so all he could do was stand up slowly.

The chief guard nodded approvingly. 'That's right, don't make a fuss, sir. We just want to ask you some questions. Unless you're going to try and bribe us . . . ?' He actually sounded hopeful.

'Bribe you?' Asaldra said in disbelief.

'It's just that if someone tries to bribe us, Mr Carradine routinely offers us the same bribe plus ten per cent,' the guard said. 'That's how he deals with all the industrial spies we get sent.'

'Nice Christmas bonus,' one of the others agreed.

Asaldra snorted. 'You've really no idea who or what I am, have you?'

'Doesn't matter,' the chief said casually, but there was unyielding steel behind the cheerful mask. 'Mr Carradine wants you questioned. Are you coming, or do we drag you?'

'I'm coming,' Asaldra muttered, and stepped forward.

They hustled him along narrow corridors and down deep, tight staircases. They were taking him via the servants' route, the network of passages designed to keep the staff invisible in the days when Carradine's home had been the dwelling place of aristocracy. They still served their purpose: as well as his private army, Matthew Carradine no doubt employed perfectly ordinary, decent people who would raise at least an eyebrow when they saw some-one clearly being held prisoner.

Asaldra wasn't sure what to expect at the end of their journey, but he knew it wouldn't match with what his imagination told him it should be, because nothing else had either. He *should* have woken up in a grimy cell somewhere – he had woken up in a lavishly furnished guest suite. He *should* have been in some windswept castle, or at the top of a wind-blown, creaky tower, or down in a dungeon somewhere – he was, he knew, in the stately home that was the headquarters of BioCarr.

But they were heading for the basement, so

maybe the dungeon scenario wasn't too far out.

The room they showed him into was just like any well-maintained, antiseptic, brightly-lit surgery, with a barrel roof that showed its origins as a wine vault. Bottles and various medical instruments were neatly stored in racks along one wall and a reclining, three-part chair sat in the middle. Various hypodermics and small ampoules of different coloured liquids were laid out on a tray next to it. In one corner, a man with a video camera was busy taking light readings.

A woman in a white coat stood next to the chair and beside her stood the little man Asaldra had seen back at the hotel, Carradine's assistant.

'Good,' the man said cheerfully. 'Let's begin.'

'What . . .' Asaldra swallowed. He had been going to say, 'What are you going to do?' but his mouth was dry and the first word came out as a squeak. He tried again and this time got the question out.

'We're going to ask you some questions,' the woman said.

'We're going to ask you a lot of questions,' the man said. 'Don't worry, it won't hurt and you'll make a full recovery. Interrogation techniques are pretty sophisticated in 2022, even for we bygoners.'

'I . . .' Asaldra couldn't take his eyes off the chair. On one level, yes, he knew it probably wouldn't hurt. And they probably weren't going to torture him or harm him – they had no need to do so, when the right concoction of pharmaceuticals

306

could get everything they wanted straight out of him. But he was going to be strapped to a chair in a distant, underground room and interrogated, and that resonated with enough images in his mind to terrify him. He so, so badly did not want to go through with this.

'I'm not sure there's so much I can tell you,' he said.

'Let us be the judge of that,' Alan said, and he nodded at the guards. They seized Asaldra by the arms and frog-marched him towards the chair. He was trying hard to remember what Field Ops were told to do in the event of their ever being captured by bygoners. They had mental blocks installed that prevented them from revealing the existence of the Home Time under interrogation . . . but he was going to be asked questions by people who already knew that the Home Time existed and he suspected the blocks weren't going to work.

His training wasn't going to be any help. He was going to spill secrets to bygoners with who knew what effect on the timestreams, and the Specifics didn't know where he was, and there was no chance of doing what he had originally planned when he contacted Carradine, which was to blank his memory once their business had been completed . . .

'Oh, God, help me,' he prayed silently as the hypo touched his skin and the chemicals flooded in.

* * *

This time Rico came awake with a splitting headache, which immediately told him he wasn't in the Home Time. It took a further half a second to work out he wasn't wearing his fieldsuit any more.

'Oh, God,' he muttered, and let his head sink back onto the pillow.

Pillow?

He forced his eyes open and looked around as best he could without dislocating his head. He took in the marbled walls; the pearly, indirect lighting; the silk sheets he lay in, smooth against his skin.

'Swish,' he muttered.

'It's one of the hall's executive guest apartments,' said a familiar voice. Alan moved into his field of vision. 'Try this.'

He put one hand behind Rico's head and helped him drink from a plastic cup. The stuff was sickly sweet but it cleared Rico's head.

'I told them to keep zapping you the moment you looked like waking up, so you've got a lot to get out of your system,' said Alan. 'You're probably a lot more dangerous than Hossein Asaldra.' He looked thoughtful. 'I imagine it's harder without that organic box of tricks you were wearing.'

'Slightly.'

'And I don't suppose you'll be surprised to hear it's almost evaporated. Holes appeared in it the moment we took it off you and now it's all but gone.'

'Of course.' Rico did feel better. He struggled slowly up into a sitting position and leaned back against the headboard. 'Can't—*aagh!*' A particularly strong streak of pain jabbed into his brain. 'Can't let Home Time tech fall into the hands of the bygoners.'

The agrav and field computer would have gone the same way, of course, and Rico knew his duty, painful though it was. He pulsed the mental signal that destroyed the symb network in his brain, reducing it to a cocktail of innocuous proteins that would be flushed out by his body. There was now nothing that could connect him with the Home Time: he was on his own in the early twenty-first century.

Or not entirely. 'Asaldra?' he said.

'Currently spilling his guts into a waiting digital recorder,' said Alan, 'and very interesting it is too.' He sat on a bedside chair and looked at Rico. Rico took exception to the half smile on his face.

'You're being very nice to me, all of a sudden,' he said.

'I've already established that Asaldra doesn't like you,' Alan said. 'I don't know about the rest of our former guests—'

'Where are they?' Rico interrupted.

'They went. You didn't. Is that what Asaldra called probability masking?'

Rico groaned. 'When they shot me,' he said, 'did I fall on top of you?'

'That's right.'

'Yeah, that's it,' Rico muttered. The recall field hadn't known what to make of two different probability frequencies – his and Alan's – so close together, and as a result neither of them had been picked up. Great. Then: 'You were saying? The rest of your former guests?'

'I don't know what their opinions of you might be, but any enemy of Asaldra might well be a friend of mine.'

'It's mutual.'

Alan raised his eyebrows. 'That sounds heartfelt.' Rico glared up at him.

'Mr Asaldra decided I'd discovered his little game,' he said, 'so he tried to discourage me, and everything he did – he got me reprimanded, he got me beaten up – it all just led me more and more to the facts. If he'd just left me alone, I'd have gone away, and I'd never have found out. And I still don't know exactly what he's up to.'

'Oh, that's easy,' Alan said casually. He crossed his legs and sat back. 'Asaldra and his friends want to save the Home Time.'

'From what?' Rico said.

'From the, um, space nations? What are they?'

'Oh, them,' Rico said. 'All the colonies that declared independence. They're way ahead of us in space technology and even though Earth's over-populated they won't let us out to join them. Yeah, there's some resentment. And?'

'And they think the technology that made the Home Time could be used in Earth's favour.'

'They're probably right, if the College would let them, which it never will.'

'Ah!' Alan looked pleased with himself. 'But apparently, in your time, the Home Time has only got twenty-seven years left to run?'

Rico was about to nod, but old habits suddenly caught up with him. Maybe Asaldra had told Alan everything, but that would have been under drugs. He should be more reticent.

'Go on,' he said.

'This man Jean Morbern created a singularity which acts as a fixed point of reference in time, and that makes transference possible. But that singularity will expire due to quantum decay in twenty-seven years, and no one knows how to make another.'

Alan looked at him as if to confirm the facts so far: Rico still said nothing. Alan shrugged.

'So Asaldra – though the Daiho man was actually in charge – and his colleagues went to where science began.'

'Huh?' said Rico.

'They sent me back, a correspondent, with a pre-disposition to seek out the philosophers. And not just any philosophers but the ones whose insights, breadth of mind, lateral viewpoints laid the foundations of science. I interviewed them, Asaldra came back to record their memeplexes in crystal, and they set up a base here in the twenty-first century so that Daiho, with all his philosophical training, could recreate the science that had led to Morbern's experiments.'

Alan finished with a satisfied smile. 'Easy, really.'

'That . . . that's it?' Rico said, astonished. 'That's it? Why all the cloak-and-dagger? Why didn't they just say so?'

'Apparently your Register is programmed to prevent this kind of thing. This Morbern character wanted the Home Time to end naturally. And they had other reasons. You don't think they were going to give the secret to the whole world, do you? Does Asaldra strike you as an altruist?' Alan's face twisted. 'No. He and his clique were going to monopolize the knowledge. Make Earth great among the space nations, yes, but at the same time they were going to set themselves up as kings.'

Rico snorted. 'That's the one unsurprising thing you've said. So, now he's told you everything, what are you going to do with it?'

Alan sighed, paused, sighed again. 'One thing Mr Asaldra is rather weak on,' he said, 'is the history of the Home Time. How it all came about. I don't think he ever really needed to know. You strike me as the kind of man who likes to find things out. How are you at Home Time History 101?'

'And what would you do with that knowledge?' Rico said suspiciously.

'Stop the Home Time from happening.'

Rico felt like laughing, but laughing required strength he didn't have, so he just shook his head, very slowly in case it fell off. He did feel strong enough to get up, so he pushed back the covers and padded in his shorts to the tall bay windows. He

312

looked out onto parkland. Tastefully landscaped gardens lay outside. Beyond them was a field with three parked helicopters; and beyond them, the rim of a natural grassy bowl where a herd of deer grazed. Trees surrounded the lip of the bowl.

'Matthew bought the hall as headquarters for BioCarr a few years ago,' said Alan behind him. 'I've got out of some prisons in my time, but even I would find this place a challenge. The grounds are crawling with guards, the security systems are absolute state of the art, and if you can't fly or make yourself invisible . . .'

'I get the idea,' Rico said. He turned back to Alan. 'Um – this plan of yours . . .'

Alan's expression went cold again. Rico recognized the look. This was obviously the correspondent's way of showing strong emotion.

'I don't know much about the Home Time,' Alan said, 'but I can guess from the clues I've got. I think the people of the Home Time are the smuggest, most amoral bunch of hypocrites that the world will ever see.'

'I'm with you so far,' said Rico, but Alan ignored him.

'They send us correspondents back, give us blithe assurances about how easy it will all be with these organic survival machines that we call bodies, but do they come themselves? Oh, no! It's far too dangerous. And, in the meantime they lie to us, they abuse us, they take advantage of us . . . and they still expect us to be loyal! I saw the way

Asaldra and his friends acted. They felt so superior to us thicky bygoners. And I saw the way they treated those two engineers they brought with them. That young man and young woman were the only two among them with any kind of useful skill, anything to contribute, and they treated them like dirt.'

'And you work for BioCarr?' Rico asked.

Alan paused, took a breath. 'BioCarr is big and powerful,' he said, 'and will become much more so over the next few years, but Matthew Carradine is one hundred per cent meritocrat. Promotion is by sheer ability and no one stays promoted without constantly proving that ability. But this is all just part of it! I've had a long, long time to work things out, Mr Garron. A long time, and I've decided the Home Time just doesn't deserve to exist. That kind of society is wrong, and if I can stop it then that can only be good.'

'You can't stop it,' Rico said quietly.

'I can try! I'll put the information on servers, I'll write it on documents, I'll carve it in stone, I'll encode it in genomes, I'll bury it in people's subconscious, I'll put it in so many places that your people could never get it all back.'

'You can't,' Rico said, more firmly. 'It doesn't work like that.'

'Then how?' Alan said.

Rico couldn't answer for a moment: the mental block against giving information to bygoners had come back. He had to force out the words with an effort of will.

'If – and it's a big if – *if* you could get enough power to change things, without the Home Time picking it up and stopping you, all you'd do is create a fresh timestream,' Rico said. 'And the stream would still inevitably end in the Home Time, because that's how it works. Morbern accidentally created several new streams when he first transferred. And every stream contains billions of people with as much right to live their own lives as you or me, so once a stream is created, you can't uncreate it without being as big a murderer as several thousand twentieth-century dictators rolled into one. So, ever since then, the Home Time has carefully been splicing all the streams together again. There's no way the Home Time won't happen.'

Alan was quiet for a few moments, digesting this. Then:

'Morbern,' he said. 'Supposing I were to look up everyone of that name now living . . . I wouldn't even have to use violence, just get them sterilized . . .'

'He's still several centuries off,' Rico said. 'I don't even know who his parents were, let alone his triple great-grandparents, and at that generational distance, all that would happen is that someone else would be his triple great-grandma instead.'

'Then I wait until that individual is born! I can—'

'But you won't be around that long,' Rico said, surprised.

'Why not?' Alan asked with a frown.

'Recall Day!' Rico said.

315

He wasn't sure what reaction he expected: Alan to slap his forehead and say he had forgotten? What he didn't expect was:

'Oh, that.' Alan could not have sounded less interested. 'That's another Home Time myth I gave up believing a long time ago, Mr Garron.'

'A myth?' Rico said. 'It's not a myth! It's—'

'It's something the Home Time told me,' Alan said, 'and therefore it's another lie, like everything else they've said.' He crossed to the table and pressed a button. 'Come in now.' He looked up. 'I was prepared to believe you were different, Mr Garron, but if you're as much a liar as your masters, you have nothing useful to tell me. Not of your own free will.'

The door opened and a group of very strong, very burly men in white coats came in.

'Oh, you're kidding!' Rico said.

'Take him,' Alan said, and they pounced.

Rico aimed low, diving between their legs in one smooth motion. He had the move neatly planned in his mind's eye: dart between the two men nearest, come out of the dive into a somersault and leap for the door. Worry about navigating the hall, its grounds and its private army in nothing but a pair of shorts later.

But his weak, drugged, zapped body betrayed him, and he ploughed into the marble tiles and stayed there. Then they were on him. He managed to get a foot into one man's solar plexus and used the half second's respite to get to his knees, and as another man laid hands on him he sent his assailant flying over his shoulder. But then a sheer weight of bodies fell on top of him and pinned him down, and he was lifted up and carried to the bed, fighting and struggling but with each limb held off the ground by a different man so that not even his training could help.

'It's true!' he shouted. 'Recall Day is true!'

Alan was deliberately not looking at him as he walked out of the door.

'It was Daiho's fall-back plan!' Rico yelled, just as the door closed. 'It was how he was going to get back if all else failed! Do you think he'd have relied on a lie to get back home . . .'

Something cold and metal touched his arm, and there was a hiss, and darkness.

Rico Garron floated in a haze. Lights flashed in his eyes, high and low frequencies vibrated in his ears and from time to time the feeling of cold metal against his skin announced the influx of another rush of fact-finding chemicals into his bloodstream. And without his fieldsuit and Home Time equipment, he could do nothing about it. He only had willpower and training to fight the constant stream of questions that dragged up information from the furthest recesses of his memory, and it was a lost battle.

– *What is a correspondent?*

Even in his haze, the question caught him by surprise. He had told them everything he knew of

317

the history of the next five hundred years, up to 2593 when the Home Time was created. He had regurgitated everything he had ever heard in his training about the theory of transference. But this was a sudden *non sequitur.*

'A reporter.' Part of Rico's mind felt smug that, though he couldn't help answering questions, he was able to give literal answers that weren't very helpful.

– What is a correspondent in the context of the Home Time?

'An individual who is sent back in time to report on history.'

– How many are there?

'Hundreds. Thousands. Don't know.'

– How are correspondents selected?

'They're citizens who fail to make the grade.'

– In what way?

'First they were the incurable psychopaths, the people who in your century would be executed or lobotomized.'

– First? What changed?

'They caused too many problems. Their conditioning broke down and they took it out on the bygoners. Termination squads had to be sent back after them.'

– So what are they now?

'The malcontents, or people who still find themselves unable to fit into the Home Time. People whose social preparation fails. Some volunteer . . .'

It seemed there wasn't one secret of the Home

Time that they didn't already know about, Rico thought, as details of the correspondents programme came pouring out of him. Their practical immortality, their enhanced physical skills, the reporting station on the moon – everything.

– *Tell us about symbing . . .*

An amazed Matthew Carradine stood with his arms folded, head shaking slowly in wonder, and watched the scene playing out on the display in his office. The captive's slow slur was annoying – it could take him a minute to come out with a whole sentence – but the recording had been spliced to weed out the junk and the content more than made up for any inconvenience.

'My God,' he said. 'So where are they now?'

'Back in their rooms,' Alan replied.

'Uh-huh.' Carradine turned back to the display. 'These correspondents. It's incredible! Hundreds, thousands of incognito time travellers?'

'Quite a clever way of getting rid of your society's rejects,' Alan said thoughtfully.

'Not if you're sending the psychos back.'

'He said they changed that,' Alan said, still more thoughtfully.

'Immortals,' Carradine marvelled. He turned to the drinks cabinet. 'There've always been legends about people who never died. They probably started them.'

'Probably. Here, let me get that, Matthew.'

'Who told them to ask about these corre-

319

spondents?' Carradine said, stepping aside as Alan moved in to fix the drinks.

'I did.'

'Oh?'

'Something the others in the hotel said. I wanted to know more.' Alan handed Carradine a drink and raised his own. 'To the future.'

'The future,' Carradine agreed, and drank. 'I wonder if anyone we know of was really a correspondent? You know, anyone famous.'

'I got the impression their conditioning forbade that. They would always be quiet, unobtrusive. Behind-the-scenes workers.'

'They'd be good to have on your staff,' Carradine said, laughing. 'They'd know the market, they'd know how things were going to turn out – just the fact that they chose to work for you at all would be a testament that you were going to succeed.'

'Exactly,' said Alan, and stepped quickly forward. With one hand he took Carradine's glass away; with the other, he caught his suddenly crumpling employer and lowered him gently to the ground.

He put the glass with its drugged contents down and lifted Carradine up onto the black leather sofa. Then he pressed the intercom on Carradine's desk. 'We're taking the private way out. No calls or visitors.'

He went into the en suite bathroom and poured the drink he had fixed, in more ways than one, into the basin. Lastly he crossed to the bookcase and pressed the spine of one of the titles: the case moved aside to reveal Carradine's private exit.

Alan took one last look around. He had said goodbye to a lot of places over the last thousand years; some with a sense of regret, others with decided relief. This place . . .

'Goodbye, Matthew,' he said quietly to the still form on the couch, and set off on his rescue mission.

Twenty-three

They solidified into the transference chamber, standing on the carryfield that provided a transparent floor within the steel sphere.

They looked at each other: Daiho bowed slightly to Su.

'Thank you for the lift, Op Zo,' he said. 'Before long, you'll realize that you've been of great help to the Home Time.' He looked around. 'Now, if you'll just open the doors . . .'

'Decon,' said Su.

'Of course.' He shut his eyes.

'That won't be necessary,' Su said. She touched a panel on the gleaming, curved wall and it dilated to show a small med scanner in the recess.

'This is ridiculous!' Daiho said. 'Just call up the decon field.'

'You were in an unauthorized area, unaccompanied by a Field Op. The standard decon field might not be enough,' Su said. She turned him and scrutinized him with the scanner. 'Hold still.'

'Listen, I insist—'

'Mr Daiho, you're legally dead and you're in a transference chamber, and in that place you are indisputably under my authority. I can keep you here as long as I like.'

Daiho sighed. 'Have your little revenge. It won't matter in the long run.'

Right, just for that . . . Su thought, but ten minutes later even she had to admit she had run out of excuses. She didn't trust herself to speak; she just signalled for the clam doors of the chamber to open and the two of them filed out, with her bringing up the rear.

And they were back in the transference hall; one small, unremarkable couple, insignificant among all the transferees coming and going through the many, many chambers arranged in tiers all around them.

'Almost an anticlimax,' Daiho said, looking around him and dusting his hands together. He turned to Su again. 'And now, I'm at your mercy. What do you intend to do with me? I can understand you might want to place me under formal arrest and turn me in, and I couldn't stop you, but I have to warn you, the matter wouldn't get much further than that.'

Su boiled within. She could grasp the obvious and she didn't need things pointed out to her.

'I'll submit my report,' she said, 'and we'll see what happens.'

Daiho nodded. 'If you don't mind,' he said, 'I'd like to hang around while you recall the others. That equipment is valuable.'

Su glared at him with pure loathing, but there would be time enough for hate later.

'Register,' she said, 'I request a recall field from this chamber . . .'

She symbed the co-ordinates of the lounge that she had acquired from Rico. A minute later the doors of the transference chamber swung open and Su dodged inside.

'Well, Rico—'

She blinked. A boy and a girl, looking as if they were ready to fall on their knees and kiss the carry-field, and a pile of equipment. No Rico.

'Where did he go?' she demanded.

Their grins vanished. 'H-he was here, miss,' the boy stammered. 'He was lying right where you're standing when the recall came on, and—'

'—here we are,' the girl said.

Su fought down the urge to look for Rico behind the equipment.

'Right,' she said. 'Wait there.' She put them through the same decon scan she had given Daiho, but this time hurrying. 'Now, help me get that stuff out of here.'

There was no need to hurry, of course; she could have waited a year and still sent a recall field back to that precise time and place again. But she was acquainted with Rico's ability to find trouble in small spaces of time and it was psychologically impossible to go slow.

With half her attention, Su uploaded her report to the Register, and then she turned her full attention to helping the kids. Jontan filled her in on his perception of what had happened just before the recall, one eye always on Daiho, who was hovering in the background.

'He made his suit shine and he blinded the guards, but then he was fighting with the correspondent . . .'

'What correspondent?' Daiho said blankly.

Jontan flushed. 'Um, the one who spoke our language, sir . . .'

'Give me a hand,' said Su, 'and keep talking.'

Even Daiho helped moved the gear out of the chamber. Five minutes later it was empty and generating a second recall field, timed for thirty seconds after the last and expanding the range by a mile in all directions.

The doors opened and Su ran in. The sodden body of Phenuel Scott lay on the floor: otherwise it was empty. Jontan and Sarai stared at the corpse with horrified fascination.

'Well, we should be getting back . . .' Daiho said.

'You stay there!' Su snapped, earning the undying respect of Sarai and Jontan. She symbed a notification that there was a corpse in the chamber that needed clearing up, then propped herself against the chamber wall with one hand. She took a couple of breaths to clear her mind, then looked up.

'Exactly where was Rico?' she said. 'What was he doing? And I mean *exactly*.'

Jontan and Sarai glanced at each other.

'He was, um—' Sarai said.

'—sitting on top of the correspondent,' Jontan said.

'No,' said Sarai, 'remember? He got shot by one of the guards.'

'Shot?' Su exclaimed.

'It would have been another stun shot.' The comment came from Daiho, who was leaning against the barrier at the edge of the tier of chambers and looking bored. 'None of them had lethal weapons.'

'And then?' Su said, looking back at the youngsters.

'He, um, fell,' said Jontan.

'On top of the correspondent,' Sarai added. Su began to suspect.

'Right on top? I mean, body to body, feet to feet, head to head?' she said.

'Um, yes, something like that, I mean, just about . . .'

'Oh, crap,' Su muttered to herself. Then: 'OK,' she said quietly. 'You can go.'

'The equipment . . .' Daiho said.

'No one's going to steal it.'

'You're quite right,' Daiho said. 'That is very valuable property of the Holmberg-Chabani-Scott combine and absolutely no one is going to wander off with it.'

'And I'm impounding it pending investigation into this entire affair,' Su said.

To her surprise, Daiho shrugged. 'It can wait a

little longer, I suppose. It'll be just as safe in your hands.'

'Just get out of my sight,' Su said.

Probability masking – it had to be. Of course, Rico and the correspondent wouldn't have stayed that close forever, but the bygoners would have learned their lesson from the last time they had Rico in their power: get him into a helicopter and just fly, fly anywhere away from the hotel at max.

Wearily, she uploaded an addendum to her report to say there was a Field Op lost upstream. So now it would be a job for the Specifics, Rico's old comrades.

'You've done it this time, Garron,' she muttered.

So, where to now?

Facing Marje Orendal was something she had no particular desire to do, but it was something that had to be done. Toning up with a shower and massage would give her the energy, she reasoned, so she headed for the Rec room.

She had taken three steps away from the chamber when a confinement field came down around her, seizing her and forcing her to stand still. She tried to move but it was like being cased in soft concrete.

'*Do not resist*,' said a voice in her head, and her eyes widened with horror as she felt something worming into her mind through the symb; a cloud that blotted out her vision and left her suspended in a dark limbo.

* * *

Jontan and Sarai walked behind Daiho, hand in hand. Jontan peeked over at her and got a radiant smile in return.

'We're back,' she whispered. 'We're safe.'

'I never want to leave the Home Time again,' Jontan agreed.

'No reason why you should, Mr Baiget,' said Daiho, and they dropped each other's hands quickly as he turned to face them. But he, too, seemed in a pretty good mood. He almost smiled at them. 'I've got catching up to do here,' he said. 'I'm sorry about your employer. I suggest you get back to the consulate, have something to eat and wait for further instructions.'

'Mr Scott was going to fine us when we got back,' Jontan murmured when they were a safe distance away.

'Sssh!'

But before they could reach the consulate, a soft wall seemed to close around them and they couldn't walk any further.

'I can't move!' Sarai said, her voice rising in panic.

'Nor can I . . .' Jontan said, and the darkness came.

Li Daiho stood in what had been his office, facing the eidolon of Ekat Hoon.

'A Field Op named Garron?' Hoon said.

'That's right. But, Ekat, he did everything he could . . .'

Hoon shrugged. 'I doubt the combine will see it that way,' she said. 'They won't be happy to lose a family member.'

'I understand he's lost upstream as well as Hossein,' Daiho said.

'So the Specifics can get them out,' Hoon said casually. 'But if I were this Garron, I'd stay there. He's made powerful enemies. So, Li, how did the mission go?'

Daiho blinked. The woman had lost a friend, and her husband was lost upstream, and she could have been talking about the weather. 'We accomplished what was planned,' hc said.

'Apart from losing Phenuel.'

'History will call him a martyr,' Daiho said, pulling an ironic face, 'which just goes to show that being a martyr isn't necessarily a big deal.'

'Can you keep the Ops quiet?' Hoon said.

'No, of course I can't keep them quiet. Garron didn't strike me as the kind of man to do as he's told. But even if he gets back, he'll find it's no good. It'll be like shouting into a space so wide open you don't even get an echo. Nothing will come of it.' He dismissed the matter with a gesture. 'And now, I really should let the others know I'm back.' He tapped his head. 'Got some goods to deliver.'

'It's all there?'

'It's all been there for a couple of days now. I was doing some final test runs when everything went pear-shaped, but I've got enough.'

'Li!'

Marje Orendal stood in the doorway, and looked as if she had seen a ghost.

'Ah, Marje. Hello.' Daiho looked embarrassed. 'Our reunion, um, wasn't meant to be like this, but now it is . . . well, hello.'

Marje took one step towards him, wonderment on her face, and suddenly froze . . .

After a period of she didn't know how long, Marje made out spots of light in the darkness. It was as if she stood in a darkened room with a handful of other people, each illuminated by a dim spotlight that showed their bodies and nothing more – a fully lit upper half, a lower half fading away into the surrounding darkness.

On her right, Daiho; opposite her, Su Zo; on her left, two young people she didn't know. All parties were looking around with equal confusion; all presumably were like her, pinned down somewhere in the College by a containment field and represented here in symb only.

Daiho seemed to recover first.

'Well, that was quick,' he remarked.

A calm, strong voice spoke to all of them out of the dark. 'Testimony has been received from Field Operative Su Zo that has led to the convening of this emergency hearing to investigate possible malfeasance.'

'And you are?'

'We are the World Executive.'

Wow, Marje thought. The World Executive was

the only thing higher than the patrician class: the collective consciousness of the ecopoloi, formed from the collective thoughts and desires and memeplexes of the millions of residence clusters and billions of inhabitants.

'And this wrongdoing is?' Daiho said.

'Endangering the security and stability of the timestreams, in violation of the first article of Morbern's Code,' said the calm voice.

'What!' Daiho exclaimed. Marje frowned: it wasn't as if he were outraged to hear of malfeasance, but that he had expected something completely different.

'We will begin. The following report was received from correspondent RC/1029 . . .'

And Marje suddenly *knew*, as the knowledge was taken from Su and symbed into her brain. This was the story that had been told to Rico Garron, and symbed to Su Zo, and uploaded in her report upon her arrival back in the Home Time. She knew about RC/1029's arrival in Persia. She knew about the interrupted interview with Avicenna, and she recognized the newcomer as Hossein Asaldra. She knew about the correspondent's further wanderings, all his other interviews, and Asaldra's attendance at all of them too, throughout the next six centuries. Until Descartes in 1646, where it all went wrong, and Asaldra told the correspondent what was happening. Marje winced as she saw the secrets of the Home Time poured out to a bygoner, but it got worse with the far chummier rendezvous after that.

Pascal in 1657. Spinoza in 1670. Malebranche in 1698. And Leibnitz in 1700.

'Oh, Hossein,' Daiho murmured, shaking his head when he saw how that last had ended. 'Oh, Hossein, you idiot.'

'How do you respond, Li Daiho?'

'I take full responsibility for the actions of myself and of all my associates in this affair,' Daiho said simply.

The testimony went on: how the correspondent had thought upon the few clues left by Asaldra as to the nature of the Home Time, and his work. How he had plotted and planned for the next three hundred years; how he had identified BioCarr as a likely target; and how, right on schedule, Hossein Asaldra had appeared to Matthew Carradine and made his proposal.

Morbern's Code lay in pieces.

The World Executive went around everyone else to take their own memories. From Daiho, the entire plan to rekindle the Home Time at the appropriate time, which had meant enlisting the help of a powerful group of patricians to deal with the nitty gritty. For one thing, the plan would lead to an open-ended disappearance from the present, with no guarantee of returning: so he had procured a clone of himself from Holmberg-Chabani-Scott and instilled his own basic brain pattern in it, so that from a forensic point of view there would be absolutely no doubt that it was the body of Li Daiho lying at the foot of the mountain.

Unavoidably, that made the clone at least semi-conscious, certainly self-aware . . . and that made what Daiho had done murder.

Daiho just looked straight ahead, calm and collected, as the story fed itself into each of their minds. Finally, he turned his head again to meet Marje's gaze and she felt that she was the only one there whose opinion mattered to him.

'I've saved the Home Time,' he said simply. 'One life for the sake of our civilization, Marje. Can't you accept that?' He held her gaze for a moment, then looked away, obviously thinking he had made his irrefutable point.

But Marje surprised them both by saying: 'Maybe.' Daiho looked back at her, eyebrows raised. He opened his mouth.

'But the choice should be informed and voluntary,' Marje went on. 'No one has the right to ordain who should make that sacrifice.'

The truth-gathering went on. From the two youngsters, their experiences of being taken from the plantation back to the Home Time. From Su came her account of the meeting with Marje in Daiho's villa; the stream of small details that weren't quite right; her constantly suspicious, volatile partner. And finally, from Marje herself, the flip-side of Su's testimony: the shock of the news of her superior's death; encounters with Op Garron; a similar sense that something, somewhere wasn't right.

And more, of course, for which Marje had

333

already steeled herself. The approach by Yul Ario, the not-so-subtle hints that she should drop the case, the attempt to recall Garron. Marje shut her eyes, knowing that not only were the others getting the bald facts but her accompanying self-loathing with it. She had been right, she had been on the right trail, and yes, there had even been a murder . . . and she had been prepared to throw it all away for the convenience of the patricians.

But lurking behind it all was the small item of knowledge – which surprised her, but for which she was glad – that, like Daiho, she was prepared to pay whatever penalties came her way. She still felt like the world's vilest traitor but there was one crumb of self-redemption in her testimony.

It stopped. The whole thing had taken only a few seconds but everyone was looking at everyone else, reassessing and re-evaluating their thoughts and opinions of the people around them. Su in particular met her eyes, held her gaze, nodded slightly and then looked away. That counted for more than anything else in Marje's opinion. Su wasn't holding her weakness against her.

And the World Executive spoke.

'We have made our decision,' it said.

'Su,' said Marje. 'Hello. Come in, take a seat.'

Marje didn't sound very interested in Su's presence. She stood with her back to the door, gazing out across the white landscape beyond the window. Su did as she was told.

'Commissioner Daiho . . . ?' she said.

'Some Security Ops came for him about ten minutes ago. They took him away.'

'I've just come from the transference hall,' Su said. 'The equipment's under guard by Security. It'll be used by the College, not Daiho's friends.'

'Good.'

'And the Specifics are going to try and get Rico back.'

'Good.' Marje still sounded numb, disinterested.

'I was just wondering . . .'

Marje finally turned round. 'Yes?'

'Will you stay on as Rico's sponsor? The thing is, Marje, Holmberg-Chabani-Scott have filed suit against him for Scott's death, they say he was negligent, and they don't have a leg to stand on, but they could make life very unpleasant for him, so—'

'No,' said Marje.

There was a silence.

'I'm sorry.' Su stood up again. 'I won't bother you again, Commissioner.'

'Wrong,' Marje said. 'Sit down, please, Su.' And while Su sat, slowly, and stayed still, something seemed to snap inside Marje at long last and she paced about the office. 'I'm not a Commissioner any more,' she said. 'I've just symbed in my resignation. No Commissioner, so no patrician membership, so no sponsorship for Op Garron. I'm sorry.'

'Marje, if it's about—'

'Su, I've been used from my very first day on this

335

job! I've been lied to, I've been blackmailed, and the worst of it is, it came damn close to working. I wanted to be a patrician so I could help others but all that happened was I got caught up in the whole sick powerplay at the top. Oh, yes, it's everywhere! They were all in on it. Yul Ario, for a start—'

Who just happens to be Commissioner for Fieldwork. Rico's boss. Su's heart hit bottom and started to dig.

'—and I suspect the rest. And will any of it come out? Will any heads roll? Of course not. Everyone involved was a patrician and they should all be above reproach. The people can't be allowed to see their failings. No, Su, I haven't been impressed by what I found out about them and I don't care too much for what I found out about myself. I'm not going to take that any more.

'And that is why I can't help.' She looked at Su and sighed, her energy expended for the time being. 'I'll be glad to offer what testimony I can, but I can't give Rico patronage. He'll have to defend himself against Hoon with the facts.'

'Marje,' said Su, 'we all know they don't need facts to make his life very unpleasant.'

One corner of Marje's mouth smiled. 'Op Garron has worked his way up from the orphan's crèche to this place, and he's done it on his own. I have a feeling he'll get through this too.'

Su quietly took her leave.

After Su was gone, Marje took a couple of deep breaths and looked again around the office. The old-fashioned bookcases and panelling; the furniture and carpet; the clash of styles she had never got round to changing.

And the hourglass on the wall, with its prominent '27'.

All someone else's problem. No more politics for her. No more manipulation. No more correspondents.

Or, in other words, no more playing God with the lives of people who couldn't make it in the Home Time. Now, she would *help* them make it in the Home Time. Her work had given her enough insight into the problems of people in the lower social levels. People who didn't have patrician power or patronage to ease their way in the system. She could set up a practice, she could help these people instead of consigning them on a one-way ticket to the past, to satisfy the needs – no, the *wants*, there was a big difference – of the present.

There were almost tears in Marje Orendal's eyes when she left the office, but also a spring in her step.

Twenty-four

The sadly familiar feel of a hypo on his skin. Hands lifting him up. Rico seemed to float in the chemical smog around his brain.

'Wha—?' he said.

'I'm not a murderer,' said a voice. Whose? He knew it, and he knew there was something he wanted to do to its owner, like kick its butt.

'Bully for you,' he mumbled.

'All that about timestreams, and what will happen if I try and stop the Home Time happening?'

'All true.'

'I know. You convinced me. Wait here.' The hands released him, and his knees buckled. He floated gracefully down to the floor and bounced slowly. The impact of his head against the tiles tickled and he giggled.

Another touch of metal against his arm; yet another blast of pharmaceuticals into his system to do battle with the cocktail already coursing through his veins.

'This should help,' said the voice.

Alan, Rico remembered. Its owner was called Alan – or rather, chose to be called Alan nowadays.

He was a correspondent.

He had handed Rico over to the interrogators.

Rico's mind told his body to lunge up and hit the man, hard. Rico's body preferred to imitate a jellyfish.

But Alan was holding a hand out to him.

'You and Asaldra both said exactly the same thing,' he said. 'You couldn't have lied with what you went through and I'm sorry I doubted you. But I've got two more questions for you.'

Rico glared at him, but took the hand and let himself be hauled up. Alan set him down into a chair. Rico looked around. He was back in what Alan had euphemistically called a guest apartment. Then Rico saw the two unconscious figures of his guards.

'They'll live,' Alan said, following his gaze. 'Just two further questions, Mr Garron, and then we get out of here.'

Rico looked from the interrogators, to Alan, to the interrogators, then back to Alan again. He shrugged.

'Shoot,' he said.

'You said there were two kinds of corre-spondents. Psychopaths and misfits. Which kind am I?'

'Dunno. I don't know when you came from.' Rico lifted his hands up cautiously and held them in front of him, wiggling his fingers. Then he held his arms out to either side – he was strong enough to do that, now – shut his eyes and touched his nose with both hands. Yes, it was all coming back. 'Still, you've been here a good thousand years. How many people have you killed?'

'One hundred and seventy-two,' Alan said at once. 'All in self-defence.'

Rico laughed weakly. 'Not even two a decade. You're the second kind. Does that make you feel better?'

'Not really. A bit, maybe.' Alan leaned closer. 'Second question. When is Recall Day?'

'I haven't already told you that?' Rico said, surprised.

'I didn't believe in it, so I didn't include it in the list of questions for the interrogators,' Alan said. 'When is it?'

'No,' said Rico.

'I beg your pardon?'

'If you want to know that, put me back under and ask, but I'm not telling you that of my own free will. I'm a Field Op and I have obligations.'

Alan was quiet for a moment. 'Well, one out of two isn't bad and I've lived through worse odds. But it must be close, or Daiho wouldn't have been counting on it, would he?' Rico just looked at him and said nothing. Alan sighed. 'All right, all right. Can you stand?'

Rico cautiously pushed himself up out of his chair. He was unsteady on his feet but he could walk.

'Good enough,' said Alan. He checked one of the unconscious guards, then the other. 'This one's about your size. Give me a hand.'

Alan was undoing the man's jacket; Rico knelt down and started on the boots.

'Where are we going, out of interest?' he said.

'You, that's up to you. Me, I'll think of something.' Alan lifted the man's torso up and began to tug the jacket off. 'A holiday. A binge at Monte Carlo. A Caribbean cruise. A golf-and-fishing holiday in Scotland. Anything to while away the time until Recall Day, when I go home.' He looked up at Rico. 'You could come with me, if you like.'

'Me?' Rico exclaimed.

'You've missed your boat back home, haven't you, thanks to me? And I want to make amends, and I got the idea from the interrogation that you don't like the Home Time that much. You'd need an identity, but I've got a few stacked up that go back for years. You can have one of them.'

'Stay here,' Rico mused. It had honestly not occurred to him and he fantasized briefly. If he stayed here until Recall Day, his savings back in the Home Time would have been growing uninterrupted for twenty-seven years while he was away. When he returned, still much the same physical age as now, then based on the date of his birth he would be that much closer to retirement. He would get off Earth, out into space, still young, and start his life all over again. It was a tempting prospect.

But . . .

'No,' he said. 'Thanks, but no. For a start, I've got to contact the Home Time and tell them what's happened here.'

Alan stopped. 'Why?' he exclaimed. 'No, don't tell me. Obligations.'

'I can't leave the situation as it is,' Rico said. 'Carradine knows about the Home Time, and so do these two, and I expect a lot of other BioCarr people, and by now that information will be stored on servers and mainframes all over the planet. I have to let the Specifics know.'

'Who are they? The time police?'

'Something like that.'

'And they take you back?'

'And they take me back,' Rico agreed, still with a tinge of regret. 'Look, life in the eleventh century was a lot simpler, but which period would you rather be living in, then or now?'

'Now,' Alan said without hesitation. 'They know about hygiene and no one tries to kill you very often.'

'Same argument,' Rico said. 'I belong in the Home Time. I'm sorry.'

'Well, it was just a thought.' Alan held Rico's gaze for a moment. 'But I am sorry for what I did to you.'

'No hard feelings. Oh, and I'm taking Asaldra with me.'

Alan seemed to deflate as the last traces of his once great plan evaporated. 'Ah, you're welcome to him. So, how do you contact your people?'

'I don't,' Rico said. He couldn't help a grin. 'You do.'

342

The road looped around the edge of the landscaped bowl in which the hall stood. The car drew
to a halt at a point overlooking the grounds. The
headlamps flicked off, its hydrogen-powered
turbine whispered to a standstill and the doors gull-
winged open with a quiet hiss. Two passengers got
out and one of them turned to give a hand to the
third, who staggered on rubbery legs and had to
lean against the side of the car.

Alan had raged. *'Call the Home Time? Me? You're*
mad! They'll just reprogramme, or—'

'Simmer down, simmer down,' Rico had said. *'You*
don't have to be here when they arrive . . .'

'You have to admit, it's attractive,' Alan said now.
He stood with his hands in his pockets, looking
down at the hall, ablaze with light. 'Wouldn't you
agree, Mr Asaldra?'

'Get on with it, for God's sake,' Asaldra
muttered. Rico remembered how he had felt on his
post-interrogation wakening and for the first time
ever he felt a measure of sympathy for the man. He
had the world's worst hangover and the only cures
for it were back in the hall or in the Home Time.

Rico was looking at the sky.

'You can see more stars on a night like this
than you could fifty years ago,' he said. 'BioCarr
had its faults but it did help clean the world up.' He
added: 'And, if you've missed it, the moon's up
there.'

'I know, I know.' Alan looked up. A couple of

seconds later: 'it's done.' He squinted at the hall again. 'It doesn't look that different.'

'Trust me,' said Rico. 'They'll have edited it into a separate stream, cleaned up, changed memories, wiped records, and then spliced the stream back into the alpha stream again. The bygoners will have a brief moment of déjà vu when the streams merge, but that will be it, and to outside observers it'll seem that no time passed at all.'

'So much for not fiddling with time.'

'They won't have caused any new people to exist, or deleted any existing ones. The Code allows that. And just in case they miss out on any records, if there's still something left, they'll implant engrams that prevent the person who sees them from making any sense of them. Or even being interested in them. It works.'

'You've done it yourself, haven't you?'

'Once or twice.'

'Freeze!' A man's voice behind them. They froze. 'Put your hands on your heads. Turn round.'

Alan, Rico and Asaldra obeyed the orders in succession, Asaldra stumbling and almost falling over. Two figures had come out of the trees behind them and were standing on the other side of the road. Their feet were apart and their hands raised, covering them.

'Stay right there,' said a woman's voice.

'Hi, Su,' Rico called. 'What kept you?'

'Rico!' A grinning Su came forward out of the darkness, tucking her synjammer into her belt. A man followed close behind. 'Well, you truly buggered up, didn't you?' He held his arms out and she fell into a hug.

'At last,' Asaldra said. His strength seemed to be returning. 'What kept you?'

'Shut up, you're being rescued,' Rico said. 'This is Mr Asaldra, if you hadn't gathered.'

'I'll just deal with the other one,' said the man, and he took a step forward. Alan moved in a blur, and then the synjammer was lying in the grass ten feet away and the man was on his front, hands pinned behind him and face pushed into the ground by Alan crouching on top of him.

'No one,' Alan said, '*deals* with me.'

'You understood me?' the man wheezed. 'But how . . .'

Rico and Su stood watching the little tableau, Rico with his arm round Su's waist. 'Brains are still a priority in recruiting Specifics, I see,' Rico said cheerfully

'He's the correspondent you were briefed on,' Su said, and it was obvious she was trying not to laugh. 'You are RC/1029, I take it?'

'At your service.' Alan stood up and let the Specific pick himself up in his own time.

'Op Bera was about to do a quick edit on you.'

'That's happened once too often for my liking,' said Alan.

'Correspondent?' Asaldra said. Alan gave him a look of pity and contempt.

345

'You still don't get it, do you, Herbert?'

'Who?' said Rico.

It took a moment to sink in. 'You?' Asaldra said. The sheer horror in his tone suggested he had gone pale in the moonlight.

'Don't worry, I think I've had my revenge.'

'Can I interrupt?' Bera was climbing to his feet. He glowered at Alan, but when he picked up the synjammer he simply put it away in his fieldsuit. 'Op Garron, Mr Asaldra, you've been identified and now we have to get to the recall field. As for *you* . . . our orders don't cover you.' Rico stepped in front of Alan, just in case Bera still intended to take the initiative in dealing with a rogue correspondent. Bera snorted. 'But there's no way you come with us,' he said.

Alan shrugged. 'As I understand it, if I go back with you, I'm still a criminal or a misfit. If I go back on Recall Day I've done my sentence. I'll hang around a bit longer.'

'Well . . .' said Rico, and stopped. He and Alan hadn't had the best of relationships but he had found himself liking the correspondent, and if they ever saw each other again, to Rico it would be twenty-seven years in the future. 'Goodbye, then. Some of it was a pleasure.' They reached out to shake hands.

A thin, high-pitched gnat's whine drifted through the quiet night air from the direction of the hall. Rico recognized the noise – a helicopter's engine starting up.

Alan was glancing back at the hall. 'No one was scheduled . . .'

Another whine, and another. Rico remembered the three helicopters parked on the lawn outside the hall.

'There's an alarm going!' Alan exclaimed.

'I don't hear anything,' Bera said, straining his ears.

'Of course you don't, but trust me.' He swung on Rico. 'I thought you said your people would fix everything!'

'They'll have left everything as it was, minus the Home Time element,' Bera said.

'Everything?'

The whine turned into a throaty mechanical roar as the first helicopter lifted off and its searchlight impaled the darkness.

'Well, yes.'

'Including Matthew Carradine lying unconscious in his study,' Alan snapped. 'Brilliant work!'

'But they won't be looking for us,' said Su.

'No, they'll be looking for Matthew's PA, who drugged him.'

The Home Timers turned for a final look back at the hall. The three helicopters were in the air, each spiralling out from the hall in a different direction. One of them was turning towards them.

'Then let's get to the recall field now,' Bera said. He set off into the trees at a light trot. Rico, Su and Asaldra turned to follow him.

As did Alan.

347

'I said you couldn't come!' Bera snapped as the leaf canopy blocked out the sky.

'I won't get out of the estate in my car,' said Alan. 'I'm taking the long way. And by the way, those choppers all have infra-red detection equipment.'

'We've got fieldsuits. We can block that out,' Bera said.

Su nodded at Rico and Asaldra. 'These two can't.'

They glanced back. Like a squadron of metallic valkyries, the three helicopters were now flying towards them in line abreast, searchlights like lances through the dark.

'Oh, *shit*!' Bera said. 'Run. And you –' he pointed at Alan – 'go somewhere else or I use the synjammer.'

They ran, pounding through the undergrowth. Branches slashed at Rico's face, brambles reached out to trip him. Bera and Su were drawing ahead.

'Come *on*!' Su urged from up front.

'You can see! I can't!' Rico shouted. Just behind him he could hear Asaldra, similarly unequipped and crashing through the undergrowth. He ducked to avoid a particularly large branch and ran into a trunk. He fell back onto the ground, dazed.

A pair of strong hands grabbed him under the arms and hauled him to his feet.

'You go on,' Alan called. 'I'll bring him. Come on, Mr Garron.'

'I've got you,' Su said behind them. She was talking to Asaldra, not Rico. 'Just follow me.'

348

For just a few moments, Su and Alan used their enhanced vision to guide Rico and Asaldra through the dark, but then light burst onto the scene as the three helicopters finally reached them and bright white light blazed down through the canopy. The downdraft of the rotors picked up the mulching leaves and swirled them about in the roar of the three engines. Branches and shadows whipped about in a crazed dance that made the going even more hazardous.

'Remain where you are.' An amplified voice echoed over the engine noise. 'We have picked you up and you can't escape. The estate is sealed off and armed guards are on their way.'

'Yeah, yeah,' Rico muttered. The three machines were directly overhead, all jostling for position and the glory of catching the fugitives, and the noise was deafening. Helicopters weren't that useful when it came to apprehending people in forests, Rico thought, as he summoned the energy for one final sprint, with Alan still at his side. There was the problem of getting through the branches.

Up ahead, maybe fifty yards off, he could see Bera. The Specific had stopped running and was looking back at them, waving, urging them on. So, that must be the recall point. Bera finally twigged that the people he was meant to be rescuing weren't doing very well and he took a step towards them.

The voice was at it again. 'I said, stay where you are. You can't get away and you're only making things worse. You— *look out, you idiot!*'

And then there was a crash, and a screech of metal tearing into metal, and the frantic *whip whip whip* of spinning metal suddenly liberated from its mounting and slicing through the air . . .

. . . And a bright orange *whoomph* as a fuel tank exploded, and the two helicopters that had collided tumbled down into the trees. The blast knocked Rico to the ground and he instinctively curled into a tight ball as bits of red hot wreckage and razor sharp, twisted steel hurtled through the air in all directions.

He picked himself up gingerly. Ahead, the forest was ablaze, an inferno that he could never get through. The flames lay between him and the recall point.

'Close one,' he commented, looking over at Alan. 'That was . . .'

He stopped. Alan was lying still. Rico reached over and prodded the man's shoulder. Still nothing.

With his heart in his mouth, Rico turned Alan over. The correspondent's chest was one large hole, gouged out by a piece of wreckage. Alan's eyes were open and blank.

Rico's world went cold and empty.

'Oh, no,' he breathed. 'Oh, no. Please. No.' He drew his knees up and wrapped his arms round them, and he sat and looked at Alan.

'Rico?' A gentle hand on his shoulder. He took it and squeezed it, without looking up.

A thousand years, almost. War, plague, famine

and Europe's Middle Ages – this man had come through them all. Convicted by the Home Time for who knew what misdemeanour, sent back to serve his sentence, innocently trusting his far-future masters, used and abused by them right from the start . . .

And it ended in a forest, with a lump of helicopter wreckage in his chest.

'Rico, I'm sorry,' Su said. He gave the hand another squeeze, then darted a venomous glare at Asaldra. The other Home Timer was picking himself up from the forest floor, brushing himself down, and he couldn't tear his gaze from the body. He had the sense to keep quiet.

Voices were shouting through the trees. Rico didn't move.

'I don't know what you did in the Home Time,' he said, his voice shuddering in his throat, 'but you didn't deserve this.'

'Rico, we've missed the recall,' Su said.

'Uh-huh.' Rico reached out for Alan's left wrist, lifted it up, glanced at the watch there. It was just past midnight. He angled the display so that Su could see it.

'Ah, well,' he said.

'Oh, God,' she said.

A light pierced the dark and picked him out.

'Don't move!' shouted a voice.

'We're not going anywhere,' Rico said calmly. Guards pounded through the bushes, wincing at the heat of the still blazing fire. They surrounded the Home Timers, guns raised, and Su and Rico just looked at them. Asaldra put his hands up and Rico at last felt the familiar feel of a recall field enveloping him.

'Hello, boys,' he said, and all three Home Timers vanished.

It was just after midnight on Saturday 21st May, 2022.

Recall Day.

Twenty-five

Rico came abruptly out of the post-transference daze when someone tripped over him. He was sitting on the floor of the transference chamber, still in the hugged-up position in which he had left the twenty-first century. It was darker for him than it usually was in a chamber because he was surrounded by people who were standing. The man who had almost fallen over him found his balance again and stumbled back into the man behind him, who stepped to one side and bumped into the woman next to him, who . . .

'Hey, hey, careful! I'm down here!'

The person next to him reached down and helped him up. Rico realized it was Su. He pulled himself to his feet, fighting the mass of people around him. The chamber was packed: men and women of all colours, shapes and sizes. There was little talking, not even murmuring. These were correspondents, conditioned to keep themselves to themselves, and not even the fulfilled promise of Recall Day was going to break them out of their usual reserve.

Asaldra was there too and his face was split by an enormous smile.

'Recall Day!' He seemed genuinely happy. 'Well, well. I'm sorry this spoils all those plans you had for me, Op Garron.'

'What do you mean? We're back in the College,' Rico said.

The old smugness was back. 'Recall Day is twenty-seven years after our own time. Assuming they haven't abolished the statute of limitations, anything I ever did wrong is long forgiven.'

'Rico,' Su whispered, and that brought Rico's mind neatly back to a far more important point than the possibility that Asaldra was going to get away with everything. Her face was ashen. Su had left a husband and child back in the old Home Time. Tong would now be almost due for retirement, her kid would be an adult, and to them, Su's non-return twenty-seven years ago would have been as good as bereavement.

Rico wormed one arm round her in the press of people and held her tight. 'Oh, Su, I'm sorry,' he said quietly. She rested her head on his shoulder and trembled.

The doors to the chamber swung open and a voice spoke. It was friendly and resonant with welcome and love.

'Correspondents, welcome back to the Home Time! Please follow the red lights.' A stream of lights appeared in the air above them, flowing from the centre of the chamber and out of the doors.

354

The correspondents waited a moment longer, then obediently began to shuffle forward.

One of them stumbled and caught herself; then another, and another. Rico glanced down. Oh, yes.

'Make way, people,' he called out, jabbing a finger down at the floor. 'Dead person.'

A few curious glances down at Alan's body, but not many.

'Yes, that's right, keep going,' Rico said. 'Follow the light. Just keep moving . . .'

Five minutes later the chamber was empty except for Rico, Su, Asaldra and the body. Rico looked down at Alan.

You're back where you wanted to be, he thought. *At least one of us made it.*

'Can I have your designations?' said a bright voice. A man and a woman in College yellow stood in the entrance, wreathed in amiable smiles.

'Sorry?' said Rico.

'Your designation?' the woman repeated. 'Is your conditioning at fault, maybe? You didn't follow the lights, you see . . .'

'Don't worry about him,' said the man, following Rico's gaze down to the body. 'We'll get a clean-up squad to take care of him.'

Rico bristled. 'He will be buried with full College honours,' he snapped. The two stewards took a step back, presumably not expecting that sort of tone from a returning correspondent, let alone a correspondent who knew what the College was. 'He will not be *cleaned up*. Got that?'

'I, um . . .'

'Please excuse my colleague, he's prone to over-excitement.' Asaldra stepped forward. 'My name is Hossein Asaldra; these two individuals and I were accidentally caught up by the general recall. Do you have any instructions concerning us?'

'Mr Asaldra?' said the woman. The two stared at him as if he had just announced his divinity to a waiting world. Rico had the horrid feeling they were about to fall down at his feet and worship. 'Yes, of course we do! And you two must be Ops Zo and Garron? Do come with us.'

'We'll see your friend is, um, looked after, Op Garron,' the man said. Rico let his gaze hold the man's eyes just long enough to impart an idea of what would happen if his friend was not looked after, and ushered Su after the woman. Asaldra had already stepped boldly forth.

The arrival scene in the chamber had been a microcosm of what was going on out in the main hall. Every chamber on every level was disgorging correspondents. ('If your designation is BC, please follow the blue lights. If your designation is AD, please follow the green lights.') No one seemed to be bothering with decon – Rico imagined this quantity of people would overwhelm the automatic systems and every correspondent would get individual treatment instead. He whistled and it was a strangely loud noise, because despite the quantity of people, the only other sound apart from the background announcements was shuffling feet and jostling bodies.

'Did we leave anyone upstream at all?' he said. The woman didn't catch his meaning.

'Oh, no, all our people will have been recalled,' she said. Then, to the air: 'I have Mr Asaldra and his companions here.'

'*This is Field Op Garron* . . .' Rico symbed to back her up, before realizing he was getting nothing in return. Of course: he had destroyed his symb implants back in the twenty-first century. It was the least of his worries right now. And . . .

What exactly was going on? 'Mr Asaldra and his companions' seemed to imply that some fame had accrued to all of them in the intervening twenty-seven years – but to Asaldra in particular.

'Hossein!' An eidolon appeared in front of them. A woman in late middle-age, red-haired, gazing at Asaldra fondly. 'Oh, how I've missed you.'

'Hello, Ekat, darling.' Asaldra's smile seemed more fixed. 'I'm back.'

'And to a hero's welcome,' the Ekat woman assured him. 'Well done.' She gave Rico and Su a glance that seemed to skim off the top of them, then looked back at Asaldra. 'Hossein, I hope you don't mind, but we arranged a press conference and everyone who's anyone is dying to meet you, or at least symb you. If you're not too tired after your ordeal . . .'

Asaldra might have been born for this moment. He seemed to puff to twice his size and his proud smile could have illuminated the entire trans-ference hall. 'Not too tired at all, my dear. I'll just need a moment to freshen up and then I'm all yours.'

'Just follow me,' Ekat said, and her eidolon drifted off. Asaldra took a moment to look back at the two Ops.

'What did I tell you?' he said quietly. 'I expect I'll see you around.'

And he was off.

It was all too obvious. Asaldra had powerful friends, and they had been laying the groundwork for his return for the last twenty-seven years. Here, he wasn't the not-especially-bright stooge of Li Daiho; he wasn't the man who had managed to be outsmarted not once but twice by the correspondent he had been so ready to use. Rico didn't know if Daiho's work had borne any fruit, but if Asaldra wasn't now the man who had saved the Home Time then he was at least the one who had busted a gut trying.

'Rico,' Su said, her voice still a whisper.

'I know, Su, I know,' he said gently.

'I can't symb. It's telling me it won't accept my connection. I can't even find out about them.'

'Hello, Mr Garron.'

It was a man's voice, and familiar enough to make Rico turn quickly. It came from a ball of marker light, hovering in the air behind him. 'Welcome back to the Home Time. And you, Ms Zo.' Familiar, yes, but Rico couldn't quite place it. 'Will you come this way, please?'

Su only looked at the light blankly. Rico still had

one arm round her and he could feel she was still trembling.

'Are you with the College?' he said. 'Op Zo has family . . .'

'I know all about both of you,' the light said. (*Whose voice was that?* It hovered just the wrong side of recognition . . .) 'Please, come this way – that's all I'm allowed to say.'

'Who . . .?' Rico said, but the light was already drifting off, so Rico and Su forced their way through the mass of correspondents, who were finally being sorted into more specific groupings ('Sixteenth to twenty-first centuries AD, please follow the yellow lights. Eleventh to fifteenth centuries AD, please follow the blue lights. Sixth to tenth centuries AD . . .'), and followed.

After a brief spell in decon the light led them out of the hall and into the corridors and chambers of the College. Rico had been wondering if there would be some kind of red carpet laid out for the returning lost Field Ops, but apparently not. No one even gave them a second glance. Maybe the enquiry into their non-return had judged them incompetent and an embarrassment to the College. Maybe, under the new version of history, they were the villains who had obstructed Asaldra in his noble work and they had been struck off the rolls.

'See, the conquering hero comes,' he muttered. The layout of the place was the same, the cut of the clothes slightly different, not one face recognizable. And the whole place was strangely quiet, subdued, as Rico thought might be expected on the last day of the Home Time.

They came to a carryfield and were whisked away, with the light following. Rico suddenly had a suspicion what was happening.

It'll be a party, he thought, with a grin. *They're laying on a welcome-home do. Maybe not everyone, but Su's family are bound to be there, maybe her grandkids too . . .*

Except that they were not heading in the direction he would have expected.

'We're going to the Outsider's Quarter?' he said.

'We're going to the Appalachian consulate, Mr Garron. All the regular College accommodation is booked up for today.'

'I haven't been having good experiences with Appalachians recently, you know,' said Rico.

The voice was amused. 'I know.'

They came to the barriers of the consulate, where Rico and Su had to get off the carryfield to walk. The light beamed a clearance code at the guards and they let the Ops through.

'Almost there,' said the light. They stopped outside an apartment and the light faded into nothingness, just as the door morphed open.

The apartment held a man and a woman, coming towards them. *Not a party, then,* Rico thought, and failed to keep the disappointment off his face.

The man was smiling broadly. 'Come in, please.' The voice was the same as the one that had led Rico here. 'How do you do, Op Zo. We met briefly, you may remember. Op Garron?' He looked Rico up and down. 'I remembered you as taller and older, but then I was slightly smaller and a lot younger.'

Rico studied the man in return. Dark hair, maybe a touch of grey, early to mid-forties . . .

The penny dropped as they stepped into the apartment and the door closed behind them.

'You're Jonjo!'

'Jontan Baiget, Mr Garron.' Jontan smiled and held out his hand. 'And this is Sarai.'

'Hello.' Sarai smiled broadly and held out her hand. 'I never got a chance to thank you.'

Jontan said, 'The Register asked us – well, ordered, but we were happy to oblige – to be here to meet you. He thought you'd like some familiar faces.'

'I never thanked you either, Op Zo,' Sarai said. Her smile was still wide and genuine as she held her hand out to Su. 'I can still remember—'

'*For God's sake!*' It was almost a scream and it made Rico, Jontan and Sarai jump. Su flung herself away from Rico and stood facing them. Her hands were balled up into fists. They quivered with emotion, her whole body shook and it looked as if she was about to throw herself at one of them and pound him to pieces. 'Will you stop nattering and tell me *where my family are?*'

'Your family?' Jontan seemed baffled. 'I've no idea, but I could find out, if you like.'

'You mean, the Register didn't tell you?' Rico said. Sarai and Jontan were completely nonplussed.

'But why should it?' Sarai said.

'Well, you know . . .' Rico stepped over to Su and gently took hold of her shaking wrists. He rubbed them together but didn't take his eyes off Jontan. 'She might have appreciated the information. She's got a lot of catching up to do with them, you know. Twenty-seven years and all that.'

'Catching up?' Jontan looked at Su in surprise. 'But, I mean, you go back, don't you? They won't miss you for a moment. Everyone knows that.'

'To use a complex legal term,' Jontan called over the hiss of the water, 'they tried to buy us off. And to use another, we took the money and ran.' He was sitting in a comfortable chair just inside the door of the bathroom. Su and Sarai were in the next-door suite, where Su had been promised an identical freshening up and debriefing.

'And you're still together,' Rico said as he scrubbed under his arms. 'I wouldn't have guessed.'

'Sorry?'

'Still together.' Rico raised his voice to get it through the shower partition. 'Ah, this is good. This is *good.*'

'Not *still* together, we got back that way. I mean, yeah, we were kids in love, but a few weeks upstream wasn't enough to make us spend the rest of our lives together. But then the Patrician's Guild paid off our service to Holmberg-Chabani-Scott to dissuade us from pressing charges of abduction against them, and Holmberg-Chabani-Scott gave us a farm each for the same reason.'

'Excuse me?' Rico said. 'They gave two kids a farm each?'

'Legally we were post-minors – young enough to still be under adult protection, old enough to own a business. But yes, sure, they were hoping we'd go under in five minutes flat, so we'd end up working for them again and they could say, well, they'd done their best for us.'

'What went right?'

'Sarai.' Even with the slightly raised voice and the partition, there was no disguising the pride and love in Jontan's voice. 'Me, I'm a biotechnician, always will be, but she's got a business head. She suggested combining the farms, which we did – I mean, I can read a balance sheet and I know when I'm about to go broke – and one thing led to another and, well, we fell in love all over again, as adults. We're due to be grandparents in four months' time and the farm's booming. We'll never be Holmberg-Chabani-Scott, but who needs it?'

'Congratulations,' Rico said. 'Tell it to stop the water and turn on the air, will you?' he added – God, he missed symb – and Jontan obliged. 'Bit warmer . . . bit more . . . that's it.' He turned slowly in the flow of perfumed, warm air. 'And now, I gather Asaldra's the big hero?'

'And how. They turned on the PR the moment Op Zo got back. She was proof it worked and he became like a posthumous hero, except that he wasn't actually dead. Ekat Hoon's still on the Oversight Committee for the College, and she'll have worked out a nice patrician post for him in the new order.'

'And the new order is?'

'Much the same as the old one,' Jontan said with a lopsided grin. 'A few different names in the top posts, but for the rest of us, life goes on. Except that transference is going to be a lot less regulated than before and Hoon's lot are full of plans for using it against the space nations. They're popular.'

'And Daiho? I mean, he did the actual work,' said Rico.

'Mr Daiho committed murder,' said a new voice. Rico popped his head around the partition in surprise. The Register's eidolon stood in the door-way to the bathroom. 'Thank you for your help, Mr Baiget, but would you mind leaving us alone now? Op Garron, your clothes have arrived. Get dressed and I'll brief you fully.'

'No!' a fully-dressed Rico exclaimed. He strode around the apartment and kicked the wall on an impulse. The Register's eidolon sat in a chair and watched him with a faint, patient smile. 'OK, so he worked out how to rekindle the Home Time, but that's not relevant! It did not excuse murder, and I mean, murder! That clone could think, it was self-aware, it had brain patterns . . . it might only have had a mind like a baby but it was still . . .'

'You're not saying anything that didn't come out at the trial,' the Register said. 'In fact, most of what you're saying was said by Mr Daiho himself.'

'But, murder?' Rico said. 'He must have known the penalty for that! I mean, it's complete brain-wipe and new personality and all that, or . . .' He stopped and his eyes went wide. 'Oh, you're kidding!' he said.

'Or induction into the correspondents pro-gramme,' the Register finished for him, with a nod. 'The Commissioner was an ardent student of ancient philosophy. He was actually looking for-ward to his sentence.'

Looking forward . . . It all clicked in Rico's mind.

'*That* correspondent?' he said. He thought back to the battered body remains on the floor of the transference chamber, and sat down heavily in a chair and put his head in his hands. Then he looked up at the Register. 'But that doesn't work. That correspondent – Alan – was sent back by him, so how could he have been him?'

'Actually, Commissioner Daiho didn't send RC/1029 back,' said the Register. 'When he first began to make plans, that correspondent was suggested to him by someone already in the know. In fact, if you will, the ringleader of the plot.'

'But who could . . .' Rico felt his insides freeze. Here he was, in a sealed apartment, unable to symb, completely at the mercy of all the technology this advanced artificial personality had at its command. 'You?' he whispered.

'Me,' the Register said. 'And now you are no doubt going to tell me why it couldn't have been.'

'It couldn't have . . .' Rico snapped, and bit his

tongue. 'OK. He was sent back by your future self. How did your past self know?'

'I've been in touch with myself for a long time. It's only an arbitrary decision on my part which keeps personnel from transferring within the Home Time. I could send people if I so chose and I can certainly send myself messages without anyone knowing. So I knew, and when the Commissioner asked me for a suitable correspondent, I gave him that one.'

'But why?' Rico said.

'I wanted to keep the Home Time going.'

'But Morbern didn't!' Rico was close to shouting. 'He expected the Home Time to lapse at the expected time, and he set you up to make sure things happened as he wanted!' Rico could feel tenets he had held since childhood crumbling under him. It was frightening. It was also, strangely, exhilarating.

'Exactly. I was set up as a mirror of Morbern's own personality, complete with his own wishes and desires. But that was four hundred years ago, Mr Garron. People can change over just a few years. How much more do you think they could change over four centuries? If Jean Morbern had lived that long, I expect he would have changed too. He'd have realized that the Home Time had to keep going. There are billions of people now alive who depend on it. It's not ideal, but the fact is, society now is so stagnant it will just collapse into chaos without the constant input from upstream.'

Rico glared at the former icon of his life. 'And was it worth it?' he muttered.

'You tell me. We're going to have a whole new Home Time, Mr Garron, and this will be very different from the last one. The last one was sprung on the world suddenly and no one expected it. This has been planned for the last twenty-seven years. Morbern's Code is to be revised, made more flexible. I was designed to expire when the Home Time expires but I'll be cloning my intelligence so there'll be something very like me still around, only it will work for the College, not run it. Above all, of course, we'll have transference again, and there'll be an opening for you – an experienced Specific. You could have your old job back.'

'Keep talking,' said Rico.

'Or,' the Register said, 'I could send you home with Op Zo.'

'Home?' Rico murmured. He was already getting used to the idea of starting a new life twenty-seven years on. Enjoying the fact that most of the enemies he had made in his career would be at, or approaching, retirement. The same statute of limitations that meant Asaldra could no longer be held responsible for events twenty-seven years ago also applied to Rico. And the future that the Register painted of the new Home Time was rosy, even if it did have Hossein Asaldra as a hero in it. To his surprise, he was already adjusting to the new situation.

But even so . . . home.

'But,' he said, 'I thought we'd already established that Su goes home, I don't.'

'Su goes home,' the Register agreed. 'She delivers the message to my earlier self that everything has worked out, and she picks up her life again without a blip. You, if you choose to go back, will be facing a tribunal and a lawsuit from Mr Scott's friends and relatives. However, the old Register would certainly offer you a new identity if you chose to return. So you see, it may just be that you go back too and Jontan Baiget hasn't heard of you.'

'You know, don't you?' Rico said. 'You know what I'm going to do.'

'I do not. I have deliberately purged all knowledge of your actions from my memory. You have to act of your own free will.'

'You know about Su, though.'

'Su's choice is a foregone conclusion. What is there for her here? Her family are back there.'

Home . . .

'It's a tough one, isn't it?' he said, but he already knew what he wanted.

The transference hall had been packed with people earlier. Now it was empty – emptier than Rico had ever known. The thirty or forty levels – Rico could never remember the exact number – were silent. No one was entering or leaving the Home Time; no technicians were working on the chambers. His footsteps rang on the metal grid beneath him.

368

'It's almost over,' said Jontan. His services had been retained for just a while longer – he could symb, Rico still couldn't – and he was tuned to a news channel inside his head. Even he had picked up on the significance of what was going on. 'This is amazing. They're actually counting down to the end of an era.'

'Uh-huh,' Rico said. The back of his neck still tingled with the recent injection of the symb seeds that were now regrowing their network inside his head.

They came to a chamber, standing with its doors open, and Jontan peered inside with interest. He had only seen one of these twice in his life, and not recently.

'You remember it as bigger and older?' Rico said.

Jontan smiled. 'Just bigger.' Then his smile faded. 'This is it. They've reached ten.'

He stepped back slightly and looked around to take in as much of the hall as he could.

'. . . Seven, six, five . . .'

He stopped speaking out loud but mouthed the words silently. And then he reached one.

Something stopped. Rico frowned and looked around. Something had been there, like the quiet, unnoticed hum of air conditioning at night, or a vibration through the soles of his feet, filtered out by the brain . . . and when it had stopped it had made just as much of an impact as a sudden bang.

'It's over,' Jontan said quietly, and Rico realized what it was. He reached out and put his hand gently against the side of the chamber. It was still, cold steel. No hum, no energy. Every chamber in the transference hall was dead. Deep beneath the College, Morbern's singularity had collapsed into nothing and the Home Time was no more.

'Now what?' he said, wishing those symb seeds would grow back more quickly. Jontan's eyes were unfocused as he followed the images inside his head.

'A lot of meaningless chatter from the commentators – right – here it comes. Another countdown. They're about to trigger the new singularity. Um, nine, eight . . .'

Again, at five he started counting silently, and at one . . .

The noise didn't just come back like that. It piled up over a couple of seconds, like being inside a vast machine that had just started up. But it was back, in a matter of seconds, to the familiar subliminal rumble Rico had always known.

Jontan's face was one huge, delighted smile. 'It worked!' he said. 'Down in Control, it's a carnival. They're shouting, dancing, whooping . . .' His eyes fixed on something behind Rico and his expression turned more thoughtful.

Rico looked round and saw Su and Sarai were coming towards them. Jontan stepped forward to intercept his wife and together they hung back slightly, so Su and Rico met up again on their own.

'Well . . .' Su said. She was smiling bravely but it didn't quite work. 'The Register told me.'

'No hard feelings?' They hugged.

'I understand. There's nothing for you back there.'

Rico hugged her more tightly. 'There's you, Su.'

'Oh, stop it,' Su mumbled into his shoulder. 'I'd never forgive you if you blew this opportunity and you know it.'

'And I'd never forgive you if you stayed just for me.'

'Oh, yeah, right, Garron. Don't flatter yourself.'

They stood close together without speaking for a moment longer.

'The co-ordinates are set,' said a familiar voice. The Register's eidolon had appeared next to the chamber. No, not the Register's eidolon, Rico reminded himself: the eidolon of the new Register, outwardly identical to the old but with important differences in what it could now do. 'Are you ready, Op Zo?'

'As I'll ever be,' Su said. She pushed herself gently away from Rico, then reached out once more to touch him. She smiled again, turned and walked into the chamber. The doors began to swing shut.

'Good luck,' she called.

'I'll manage.' Rico knew his own smile was twisted.

'Give Asaldra a hard time.'

'Why do you think I'm staying?'

'I'll miss you,' Su called, and then the doors finally closed.

Rico stepped back and looked at the transference chamber. He felt a sudden surge of irritation at its smug, shiny, spherical complacency. The chambers just sat there while Field Ops came and went and technicians tended to their every need. They swallowed people up and, in their own good time, returned them. It was as if Su was held in one of them, and all it had to do was open its doors . . .

'Mr Garron?' said Sarai behind him. He turned round. She and Jontan were still standing a discreet distance away, arms around each other's waists. And more people were approaching, borne by a carryfield.

'We called some people, once we learned you were staying . . .' Jontan said, but Rico had already twigged. The banner saying 'Welcome Rico' was one clue. And the faces.

Tong, Su's husband – hair shorter and greyer than it had been. A man and woman in their thirties, with a couple of toddlers – grief, that must be Su's descendants – and, at the forefront . . .

They stood face to face as, for Rico, they had just been doing, each savouring the sight of the other, drinking it in. Then:

'Those twenty-seven years have been good to you,' he said.

'Hello, Rico,' she said, and for the second time in a couple of minutes and twenty-seven years, Su Zo walked into his arms.

Author's Note

The Marconi Monument does exist, exactly as described in Chapter Eleven, and Daiho is entirely correct about its significance in human affairs. There is also a hotel at the location depicted in the book, and I leave its identity as an exercise for readers with an interest in telecommunications, the directions given in Chapter Eleven and a handy guide to the Lizard peninsula. However, the real-life hotel and its staff bear no resemblance at all to their fictional counterparts.

Acknowledgements

Many thanks to everyone who helped, criticized, gave advice, just plain suffered or any combination of the above: Chris Amies; Tina Anghelatos; Paul Beardsley; Molly Brown; David Fickling; Liz Holliday; Andy Lane; Ben Sharpe; Gus Smith; Jonathan Tweed. The drowned kitten lives again.